DRAGONS OF DELTORA

Special Edition

Books 1 & 2

DRAGONS OF DELTORA

Special Edition
Books 1 & 2

EMILY RODDA

SCHOLASTIC INC.
New York Toronto London Auckland Sydney
Mexico City New Delhi Hong Kong Buenos Aires

For Reuben Jakeman

Dragons of Deltora #1: Dragon's Nest, ISBN 0-439-63373-7
Text and graphics copyright © 2003 by Emily Rodda.

Dragons of Deltora #2: Shadowgate, ISBN 0-439-63374-5,
Text and graphics copyright © 2004 by Emily Rodda.

Graphics by Kate Rowe.
Cover illustration copyright © 2003 by Scholastic Australia.
Cover illustration by Marc McBride.

12 11 10 9 8 7 6 5 4 3 2 1   6 7 8 9 10/0

Printed in the U.S.A.   23

This edition created exclusively for Barnes & Noble, Inc.

2006 Barnes & Noble Books

ISBN 0-7607-9611-4

First compilation printing, April 2006

Contents

DRAGON'S
NEST

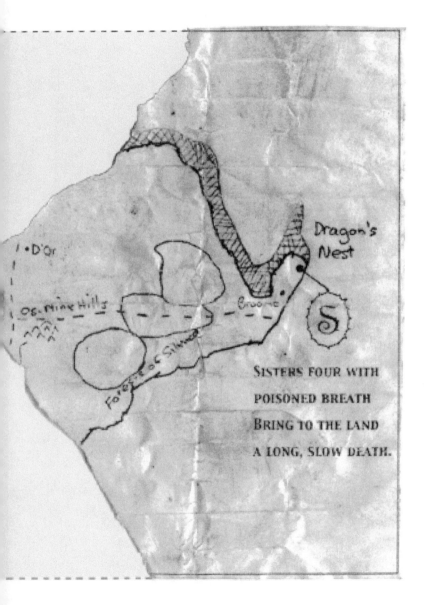

SISTERS FOUR WITH

POISONED BREATH

BRING TO THE LAND

A LONG, SLOW DEATH.

Contents

1 - The Voice in the Crystal

Unwillingly, Lief joined the crowd flocking up the sweeping stairs to the palace of Del. His legs felt heavier with every step. The sweet morning air was cool, but his hands were slippery with sweat.

The other people on the stairs stood back respectfully to let him pass. Some bowed low. Many smiled and waved, thrilled to see their king among them. All whispered and pointed at the glittering jeweled Belt he wore — the magic Belt of Deltora.

Lief forced smiles and waves in return, but his heart sank as he saw how thin the people were, how shadowed were their eyes.

He looked up. The great carved doors of the palace yawned wide above him. Through the doorway he could see only darkness. And from the darkness . . .

1

I am waiting for you, little king.

The voice of the Shadow Lord struck, hissing, in his mind. He had been prepared for it but still he froze.

Are you greeting your miserable people, little king? the jeering voice whispered. *Fools! They look at you and think, King Lief and his brave companions Barda and Jasmine rid Deltora of the Shadow Lord's tyranny, and drove him back to the Shadowlands. King Lief rescued the prisoners the Enemy was keeping in slavery, and returned them to their homes. Now, surely, King Lief can make us live happily ever after . . .*

The voice trailed away in mocking laughter. Lief gritted his teeth and kept climbing.

He could not let the voice drive him away, back to the blacksmith's forge that was once again his home.

Tonight it would be a full moon, and that meant that today was the day of the monthly public meeting. People had come from far and wide to speak to their king. He could not disappoint them.

At the top of the stairs he looked back, as if to catch one last glimpse of the morning before the cold shadows of the palace closed around him.

A black bird was swooping down towards him from the pale blue sky. It was holding something in its claws.

Kree! Lief thought, his spirits lifting. *Kree, bringing me word from Jasmine! Perhaps Jasmine has decided to leave Mother and Doom in the west, and return to Del sooner than expected. Perhaps she is here now!*

Eagerly he looked towards the road. But he could see no familiar black-haired figure among the people streaming towards the palace. And as the bird plunged downward he realized that it was not Kree at all.

He stood motionless, watching it. The bird wheeled above him, its yellow eye marking his position. Then a tiny package dropped at his feet with a muffled clang.

He picked up the package and raised his hand. The bird gave a harsh cry and soared away, towards the northwest.

The people on the stairs eyed the package nervously. Jasmine had begun training messenger birds not long ago, so they were still an uncommon sight in Del. And black birds had not always meant well in the days of the Shadow Lord.

"It is just a message from Dread Mountain," Lief called as casually as he could. He pulled off the package's outer covering and showed the note wrapped tightly around an arrowhead and tied in place with twine.

You have stopped again, coward. Very wise. Now turn and run, like the sniveling blacksmith's son you really are.

Lief moved quickly through the palace doors, into the vast, echoing space of the entrance hall.

3

The hall was already crowded with chattering people. Lief knew that the noise must be great, but to him it seemed nothing more than a low drone. It was as though he were trapped inside a bubble.

Every sound outside the bubble was muffled. Only the evil whisper inside it seemed real.

Ah, you are closer to me now. Do you see your people before you, swarming like starving rats?

Lief looked down at the jeweled Belt. The ruby was pale. The emerald was dull. The gems felt danger. Evil . . .

"Lief! What news?"

The voice rang out, confident and strong, shattering the bubble, setting him free.

Lief looked up and saw Barda striding towards him, dressed for the meeting in his uniform of chief of the palace guards.

The pale blue uniform trimmed with gold was very different from the rough clothes Barda had worn when Lief had first met him. But Barda's brown, bearded face was the same, though his broad grin was a little forced. He looked at Lief closely as he clasped his hand.

Wordlessly Lief showed him the arrowhead.

Barda glanced around the crowded entrance hall, then jerked his head towards a roped-off hallway at one side. "We will get some peace in the new library," he murmured. "Old Josef is still at breakfast."

Lief nodded and together they stepped over the

rope barrier and hurried down the hallway. Soon they were standing in the huge, box-filled room that was Josef the librarian's despair.

Josef had not wanted to move the library down to the ground floor. The old library on the third floor of the palace had been his pride and joy. He wanted it to stay exactly as it had always been.

But Lief had insisted. The third floor of the palace was not safe. It had to be closed and never used again. For on the third floor, at the end of a sealed hallway, in the center of a bricked-up white room, was . . .

You will never be free of me, Lief of Deltora. Whenever I wish I can speak to you — and to others, when I am ready. Ah, I look forward to playing with those weaker, flabbier minds. They bend and break so easily. So easily . . .

Lief felt Barda's hand grip his shoulder.

"Do you hear him too?" Lief asked dully.

The crystal is the window through which my mind and voice can reach you. You will never be free of me. Never . . .

"Not as you do, I think," Barda said. "For me, there is only a feeling. A bad, bad feeling . . ."

Lief looked at his friend. Barda's face was grim.

"You should not be sleeping at the palace, Barda," he said. "This is getting worse."

"Far worse for you than for me," Barda said. "You should not have come."

"Even at the forge the whisperings enter my

dreams," Lief muttered. "And, in any case, the palace is the only place big enough for the monthly meeting."

"Then stop the meetings for a time," Barda said. "Until we can build — "

"No!" Lief broke in. "That is what he *wants*, Barda! He is trying to make me break faith with the people. Things are bad enough as it is. I should not be holding these meetings only in Del, leaving all the traveling to Mother and Doom. But I cannot take the Belt away, leave Del unprotected from that — that *thing* upstairs!"

Blindly he tore at the twine around the arrowhead and freed the note. As he smoothed the paper out, Barda gave a snort of disgust.

"Why does the old fool write in code?" Barda exploded. "We are supposed to be living in a time of peace!"

"The Dread Gnomes have always been suspicious folk," Lief said. "Perhaps the young ones will change in time, but old ones like Fa-Glin never will."

He shrugged. "And in any case, this code is as simple as can be — only intended to baffle the quick glances of strangers. See? Fa-Glin has just written out his message putting all the letters into groups of four, with no full stops."

Barda snatched the note, cursed under his breath because he had not seen the trick at once, then haltingly began to read the message aloud.

GREETINGS, dIEF, KING oF DELTORA!
THIS IS THE REPORT OF FA-GLIN
OF THE DREAD GNOMES.

IGRI	EVET	OTEL	LYOU	THAT
THEN	EWOR	OPON	WHIC	HWEP
INNE	DOUR	HOPE	SHAS	BEEN
DISA	PPOI	NTIN	GTHE	VINE
SWER	ESIC	XLYF	RIMT	HEFI
RSTA	NDON	LYSI	XBAS	KETS
OFSM	ALLS	OURF	RUIT	RESU
LTED	FROM	ALLO	URCA	RETH
EYAM	HARN	ESTW	ASAL	SOVE
RYBA	DMAN	YOPT	HEYA	MSHA
VING	ROTT	EDIN	THEG	ROUN
DHUN	TING	ISFO	ORTH	CREA
REFE	WFIS	HINT	HEST	REAM

IFON	LYWE	COUL	DEAT	THEF
RUIT	OFTH	EBOO	LONG	TREE
SLIK	FOUR	NEIG	HBOU	RSTH
EKIN	THEB	OOLO	NGTR	EEST
HRIV	ELIK	ETHE	WCED	STHE
YARE	BUTA	LLPA	RTSO	FTHE
MDIS	AGRE	EWIT	HUSI	TWIL
LBEA	NOTA	ERHA	RDWI	NTER
ONDR	EADM	OUNT	AINI	FEAR

YOUR RESPECTFUL SERVANT,

FA-GLIN

" 'I grieve to tell you that the new crop on which we pinned our hopes has been disappointing. The vines were sickly from the first, and only six baskets of small, sour fruit resulted from all our care. The yam harvest was also very bad, many of the yams having rotted in the ground. Hunting is poor. There are few fish in the stream.' "

He broke off, shook his head, then read on:

" 'If only we could eat the fruit of the boolong trees like our neighbors the Kin! The boolong trees thrive like the weeds they are, but all parts of them disagree with us. It will be another hard winter on Dread Mountain, I fear.' "

He handed the note back to Lief, his face very grave.

"So," he said. "More bad tidings. North, south, east, and west, it is the same story. But Fa-Glin did not ask for food to be sent, as the other tribes did."

"He is too proud for that," said Lief. "He would rather starve than ask for help. And perhaps he guesses that we have little to send, in any case."

Suddenly, he crumpled the note into a ball and threw it across the room.

"Oh, what are we to do?" he groaned. "The people have worked so hard, and we have given them every help we can. But it seems that nothing thrives in Deltora except weeds and thorns. It is as if the land is poisoned!"

"Or cursed," said a quavering voice behind him.

2 ~ Tales of Dragons

Lief and Barda spun around. Josef the librarian was standing there, leaning heavily on his stick. He had crept into the room so silently that they had not heard him.

"What foolishness are you talking, Josef?" snapped Barda, glancing at Lief's strained face in concern. "Crop failures are nothing new in Deltora. We were half-starved all through the years of the Shadow Lord's terror, but we hardly noticed it then. It is only after a battle, when you are safe, that you have time to fret about the sting of a small wound or the tightness of your boots."

Josef followed the big man's eyes to Lief's fixed, dread-filled expression. His face fell.

"Forgive me," he said, hobbling forward. "I am tired, and spoke hastily. Barda is quite right. The threat of famine has plagued Deltora for centuries."

"Yes," said Lief in a low voice. "But it was not always so, Josef. You and I both know it."

He pointed at the one tidy shelf in the great room — a shelf holding a row of tall, pale blue books.

"The early volumes of the *Deltora Annals* are full of tales of giant harvests, prizewinning melons, hauls of fish so heavy that the nets of the fishermen tore," he said. "When did things change? And why?"

Josef looked anxiously from his king's drawn face to Barda's, and back again.

"I . . . I do not know," he stammered. "It — just happened. Little by little. But I have sometimes thought . . ."

"Yes?" Lief leaned forward. "What, Josef?"

Josef wet his lips. "Only . . ." he quavered, "only that the land's decline seems to — to have followed the decline of Deltora's dragons."

Lief and Barda glanced at each other. In both their minds was a vision of the golden dragon they had seen in the Os-Mine Hills.

The dragon had been deep in an enchanted sleep, and they had not breathed a word of it to anyone, for its cavern guarded a secret underground world they had sworn never to reveal.

Barda cleared his throat. "I do not see how the land could have suffered from the dragons' extinction," he said roughly. "The beasts were a menace, by all reports."

Josef drew himself up. "I beg to disagree," he said. "Look! I will show you!"

He tottered to the shelf where the many volumes of the *Deltora Annals* were stored.

Barda clicked his tongue impatiently. "Oh, why did I give him an excuse to start messing around with those cursed books?" he said to Lief under his breath. "Now there will be no stopping the old bore."

"Josef," said Lief, "the meeting is about to begin. We really do not have time for — "

But the old man had already thrown aside his stick and seized a pale blue book from the shelf.

"I have always believed that the dragons of Deltora were linked to the land more closely than most people understood," he said, flipping eagerly through the book's yellowed pages. "Do you know, for example, that the dragons were divided into seven tribes, just as the original peoples of Deltora were?"

"No! Nor do I care," said Barda rudely.

"If you would prefer ignorance to knowledge, that is your affair," said Josef, turning from his book with a frown. "But the king, who has read my small work, *The Deltora Book of Monsters*, knows exactly what I am talking about. Is that not so, your majesty?"

"Oh — yes!" stammered Lief.

In fact, though he had glanced at the remarkable pictures in Josef's book, he had not yet found time to read the closely written words.

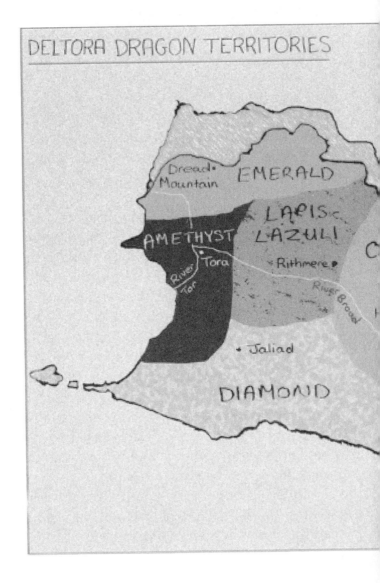

DELTORA DRAGON TERRITORIES

- Dread Mountain
- EMERALD
- LAPIS LAZULI
- AMETHYST
- Tora
- River Tor
- Rithmere
- River Broad
- Jaliad
- DIAMOND
- C

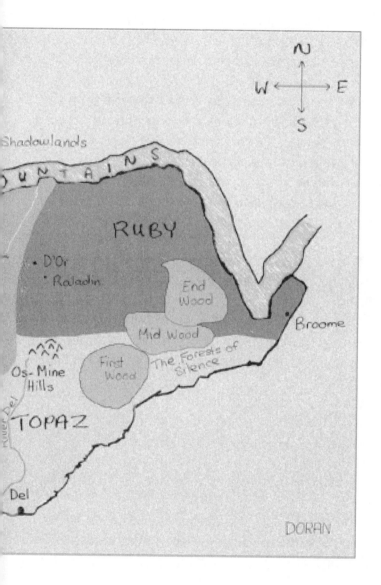

Fortunately, Josef did not notice his confusion. He had found the page he was looking for. On it was a map of Deltora — one Lief only vaguely remembered.

Curious despite himself, Lief moved to the old man's side and looked.

"This map was made by the explorer Doran the Dragonlover, long ago," said Josef, tapping the page with a bony finger. "Doran's maps were never elegant, but they were always accurate. This one shows the borders of the seven dragon territories. Doran drew it often, but sadly only one of the loose copies he made for travelers still survives. I keep it safely locked away."

"The borders look the same as the old borders of the seven tribes," said Barda, looking over his shoulder.

"They *are* the same!" exclaimed Josef excitedly. "That is just the point! The territories of the people, the dragons, and the gems of Deltora correspond exactly."

"And so?" Barda enquired in a bored voice.

"Do you not see how important this is?" exclaimed Josef. "You are not thinking, captain of the guards! Why, you of all people should understand!"

Barda remained silent. Josef looked at him severely.

"The magic Belt of Deltora, created by our first king, the blacksmith Adin, and worn by his heirs, protects the land from the Shadow Lord," he said in the patient tone of one speaking to a very small child. "Each of its great gems — the topaz, the ruby, the opal, the lapis-lazuli, the emerald, the amethyst, and the diamond — came from deep within our earth, and each was the talisman of one Deltoran tribe."

"Barda knows this very well, Josef," said Lief gently. "Now, we really must — "

"Wait!" Josef commanded, stabbing at the writing beside the map. "Read what Doran says here. Read it!"

Once, the seven Dragon tribes encircled Deltora with their strength. The most ancient and wise of beasts, the Dragons were the guardians and protectors of their territories. Now I fear their time is ending. They are being attacked and killed in great numbers by the monstrous, vulture-like birds from the Shadowlands known as the seven Ak-Baba. Despite my pleas, the King does nothing, and the magic Belt remains locked away from him, in the tower.

The people are glad, because they can ill spare the beasts they lose to the Dragons. But I am certain that the Dragons' loss is disastrous for Deltora, and was meant to be so. They are being destroyed for a reason. I am determined to search out the last of them, and find a way of protecting them if I can.

I leave on the morrow, and pray I will not be too late.

Lief frowned. "Josef, Doran was a great explorer. But he was not called 'Dragonlover' for nothing. He was fascinated by dragons. He would have said anything to rally support to save them."

Josef sighed, and much of his excitement fell away, leaving him a frail old man again. "No doubt you are right," he said. He rubbed his chin with a hand that trembled slightly. Then he looked up.

"I am sorry to have wasted your time, your majesty," he said with dignity. "It is just that — I want so much to help you. Forgive me for saying so, but you are bearing great burdens for one so young."

Suddenly, Lief could pretend no longer. "I fear I am not bearing them very bravely at present, Josef," he said. His throat tightened and he bowed his head.

Timidly Josef put a hand on his arm. "I have lived long," he said. "I have lived through terrible times, and seen terrible things. But I have never lost faith. That is what saved me. You must have faith in yourself, your majesty, faith in your destiny."

"Destiny," Lief muttered.

"Yes!" The old man nodded violently. "You are the true heir of the great Adin, and not just because his blood runs in your veins. Surely it is no accident that you were born and raised not in this grand palace, but in Adin's old home? Why, day after day you worked with your father at the very same blacksmith's forge where Adin beat out the steel that was to become the Belt of Deltora!"

Lief gave a muffled exclamation, but Josef rushed on.

"You are heir to all the Belt's magic and power, my king," he said. "Surely it will aid you now. See how Del's topaz, the symbol of faith, shines for you?"

Lief's fingers slid down and touched the golden topaz in the Belt of Deltora. But still he did not raise his head or speak.

Josef glanced nervously at Barda, who was looking puzzled and almost afraid.

They both started when there was a timid knock. They turned to see the fluffy golden head and small face of Josef's assistant, Paff, peeping around the door.

"Forgive me, Josef, your majesty — oh! — and captain of the guards!" Paff gasped, her pink-tipped nose twitching nervously. "But — the people are growing restless. I was sent to ask you — "

"The full moon," Lief murmured. "Full moon . . . of course! But I need Doom. And Doom is in the west, in Tora. I must . . ."

Paff's eyes grew very wide. Her small mouth dropped open.

"Paff!" said Josef. "Leave us! His majesty is not — "

But Lief had raised his head. His eyes were clear and bright.

"Josef! A pen and paper, quickly, if you please!" he said. "Barda, I need the fastest messenger bird we have — Jasmine's favorite, Ebony, if she is here. And Paff, please let the people know that I will be with them in one moment. We will have our meeting and then — then I have something of great importance to tell them."

3 - The Full Moon Meeting

The meeting ran its usual course through the day. Reports and complaints were made, questions were asked and answered. None of the news was good, but Lief kept nothing back.

He knew that it was no use trying to give the people false comfort. They had eyes and ears. They knew only too well that times were hard. They would see through any pretense in a moment.

To be seen by all, he had to stand on the stairs that led to the upper floors of the palace. Just a little closer to the source of the voice that soon came back to torment him.

He fought it by keeping his hands on the Belt of Deltora — using the power of the gems, keeping his fingertips on the amethyst that soothed, the diamond for strength, the topaz that cleared the mind.

But the voice was relentless. Its poison dripped

into his mind hour after hour, till his stomach was churning and his clothes were damp with sweat.

Soon, he told himself. Soon . . .

The Belt cannot save you, little king.

Abruptly the voice left him. His head reeled with the sudden freedom. He became aware that Barda had taken his arm, that the people were staring up at him in fear. He realized that he must have staggered.

"I am sorry," he said. "I . . . am a little tired."

"The king must rest now," said Barda. "Thank you all — "

There was a stir from the crowd as a woman holding a sleeping baby scrambled quickly to her feet. The woman was gaunt, and her clothes, though carefully washed and pressed, were ragged. She looked nervous, but stood very straight, with her shoulders back.

"I am Iris of Del, bootmaker and mender, wife of Paulie and mother of Jack," she began, identifying herself as was the custom at these meetings. "I have a question."

As Lief met her determined eyes, he knew exactly what she was going to ask. Plainly Barda knew it too. The big man stiffened and began to raise his hand as if to say that it was too late, that no more questions could be answered.

"Yes, Iris," Lief said quickly.

The woman hesitated, biting her lip as though suddenly regretting her boldness. Then she looked down at the baby in her arms and seemed to gain confidence.

"There is something worrying my husband and me, sir," she said. "I am sure it must be worrying many others, too, but no one has yet spoken of it."

Lief saw that many people in the crowd were nodding and murmuring to one another. *So — the word has spread*, he thought. *All the better. It will make what I have to tell them easier, if they are prepared. I only wish . . .*

He opened his mouth to speak, then froze as there was a sudden stir near the doorway. Two women shrieked and ducked, a man shouted, and a small child gave a high-pitched cry of excitement.

Then the whole crowd was exclaiming, looking up.

A messenger bird had soared through the doorway and into the palace. Lief's heart gave a great leap as it sped towards him.

"Kree!" Barda muttered.

Kree landed on Lief's outstretched arm and waited until Lief had taken the scroll from his beak before squawking a greeting. Lief unrolled the note.

Your message received.
Jasmine and I will be
with you within the hour.
DOOM

"Thank you, Kree," he said, passing the note to Barda. He did not know how to feel. He needed Doom urgently, and was filled with relief at the thought that Toran magic was speeding him to Del. But he would rather Jasmine had remained in the west, in Tora, where she would be safe.

Then he shook his head. How could he have thought Jasmine would agree to that?

"I must have been mad," he said aloud. Barda nudged him, and he glanced up. Iris was still standing in the center of the crowd, looking bewildered.

"Go on, Iris," he said, smiling at her. "I am sorry for the interruption."

The woman swallowed, tightened her grip on her child, and spoke again.

"It sounds foolish, but Paulie and I half feared to come here today, sir," she said. "Especially as we had to bring our little Jack with us. We have heard rumors that somehow the Shadow Lord has returned — that he lurks here in the palace, in a locked room above stairs. Is that — could that be — true?"

"No, it is not!" barked Barda, before Lief could speak. "The Enemy has been exiled to the Shadowlands, as well you know."

But Iris's anxious eyes had never left Lief's face.

"We have heard that the Enemy talks to you, sir, in your mind," she said in a low voice. "And perhaps to others, too, for all we know."

"That is so," Lief said quietly, ignoring the pressure of Barda's hand on his arm. "And it is time to tell you about it. I was going to do so today in any case, as soon as the time for questions was over. Thank you for giving me a way to begin."

Very flustered, not knowing whether to be pleased or afraid, Iris sank back down beside her husband. He put his arm around her and gently touched the baby's cheek with a work-stained finger.

The room was very still as Lief began to speak.

"On the third floor of the palace, in a sealed room, there is a thing called the crystal," he said. "It is a piece of thick glass set into a small table, and it has been in the room where it now stands for hundreds of years. The Shadow Lord can speak through it, as you or I might speak through an open window."

A murmur of dread rippled through the crowd.

"The Enemy once used it to talk to his palace spies," Lief went on. "Now he has begun to use it to taunt me, to distract me from my work, and, above all, to try to make me despair. He torments Barda and Jasmine too. And as he gains strength, I fear he will begin on others."

"But can this evil not be destroyed?" someone called from the back of the room. "If it is made of glass — "

"I have tried to destroy the crystal many times, without success," Lief answered.

His calm voice gave no hint of what those grim, exhausting struggles in the white room upstairs had cost him. But everyone could see it, everyone close enough to see the sheen of sweat on his brow, and the shadows that darkened his eyes at the memory.

He took a deep breath. "The crystal was made by sorcery, and can only be destroyed by — by something just as powerful. The Belt of Deltora alone is not enough. But just before this meeting began, I suddenly saw another way. Tonight, I am going to try one last time to destroy this thing that threatens us all."

"Lief, what are you saying?" Barda muttered.

The murmur in the crowd had risen to a dull roar. Before him Lief saw a sea of frightened, exclaiming faces. The people were afraid. Afraid for him, and for themselves. They were right to be so, but panic would help no one.

"I cannot do this without your help," he called over the din. "Please hear me!"

Utter silence fell.

"These are the things you all must do," Lief said. "When you leave here, go directly to your homes. Bolt the doors, put up the shutters, and do not stir outside again until you hear the bells ring to tell you all is well. This is for your safety. Do you understand?"

The people nodded silently, awed by his seriousness.

Lief nodded. "Good," he said. "Now — there is

something else that can be done by those who want to help further. Make yourselves as comfortable as possible, and stay awake. Stay awake through the night and — as often as you can — think of me. Send me your strength."

"And is this all you ask of us, King Lief?" cried a man from the back of the crowd. "Our thoughts? Why, we would give you our lives!"

A great cheer rose up, echoing to the soaring roof of the great hall.

Lief felt a hot stinging at the back of his eyes. "Thank you," he managed to say. "I will carry your words with me. They will help me more than you can know."

✳

The sun had dipped below the horizon, and a huge full moon was rising, when six of Barda's strongest guards carried a shrouded burden from the sealed room on the third floor of the palace.

The guards were grim-faced. Each one of them was astounded at the enormous weight of the small thing they carried. Each was filled with a nameless dread.

Lief walked in front of the guards, Barda walked behind. Both of them were bent forward, as if in pain. But neither paused or uttered a word as they moved along the hallway, towards the stairs.

And because they did not falter, the guards did

not falter either. Suffering but uncomplaining, they heaved their hooded cargo forward, over the rubble of the bricks that had once blocked the hallway, past the old library, down the great stairway, across the deserted entrance hall, out of the palace.

Only when they had crossed the palace lawn and were moving down the hill did one of the guards speak. He was a guard called Nirrin, rescued not so long ago from slavery in the Shadowlands.

"Where are we going, sir?" he gasped. "It would help — I think — if we could know. Is it far?"

Lief turned to him. Later, Nirrin would tell his wife that never had he seen such a tortured face as when the king turned to him that full moon night. Only the heavens knew what the boy was going through, what was pouring into him from that nightmare beneath the cloth.

Nirrin had volunteered for this task, and never regretted it for a single moment, though he had bad dreams for months after that terrible journey.

He had heard nothing from the crystal, but still it had touched him. Long after he carried it, the weight of its evil seemed to press him down, to make it hard to breathe, even in his own safe bed.

And never would he forget Lief's eyes.

"The king just stared at me for a moment," he told his wife. "His eyes were like — like deep wells. His mouth opened, but no words came. It was as if he had forgotten how to speak. Then, he croaked out an answer.

" 'Not far,' he said. Then he pointed down the hill and across a bit, and I could see a sort of glow through the trees. 'Only to Adin's old home, and mine, Nirrin. Only to the forge.' "

4 ~ Act of Faith

Jasmine was waiting at the partly open forge gates, Kree motionless on her shoulder. Both were lit by a weird red glow, and shadows leaped behind them. Above, the great golden circle of the moon floated just clear of treetops that looked like black paper cutouts against the gray sky.

As the strange procession from the palace stumbled into view, Kree gave a harsh cry. It was plainly a signal, for it was answered by a shout from within the forge. The red glow brightened. Jasmine pushed the gates fully open.

Now the struggling guards could see the fiery blaze within, and the powerful figure of the blacksmith working the bellows, increasing the heat, the muscles of his bare arms gleaming with sweat.

"Jasmine! Stay — back," Lief gasped as the men behind him pressed forward, groaning under the weight of their terrible burden. But either he spoke too softly for Jasmine to hear or she chose not to listen. She darted towards him. In another moment her arm was around his waist, and she was half-supporting him as they moved through the gateway.

Feebly he tried to push her away.

"Don't, Lief," she snapped. "If Barda can stand against him, so can I!" Even as she spoke, the blood was draining from her face, but she held him tightly, and together they moved on.

They drew closer to the fire, and closer, till they could feel the burning heat on their faces. The black-smith looked up as they approached. But still he worked the bellows, and the fire in the forge was like liquid flame.

"It is as hot as I can make it," he shouted over the roaring sound.

The faces of the guards changed as they recognized him, as they saw with awe that this man with the strip of rag bound round his brow, the blacksmith with sweat pouring from his black-streaked face, was the legendary Doom.

Doom. The strange name moved between them, whispering in the heated air. *Doom. It is Doom.*

Doom, the mysterious, scar-faced leader of the Resistance in the time of the Shadow Lord. Doom, the stern, solitary traveler. Doom, the ruthless one, who still held the ruffians of Deltora in the palm of his hand.

Doom, who had once sacrificed his whole world for his king.

And here he stands, Lief thought. *In the place where he belonged, before the Shadow Lord came, and everything changed. Where once he mended plows, forged swords, and made shoes for horses. Where my gentle, gallant father stood, too, in his time. And where, long ago, Adin made the Belt of Deltora.*

He stared at the glaring forge. Always before, it had been used to create. Now it was to be used to destroy. If he could find the strength.

You cannot defeat me . . .

He saw that the guards had begun to struggle. It was as if the thing they carried had suddenly become ten times heavier. They were dragging it now. Two were already on their knees.

You cannot defeat me . . .

Through a fiery haze Lief saw Barda push between the men and grasp their shrouded burden with his own hands. Veins stood out in his neck as he heaved, his teeth bared, the great muscles of his arms and shoulders bulging through his shirt.

The thing shifted a little. Barda heaved again. Closer to the flame, a little closer . . . close enough. But now . . .

They will never be able to lift it onto the forge, Lief thought suddenly.

Pain pierced his head, doubling him over, tearing him from Jasmine's grip.

Dimly he heard Doom and Barda shouting, Jasmine calling his name, but their voices were distant. The only voice that was strong and real hissed viciously in his mind, in the still center of a whirlwind of pain.

I am too strong for you. You cannot win.

Blindly, instinctively, Lief felt for the Belt of Deltora. His fingers found the topaz. The gem seemed to quiver at his touch. It seemed to melt into his fingertips, golden and warm. It seemed to become part of him.

Topaz, symbol of faith, he thought hazily. And into his clouded mind sprang an image of words on a printed page. Words he had suddenly remembered that morning in the library. Words from *The Belt of Deltora,* the small blue book that once he had carried like a talisman:

The topaz is a powerful gem, and its strength increases as the moon grows full. The topaz protects its wearer from the terrors of the night. It has the power to open doors into the spirit world. It strengthens and clears the mind . . .

The pain in Lief's brain began to ease. And as he slowly straightened and stood upright once more, it seemed to him that many others were crowding around him. Faces, clear and hazy, serious and serene. Shapes from the present and the past. Dozens of voices, hundreds, drowning out that other voice, speaking separately and together . . .

Have courage, my son. We are with you.

We will help you, boy. Have faith . . .

King Lief . . . we are thinking of you, as you asked.

We would give you our lives . . .

Lief bent and seized the shrouded thing that stood before the forge, and it was as if hundreds of invisible hands were beside his own. He looked up, caught a glimpse of the panting, exhausted guards, Barda's baffled face, and Jasmine's green eyes dark with fear.

"Stand back!" he shouted. And with one movement, he swung the evil thing up, up and slammed it upside down on the fiery forge.

Doom shouted in savage triumph. The guards groaned in amazement and terror.

The thick cloth covering burst into flames and disappeared in a cloud of ash. The wooden frame of the table, its stubby legs sticking upward, began to burn.

"Get it off!" shouted Doom. "The wood will choke the coals."

Jasmine sprang forward and pulled the table frame up and away from the sorcerer's glass it had supported for so long. She threw it aside, into the shadows, and it lay there, smoldering.

And then the crystal lay on the forge alone, revealed to all. It lay on the fiery coals, twisting like a live thing. Gray spirals edged with scarlet swirled on its rippling surface, and in its center was a hollow, whispering darkness.

Barda turned to his guards. "Get out!" he bawled. "Run! I order you!"

The guards scrambled up and did as they were bid. They were strong, brave men, every one, but afterwards none was ashamed to admit that he had taken to his heels and run for his life, the night the crystal burned on the forge in Del.

Only Lief, Barda, Doom, and Jasmine witnessed what happened next.

The crystal writhed, its center darkened. Then, with a hideous, grinding sound it cracked from corner to corner. Red sparks flew upward from the crystal's core, and a terrible howling filled the air.

Barda, Jasmine and Lief were thrown back, their hair flying around their faces as if blown by a fierce, hot wind. The bellows dropped from Doom's hands and he clapped his hands over his ears, his face a mask of agony.

But the fire of Adin's forge, where the Belt of Deltora had begun its life, burned on, relentless. The great topaz, which had summoned both the living and the dead to Lief's aid, gleamed golden as the full moon. And slowly, slowly, the howling died to a moaning hum, and the crystal began to cloud and soften.

Lief, Barda, and Jasmine crawled to their feet.

They saw that Doom had picked up the bellows and was moving back to his place by the forge. Doom's face was drawn but, gritting his teeth, he lifted the bellows and began raising the heat of the fire once more.

There was a sharp cracking noise. The humming abruptly changed to a low buzz that rose and fell as if hundreds of flies were trapped within the glass. Then, horribly, a thick, dull gray liquid began bubbling from the crack in the crystal, oozing across the glass surface.

Filled with disgust, Lief stumbled to where the huge hammer lay beside the forge. He picked it up, feeling its mighty weight. He took a sure grip on the familiar handle that had been polished to silken smoothness by so many hardworking hands. He turned . . .

"Come closer, Slave!"

The Shadow Lord's voice hissed from the crystal. Lief jumped, almost losing his footing as the weight of the hammer dragged him off-balance. He felt a split second of shock mingled with crushing disappointment. Then he heard the second voice.

"Yes, Master."

It was a thin, cold voice — faint, but clear. And it, too, had come from the crystal.

Lief heard Jasmine and Barda exclaiming behind him. He saw Doom's eyes widen in disgusted horror. The oozing liquid on the surface of the crystal was forming into the shape of a thin, cruel face. The shape's writhing lips moved.

"I am here, Master. What is your will?"

"Is the idiot boy Endon proclaimed king, Slave?"

"Yes, Master."

"And the Belt?"

One side of the gray face sliding on the glass bulged hideously, then shrank back into place. The thin lips curved into a smile. "The Belt has been returned to the tower. It awaits your pleasure."

"Ah . . . " The hissing voice sighed with evil satisfaction.

5 - The Four Sisters

A wave of fury swept over Lief, burning like the coals of the fire. He swung the hammer high and smashed it down with all his strength. The hammer head sank deep in the softened glass of the crystal, bending rather than breaking it. Gray ooze ran into the hot coals, sizzling, burning.

Lief wrenched the hammer free and prepared to strike again.

"No more, Lief," Doom said quietly. "Let the fire finish its work."

The buzzing was patchy now, coming in short, harsh bursts. Somewhere deep inside the glass, a feeble red light flickered.

"What was that other voice?" Jasmine shivered. "Why did it speak of Endon — of your father, Lief?"

Lief wet his lips. "It was a memory," he said. "It was my father's chief advisor, the spy Prandine, talking to the Shadow Lord just after Father became king."

"The crystal must somehow keep a record of everything that has passed through it," said Jasmine in wonder. "But now it is broken and dying, and it is spitting out snatches of talk meant to be locked up for-ever. Those buzzing sounds . . . I think they are voices."

"The sounds of centuries of plotting, betrayal, and wickedness, no doubt," said Barda grimly. "I have no wish to hear them."

He leaned over the slowly melting glass and spat on it, his face heavy with hatred. Then he moved to Doom's side.

"Your arms are tired," he said abruptly. "Give me the bellows. We need more heat."

Doom nodded, and Barda took his place beside the forge and began working the bellows steadily.

The glowing coals flared. The crystal began to lose its form and color. There was a faint clicking sound from deep within the clouded glass. Then the red light flickered dimly, and the voice of the Shadow Lord came again.

"The Four Sisters are in place, Slave. The Sisters of the north, south, east, and west. Have you done your part?"

"Oh, yes, Master. Everything you ordered." This voice was different from Prandine's. It was higher and more whining.

An earlier chief advisor to an earlier king or queen, Lief guessed. He felt ill, and began to turn away.

Then he heard something that turned his blood to ice.

"Good. The Sisters will do their work well. And the wretches of Deltora will never know what killed their land, even as they leave it, or die," hissed the voice of the Shadow Lord.

"But you will know, Master. And I," said the other speaker eagerly.

There was a long, low laugh. "You, Drumm? Oh, no. Like all good plans, this will take time to bear fruit. By then, I will have tired of your flattery, and you will be long dead."

Drumm whimpered, but wisely made no other protest.

"I have many plans, Drumm," the harsh, whispering voice went on. "Plans within plans, and all of them with one aim. Deltora must be mine. I need it for the gems and metals beneath its earth, and for its calm southern harbors, perfect for launching ships of war."

"I — I understand, Master," stammered Drumm. "And Deltora *will* be yours, as you wish. The Four Sisters will ensure that — "

"You understand nothing!" hissed the Shadow Lord. "If all goes well, Deltora will be mine without the Sisters' help. I would prefer to take the people alive. Even miserable wretches like them can work, and provide . . . entertainment."

Lief pressed his hand to his mouth to stifle a groan. He felt Jasmine grip his arm, heard Barda and Doom whispering curses. Straining every nerve, he bent towards the melting, collapsing crystal, shut his eyes, and listened.

Barda had let the bellows fall, but the coals still raged with heat, and the hissing voice of the Shadow Lord was growing more faint, more jerky and buzzing every moment.

"But if what that idiot soothsayer dared to say, before I tore out her tongue, is true," the evil whisper went on, "if there should come a time when a king rises from the people, like the accursed Adin, to wear the Belt and overthrow my plans . . . then, Slave, I will have the pleasure of knowing that this king defied me only to watch his land sicken and his people die. And I will have Deltora despite him."

"But — " There was a muffled sound, as if Drumm was clearing his throat nervously. "But, Master, if such a king should ever exist — which of course I hope he will not — perhaps he will hear of the Four Sisters, and try to find and destroy them. The enemy, the upstart whose name you have forbidden me to utter, dared to mark their places on a map, and — "

"That has been dealt with," his Master whispered. "The upstart has the fate he deserves. Also, the map has been removed, and my marks have been put upon it."

"But it was not destroyed!" wailed Drumm. "Surely it should have been — "

Too late he realized he had spoken too hastily. His next sound was a high-pitched scream of agony.

"Do not question my decisions," the voice of the Shadow Lord hissed. "Did you not tell me that you had followed my orders? That the part of the map you were given is safe?"

"Yes, Master, yes!" sobbed Drumm. "It is in a place where it could not be safer. Under my eye — and yours."

"Then this king will never find it. I dare him to try, and go more quickly to his death," sneered his master, and laughed.

The laughter was still echoing in Lief's ears when the glass of the crystal began to boil, and the red light, at last, went out.

✳

. . . this king will never find it. I dare him to try, and go more quickly to his death.

The ancient sneer burned in Lief's mind.

He knew that he was the king who had been foretold by the unfortunate soothsayer. He was the one for whom the Shadow Lord had laid a trap. He was the one who was destined to save his people from tyranny, only to watch them die.

It was long past midnight. The twisted lump of

melted glass that had once been the Enemy's crystal had been cooled, then smashed to powder and trodden underfoot. But the triumph the four companions in the forge should have felt had been snatched away from them.

They knew they should hurry to the palace, ring the bells to signal to the people that they were safe and the crystal had been destroyed. But none of them had the heart to do it.

They wandered into the forge yard and sat down together in the moonlight.

"It seems we keep solving one problem only to be faced with another," said Barda wearily, "It reminds me of those painted wooden birds travelers sometimes show — the ones that you can pull in half. Open one bird and there is a smaller one inside. Open the smaller bird, and you find one still smaller. And so on, until there is a bird no bigger than your thumbnail. And inside that is a tiny egg."

I have many plans. Plans within plans . . .

Lief stiffened. But the voice in his mind was only a memory.

The crystal is destroyed, he reminded himself. *That menace, at least, is gone. My mind is my own again.*

"The Four Sisters," muttered Doom. "Sisters of the north, south, east, and west. It is like a riddle!"

"The man they called enemy and upstart knew the answer, for he drew a map to show where the Sisters were," said Lief. "If only we could find out who he was! Our one clue is that he lived in the time of a chief advisor called Drumm. Josef can surely tell us when that was."

"The man himself is not important, Lief!" exclaimed Jasmine. "The important thing is his map! Drumm had part of it, hidden in a safe place. It may still exist."

"After hundreds of years?" jeered Doom.

"Why not?" Jasmine flashed back. "The palace is *full* of things that have been there for hundreds of years. That is one of the reasons it seems to me a tomb! And surely the palace is where Drumm would have hidden something valuable. He lived there."

"Yes. And he told the Shadow Lord that his part of the map was under his eye," Barda put in.

" 'Under my eye and yours,' " said Lief slowly. "That is what he said."

Suddenly, a startling idea came to him.

He jumped up. His heart had begun to beat very fast.

"And what was under the Shadow Lord's eye?" he exclaimed. "Under the Shadow Lord's eye, as well as Drumm's?"

"Is this another riddle?" growled Barda. "If so, I am in no mood for it."

But Lief was already running towards the forge. In moments he was back, dragging the blackened table frame that had supported the crystal.

"Under their eyes!" he panted. "What else can that mean, but this?"

"But it was in the fire!" cried Jasmine in horror. "If the map was fastened to it — "

Lief shook his head and threw the table frame onto the ground in the full glare of the moonlight.

"Drumm would have been more careful than that," he said. "If the map is in this frame, there must be a secret compartment somewhere."

He crouched and began running his fingers over the scorched wood. In moments Jasmine, Doom, and Barda had joined him.

The search was long. The varnish on the wood had swelled and bubbled in the fire, leaving the surface of the table frame so rough that Lief soon despaired of finding a secret compartment by touch, as he had hoped.

Then Jasmine cried out excitedly. As they all crowded to look, her finger traced a small rectangle on the inside of one of the table legs.

"A piece has been cut away here, then replaced," she said. "Do you see? The patch fits very tightly, but the grain of the wood does not quite match."

Lief, Barda, and Doom stared blankly at the table leg. They could see no change in the grain at all. But none of them doubted Jasmine. She had grown up in the Forests of Silence, and knew trees in all their forms as no one else did.

They watched as she fitted the point of her dagger into the edge of the patch only she could see. Soon a small block of wood had fallen to the ground, and Jasmine was slipping her fingers into the shallow hole now visible in the table leg.

"There is something in here," she whispered. "I — I have it!" Very carefully, she withdrew her fingers.

Between her fingertips was a folded scrap of yellowed paper.

"I cannot believe it," breathed Barda.

Gently, Jasmine unfolded the paper. It was a fragment of map, old and creased but strangely familiar.

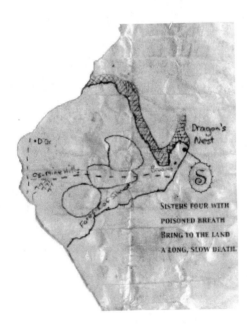

"It is Deltora's east," Lief breathed. He pointed to the large "S" marked on the map fragment. "And that, I imagine, shows where the first Sister lies."

"In a place called Dragon's Nest," said Barda. "I do not like the sound of that."

"It is the rhyme I do not like," said Doom.

And they all stared at the two lines of verse, which had been added to the map in a strange, bold hand.

Sisters four with poisoned breath
Bring to the land a long, slow death.

6 - The Upstart

When Lief, Barda, Jasmine, and Doom at last returned to the palace, they found it ablaze with light. The entrance hall was crowded with waiting people.

Guards and palace workers alike had crept out of their rooms and gathered together as soon as the crystal left the palace. All had stayed awake, to send strength to their king. The story told by the six guards who had run from the forge had only made them more determined to continue their watch.

Lief's heart twisted with pain as he saw the gladness on their faces, heard their shouts of triumph and relief as he told them that the crystal was no more. The yellowed scrap of paper tucked away inside his jacket seemed to burn him. The words of the evil rhyme tormented him.

As the bells began to ring and celebrations began, he slipped away to the new library. It was shadowy and seemed deserted, but a light glowed at the end of the room, from Josef's private chamber.

The old librarian was sitting at his worktable, with his back to the open door.

The table was cluttered with paints and brushes, and a half-completed illustration for a new book lay at Josef's hand. But the brushes were clean, and the jars of paint sealed.

Plainly, Josef had not been working, but had been sitting at the table out of habit. He, too, had been keeping watch.

Lief knocked gently on the edge of the door. Josef turned stiffly in his chair, frowning slightly. When he saw who his visitor was, however, his face broke into a radiant smile.

"Your majesty!" he cried, struggling to his feet. "I thought it was Paff. How wonderful to see you safe! I knew you would succeed!"

"It was thanks to you that I dared to try," Lief answered.

He moved into the room and took the old man's outstretched hands, shaking them warmly. Then he hesitated, not quite knowing how to go on.

"Josef, there is something I need to — " he began.

"I know," Josef broke in. "Ever since I first heard

the bells I have been thinking about it. And — you will be surprised — I have decided that we should stay where we are."

He saw Lief's confusion and looked surprised. "Did you not mean to ask me about the library, your majesty?" he asked. "About moving it back to the third floor, now that the menace has been removed?"

"Oh, yes, that, too, Josef, of course," said Lief hastily and quite untruthfully.

"It has taken a very long time to move all the books downstairs," Josef said. "I cannot bear the thought of carrying them all back again. Paff tries her best, I daresay, but I fear she will never be half the assistant Ranesh was. And she *chatters* so!"

Lief smiled, despite his impatience. Paff annoyed him, too, though at the same time he felt rather sorry for her. Josef was not much of a companion for a young girl.

But when Ranesh, Josef's foster son, had left Del and gone to the west to marry his true love, Marilen, Paff had timidly come forward and asked if she could replace him.

Josef had been pleased enough to have her. Paff could read and write, which was sadly uncommon among the young people who had grown up under the rule of the Shadow Lord. And there had been no other applicants for the job.

No wonder, thought Lief. Everyone knew that Josef was a fussy and demanding employer. But Paff, a released prisoner from the Shadowlands and the only surviving member of her family, had been anxious to find work as quickly as possible.

"At least Paff is hardworking, Josef," Lief said soothingly. "And we could give you other help to move again. Are you sure about staying here? I know how much you miss the old library."

Josef shrugged and grimaced. "I have complained very much, I know," he said. "I am too set in my ways. The fact is, your majesty, in the past weeks I have realized how isolated we were on the third floor. Here, we are in the thick of things. I think that the library will have many more visitors if it is placed where everyone can see it."

"That is certainly true," said Lief heartily. "Well, then, that is settled. Now . . . Josef, can you help me with some — some research I have to do, about Deltora's past?"

"Why certainly!" beamed Josef, rubbing his hands delightedly. "How can I be of service?"

"First, I need to find out when a chief advisor called Drumm lived," Lief said. "Do you know of him?"

Josef frowned. "I know the name. I just cannot recall where I have seen it," he muttered in annoyance. "But I will soon find it in the *Annals*, your majesty, never fear."

He began shuffling rapidly to the door.

Lief caught his arm. "Not now, Josef. It is late,

and we must both get some sleep. In the morning, perhaps. But here is something else to think about. Have you ever heard the phrase 'The Four Sisters'?"

"Ah!" Josef's face brightened. "Why, of course! *The Four Sisters* is an old Jalis legend — one of the Tenna Birdsong tales. It is about four sisters who loved to sing together. They sang so sweetly that they annoyed a wicked sorcerer, who banished them to the four corners of the land. But still they sang to one another, though they were far apart."

Lief nodded gloomily. *No doubt the Shadow Lord thought it amusing to name his sources of poison after four sweet sisters in an old Deltoran folk story,* he thought. *But this does not take me much further.*

"Yes, *The Four Sisters*. A charming little story, as I recall," Josef chattered on eagerly. "I have not read it for years, but planned to do so very soon, to see if it is worthy of inclusion in *Tales of Deltora* — my new book, you know. I will look it up for you now!"

This time he would not be stopped. He hurried out of his room and, with Lief following reluctantly, hastened to the shelf where the *Deltora Annals* stood.

Pulling the first thick volume from the shelf, he began leafing through it.

Suddenly, Lief could not bear it. He was bone weary, and even to please Josef he knew he could not stand and read an old folktale now.

Firmly he put his hand on the old man's, to stop the restless flipping of pages.

"Not now, Josef, please," he said. "I will look at the story in the — His voice broke off as, suddenly, his stomach seemed to turn over.

He was aware of Josef looking at him in puzzlement, but for a moment he could not speak. He stared down at the closely printed page on which his and Josef's hands rested. Was it a coincidence? Could it be . . . ?

"What is it, your majesty?" Josef asked nervously.

Slowly Lief straightened. He slipped his hand into his inside jacket pocket, and brought out the torn part of the map.

"Josef," he said, trying to control the excitement in his voice. "Before I show you this, you must promise me that you will speak of it to no one."

Josef bit his lip. "I know I have let my tongue run away with me in the past, your majesty," he mumbled. "But I have learned my lesson, I swear it. Any secret you share with me now, I will take to my grave."

"I hope it will not come to that," said Lief lightly. And, still wondering if he was doing the right thing, he unfolded the map.

Josef's eyes widened. "Why, how did you come by this!" he exclaimed in excitement.

"You recognize this paper?" Lief asked quietly.

"Of course!" Josef cried, touching the map with reverent fingers. "Doran the Dragonlover's mapping style is unmistakable! Ah, but what a tragedy that only a fragment remains."

Lief stared at him in astonishment. This was not what he had been expecting the old man to say. But . . . Doran the Dragonlover! Of course!

That was why the markings on the fragment of map — all but the verse — had looked familiar. They were almost exactly like those on the map of Dragon Territories Josef had shown him just before the meeting.

"What a fool I was not to have seen it," he murmured.

But Josef was not listening. His eyes had moved to the verse printed at the bottom of the paper.

"Not only has it been torn, but someone has dared to scrawl their own words here!" he said furiously. "What is this drivel? *'Sisters four with poisoned breath, Bring to the land a long, slow —'* "

He stopped, his mouth gaping. He swallowed hard.

"Four sisters," he whispered. "The Four Sisters . . . Doran . . . Oh, how could I have forgotten? Why did I not think of it! How could I — "

Frantically he pulled the fifth volume of the *Deltora Annals* from the shelf. He flipped through the pages until he came to the Dragon Territories map. Then he slowed, and began turning the pages more carefully.

"Josef, what are you looking for?" demanded Lief in a fever of impatience.

But still the old librarian did not answer. He was muttering to himself, completely wrapped up in his own thoughts.

"Now, where is it?" he said, glancing rapidly at every page. "It cannot be far now. Not far now . . . Aha!"

Recklessly he pressed the book wide open and pointed triumphantly at the left-hand page, which was covered with Doran's writing.

"Here it is!" he said. "Doran's final entry in the *Annals*. Read it!"

"Josef, what—?" Lief began.

"Read it!" roared Josef, his eyes wild. "Read all of it! You will see!"

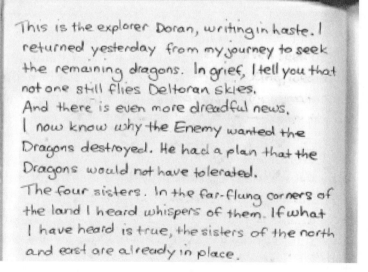

This is the explorer Doran, writing in haste. I returned yesterday from my journey to seek the remaining dragons. In grief, I tell you that not one still flies Deltoran skies.
And there is even more dreadful news.
I now know why the Enemy wanted the Dragons destroyed. He had a plan that the Dragons would not have tolerated.
The four sisters. In the far-flung corners of the land I heard whispers of them. If what I have heard is true, the sisters of the north and east are already in place.

The south, and the west, will surely be next, and I can guess where, if the rumours of the locations of the others are to be believed.

Whoever reads my words, show them to the King if you can. The King, wearing the Belt of Deltora, is Deltora's only salvation now. No-one will listen to me. They think I am mad. I hurried to Del without pausing to eat, wash or sleep. To these palace fools, with their soft hands and painted faces, I look like a wild man.

I must set out once more, to seek proof of what I say. Another long journey... perhaps my last, for I fear the Enemy is aware of me.

If I do not return, seek me where the Four Sisters lurk...

That was all. On the opposite page there was only a beautifully neat report of a palace dinner, written by one of the librarians. Heading the list of people who attended was the name of Drumm, the king's chief advisor.

Lief felt sick.

"Doran's words are wild, I know," said Josef softly. "It was said that his last, hopeless dragon hunt had sent him mad with grief. There are many references to it, later in the *Annals*. The thought of it always grieved Ranesh and me very much. Doran was a great man."

"Indeed he was," said Lief, looking down at the hastily written words. His stomach was churning as he imagined the desperation of the man who had written them. "And he was not mad, Josef. Unless being the only one to see the truth is a kind of madness."

He pressed the book even further open and pointed to a few tiny, jagged rags of paper clinging to the binding.

"Look," he said softly.

Josef squinted shortsightedly, then recoiled.

"But — but it looks as if a page has been torn out here!" he exclaimed. "That is impossible! Once a thing was written into the *Annals*, it was written! It was strictly forbidden for anything to be removed."

"Drumm would not have cared what was *forbidden*," said Lief. "He was following the Shadow Lord's orders. I think this is part of the missing page."

He put the fragment of Doran's map on top of the open book. It was clear at once that the thick, yellowed paper of the map was the same as the paper used in the *Annals*.

Josef stared, aghast. "Doran drew a map on the page opposite his words, to show where he thought the four sisters lurked," he breathed. "And that page was torn out! No doubt very soon after he wrote it, too, because the back of the map is blank. But how did you know?"

"I only suspected," Lief said. "When you were looking for the story of the Four Sisters, I realized that the paper of the map was the same as the paper always used in the *Annals*. It could have been chance — but it was not."

Again he stared at the final lines of Doran's message.

. . . the Enemy is aware of me . . .

He swallowed. "You said that this was Doran's last entry in the *Deltora Annals*?"

"Oh, yes," said Josef unhappily. "He set out to find the Four Sisters of whom he speaks. But he never returned, and no one knew where to look for him. He was never seen again."

7 ~ Dragon Hunt

A few days later, Lief, Barda, and Jasmine set out from Del on horseback, accompanied by a troop of palace guards. Lief carried with him both the fragment found in the table frame and Josef's precious copy of Doran's Dragon Territories map.

As far as the people of the city knew, their king and his companions were going on their long-delayed tour of the kingdom, beginning in Broome, far to the east.

Only Doom and Josef knew their real purpose. To find the Sister of the East at Dragon's Nest, to destroy it if they could, and perhaps, through knowledge of it, to guess at the hiding places of the other three Sisters.

"I would give much to be going with you,"

Doom said as he farewelled them at the city gates. "But someone must stay to deal with things here."

His mouth twisted in the familiar mocking smile.

"And in any case, the three of you have done well enough without me in the past," he added. "I might spoil your luck."

"I doubt it," said Lief, clasping his hand warmly. He knew what it cost Doom to jest at this moment.

They were now all convinced that the kingdom's future hung on this perilous quest. Hundreds of last-minute words of advice and warning must have been trembling on Doom's tongue. But he held them back.

He knew that nothing he could say could help Lief, Barda, and Jasmine now. He could only offer them his trust.

At a shout from Barda, the guards moved off, their heavy gray horses breaking into a steady trot.

With Kree swooping above them, the three companions followed. Their lighter, faster mounts, carefully chosen by Barda, snorted with pleasure, puffing mist into the crisp dawn air.

Lief rode Honey, a spirited golden mare with a flowing white tail and mane. Barda rode his favorite, a strong, sweet-tempered chestnut called Bella. Jasmine's horse was the coal-black Swift.

Lief looked back, lifted his arm to return Doom's wave, and felt a pang of guilt.

"Cheer up. What Doom does not know will not hurt him," said Jasmine's voice beside him.

Jasmine was grinning, relishing her freedom from the city. Her long black hair was already tangling in the breeze. Filli peeped out from under her jacket. His tiny paws were clutching her collar tightly, and his black eyes were very wide. Plainly, he found horse-riding very alarming.

"I am leading you into danger," Lief muttered. "And you are Doom's child."

"Quite!" Jasmine snapped, her grin disappearing. "Like father, like daughter. Have you ever known Doom to tell all his secrets? Or to shrink from peril, for any reason?"

Lief said nothing. The relationship between Jasmine and her father, that strange mixture of love, respect, and rivalry, was something he would never understand.

"Besides," Jasmine said, in a milder tone, "Doom thinks we are going directly to Dragon's Nest. There we will be facing the Shadow Lord's evil. Nothing we could do on the way could be more dangerous than that."

Lief was not so sure. He fought back a shudder as he remembered . . .

Barda rode up on his left. "As soon as we are well out of sight of Del, I will give the order to turn north," he said in a low voice. "If you are still determined to do this, Lief."

Lief moistened his lips. "I am," he said. "I feel it is the only thing that might help us. We need a weapon the Shadow Lord did not plan for. Powerful as the Belt of Deltora is, it may not be enough."

"Very well," Barda said grimly. "North it is. To the Os-Mine Hills. And the dragon."

✳

A day and a half later, they left their horses and the confused, nervous guards in a grassy space sheltered by the first rocky slopes of the Os-Mine Hills. Barda had put his men under the orders of Brid, his second in command, telling them that he, Lief, and Jasmine wished to walk into the Hills alone, to gather healing herbs.

"Did you have to tell that story?" hissed Jasmine as the three companions tramped away, the guards staring after them. "Herbs! Now Brid and the others will think this trip to the Os-Mine Hills is my fault! Already most of them believe I am a witch because I speak to birds and trees. Now, no doubt, they think I need rare ingredients for my spells."

Barda shrugged. "All the better," he said. "The important thing is that they do not suspect our real reason for being here."

"Why can't we just tell them the truth?" Jasmine exclaimed. "They will find out soon enough, if we come back to them leading a golden dragon!"

"*Leading* it?" growled Barda. "It is more likely that we will be running from it in terror."

"We have to keep the entrance to the underground world secret, Jasmine, you know that!" said Lief. "And, in any case, the guards would panic if they knew what we planned. Dragons have an evil reputation. If the topaz dragon *does* rise, and *does* agree to help us fight the Sister of the East, it must seem a complete surprise."

"It *will* be a great surprise, as far as I am concerned, if the dragon does anything but try to eat us," Barda snorted. "That is, if it wakes at all."

"It will wake," said Lief, with a confidence he did not feel. "The presence of the Belt of Deltora in its territory will make it stir. I am sure of it."

"I am hoping that the Belt will also protect us from our old friends the Granous," Barda said. "It has killed evil creatures before, at the height of its power."

Lief remembered the sharp yellow teeth and stinking breath of the bloodthirsty, game-playing creatures that hunted in packs over these hills.

He did not relish the idea of becoming a prisoner of the Granous again. But he knew he could not depend on the Belt to save him.

"The Granous are wicked, but they are not creatures of the Shadow Lord," he said in a low voice. "They are of Deltora. The Belt may weaken them, but that is all, I fear."

They had walked for an hour. The sun was high in the sky when Jasmine stopped abruptly, lifted her head, and seemed to listen.

"What is it?" Lief whispered.

Jasmine murmured to Kree, and the black bird took flight. He wheeled overhead, and in moments was back on Jasmine's shoulder, squawking rapidly.

"Granous," Jasmine said briefly. "In a clearing not far over the next rise."

"We must find a way around them," said Barda. "We cannot afford a fight now. Tell Kree — "

He and Lief froze as suddenly a wail of terror echoed through the hills.

"If we are careful, the creatures will not hear us, or smell us either," Jasmine said calmly. "They are well occupied. They already have a prisoner."

Her companions stared at her in dismay.

She met their eyes coolly. "It is good fortune for us," she said. "We would be well advised not to interfere."

"But we cannot knowingly leave someone at the mercy of the Granous!" Lief hissed. "They will ask him their infernal riddles, and when he cannot answer them they will start biting off his fingers and toes. They will kill him, Jasmine!"

"Better that they kill a stranger than that they kill us," Jasmine said. And Lief knew that she was repeating a lesson she had learned only too well in the terror that was the Forests of Silence.

For a moment he hesitated. He knew that he should not let his heart rule his head in this. But then the piteous cry came again, followed by a scream of pure agony.

"No!" Lief breathed. He started forward.

"Wait! I will go back and fetch the guards," said Barda, catching at his arm.

Lief pulled himself free. "There is no time for that!" he muttered. "Come with me or not, as you like."

He began to run, and Jasmine and Barda followed, as he knew they would.

Panting, the three scrambled up the next hill. When they reached the top they flattened themselves on the ground and crawled forward until they could see the ground below.

The other side of the hill fell away into a treacherous, pebbly slope ending in a tumble of parched rocks. Beyond that was a grove of stunted trees, from which came the faint sounds of moaning and sobbing mingled with rough laughter.

They began picking their way down the slope. Their progress was agonizingly slow. The sounds from the trees were growing louder and more disturbing.

Lief's heart was pounding. He was sickened by the thought of what was happening in the grove. As soon as he reached level ground and the trees were straight ahead, he reached for his sword.

"Do not even *think* of charging in there, Lief!"

Barda whispered fiercely in his ear. "We will have no chance in hand-to-hand combat with twelve Granous! We must try to separate them."

Lief gritted his teeth and nodded. Desperate as he was to free the sobbing, groaning man within the grove, he knew that Barda was right.

"Jasmine, you come with me," Barda ordered. "We will try to lure some of them away. Lief, there is probably a clearing in the center of the grove. Move around it and get behind the prisoner. Cut his bonds if you can, but keep out of sight until I give the signal."

They separated. Lief crept around the trees until, through a gap, he saw movement. He moved in a little, and his stomach turned over as he suddenly gained a clear view of what was happening in the clearing.

The Granous were gathered around someone who was sitting at the clearing's edge. Their shaggy gray bodies almost hid their victim. Lief could only see a mop of curly brown hair, hunched shoulders shrouded in a brown cloak, and a hand clutching another hand, from which bright red blood streamed.

"Time for the next question!" the biggest of the Granous cackled. "Another question, another finger!"

The others danced backwards, screaming with pleasure and snapping their jaws. Then Lief saw the sobbing victim clearly for the first time.

He was sitting propped against a tree, bound in place by strong vines. From the waist up, he looked like a man. But from the waist down he was covered in thick brown fur, and he had delicate, pointed black hoofs instead of feet.

Astounded, Lief realized that he was looking at a being he had thought was merely a legend. The Granous had captured a Capricon.

8 - Deadly Games

The Granous pack was still shrieking and howling. Taking advantage of the noise, Lief slipped quickly through the trees, circling until he was directly behind the bound Capricon.

He took out his knife, lay down, and wriggled through the undergrowth. Soon he was pressed against the back of the tree to which the Capricon was tied.

The tree trunk was broad and hid him well, but in turn he could see nothing. The noise in the clearing was dying down. He knew he had to find out where all the Granous were before trying to cut the vines.

A straggly bush grew beside the tree. Lief eased himself to his knees. He peered cautiously around the tree, using the sparse branches of the bush as a screen.

The head Granous was squatting on the ground in front of its prisoner, arranging something in the dust.

"Very well then, creature," it cackled after a moment, shuffling back. "Are you ready for your next question?"

The Capricon moaned and struggled vainly. Lief saw that the Granous had arranged some sticks in the dust, to make a crude fish shape.

"Here is a fish from our stream," said the Granous, flexing its thin, wiry fingers. "There are precious few of them, but this is one."

The other Granous tittered.

"Now," their leader said. "This fish is swimming to the left. If it goes on doing that, it will escape our nets, and we do not want that. Do we, friends?"

"Oh, no!" chorused the other Granous, grinning hideously.

"So, creature," said the head Granous. "By moving three sticks — no more, no less — you must make our fish turn around so it is swimming to the right."

The Capricon moaned, shaking his head help-lessly.

The Granous laughed and snapped their jaws.

His mind racing, Lief eased himself back behind the tree and began sawing at the vines. They were very tough, and there were three lengths, knotted separately so that if one broke, the others would still hold.

He was sure that the Capricon would feel what he was doing, and prayed that he would make no sign. But the prisoner was too panic-stricken, it seemed, to notice anything. The low moaning did not change or falter.

"Don't give up so easily!" Lief heard the head Granous jeer.

"Please!" mumbled the Capricon. "Please . . ."

One vine was almost cut through. Leaving a few strands in place so that the bond would not fall and alert the enemy, Lief began on the next.

"You have till we count to twenty to solve the puzzle," said the Granous. "As before, if you do not solve it, the penalty is one finger. Ready? Go!"

The other Granous began to chant. "Twenty. Nineteen. Eighteen . . ."

Lief risked another glimpse around the tree.

The Capricon was gaping wildly at the diagram. Clearly he did not have the faintest idea how to solve the puzzle.

The Granous shouted and stamped. "Fourteen. Thirteen . . ."

Grinning, their leader turned and began triumphantly conducting them. Their eyes were fixed on him.

None of them are watching, Lief thought. *Now is our chance. But I will never cut these vines in time!*

He stared at the diagram, forcing himself to think.

"Ten. Nine. Eight . . ."

Then, suddenly, Lief saw the answer. Recklessly he leaned forward and whispered in the Capricon's ear. The Capricon jumped and cried out in shock.

Luckily the Granous were too busy stamping and counting to notice.

"Do as I say!" Lief whispered urgently. "Make haste!"

But the Capricon, whimpering and trembling, seemed unable to move.

"Six. Five . . ."

Abandoning all caution, Lief ducked out of cover, reached forward, and rearranged the sticks himself.

"THREE! TWO!"

Lief jerked back behind the bush with a split second to spare. The lead Granous turned around, sharp, yellow teeth grinning and snapping.

"ONE! . . . Oh!"

The pack howled in disappointment as they saw that the stick fish was now facing to the right. Shallow grooves in the dust showed where the three moved sticks had been.

The head Granous lumbered forward. Gnawing at one of its grimy yellow nails, it stared down at the diagram. Then it looked suspiciously at the prisoner, who was cringing against the tree trunk.

"You cheated!" it accused. "The penalty for cheating is five fingers!"

"No!" the Capricon wailed, cradling his injured hand. "No, please! It wasn't my fault! It was . . ." He half-turned to look behind him.

Lief stiffened.

"Get on with the game!" shouted one of the pack.

"The game! The game!" chanted all the others.

Furiously, the head Granous kicked the sticks aside, showering the Capricon with dust.

"The next puzzle will not be so easy, creature," it

growled. Then it turned and slouched out of Lief's sight.

Lief began cutting the second vine, every now and then peeping out at the clearing.

The other Granous waited, muttering to one another in low voices. Then there was a sound from the trees at the other end of the clearing. They all swung around to look, and two went to investigate, quickly disappearing into the undergrowth.

Lief left a few strands of the second vine, to hold it in place, and began on the third. This time the Capricon felt it and whimpered.

"Be quiet!" whispered Lief, sawing desperately. "I am releasing you!"

He heard a chorus of rasping calls and again peered through the bush. The Granous had all moved to the other end of the clearing and were calling their invisible companions. When no answer came, two more lumbered into the trees.

Jasmine and Barda are doing well, Lief thought.

But there were still seven Granous in the clearing — eight, counting the leader.

Too many. Far too many to fight.

He returned to his work with new energy. When the third vine was almost cut through he moved to look through the bush once more.

The head Granous was returning with something clutched in its hand.

"I have cut the vines almost through," Lief

breathed to the Capricon. "Stay absolutely still or you will break them and alert the Granous. But when I give the signal, leap up and run!"

"I cannot run!" whimpered the prisoner. "They bit off my finger! I am in agony!"

"There will be far worse pain for you if you stay here," Lief whispered furiously. "And keep your voice down!"

The head Granous reached the tree and stood grinning at his cowering prisoner.

"One of our visitors left this trinket with us," he said with an evil grin, holding out a small wooden box, richly carved and painted in a complicated pattern of scarlet and gold. "All you have to do is open it. We humble Granous have never found the trick. But I am sure a fine, clever creature like you can do it with ease."

He leaned forward and tossed the box into the Capricon's lap.

"No!" screamed the Capricon, throwing himself violently to one side. The weakened vines snapped and fell in a tangled heap into the dust.

The Granous roared in surprise and anger. The Capricon clawed at the bush that was Lief's shelter, bending and breaking the flimsy branches.

"Save me!" he screamed. "Save me!"

Lief tried to scramble back, but the Capricon caught his cloak and held it fast, sobbing and crying.

"Enemy!" howled the Granous. It hurled itself forward, snapping and snarling.

In dismay, Lief felt wiry fingers fasten on his ankle. He was jerked backwards with such tremendous force that he could do nothing to save himself.

The next moment he was lying dazed in the clearing, with the hot, foul breath of the Granous in his face and the great weight of its body on his chest, pinning down his arms.

The rest of the pack had come running and now stood in a tight circle around their leader and his captive.

Two of them had seized the Capricon, who sagged motionless between them. His head hung down, so that Lief could see the small horns beneath his curly hair. His eyes were closed.

The head Granous bent lower, its wet, black nose snuffling in Lief's face, its tiny eyes burning with fury.

"I have seen you before," it snarled. "You are the one who calls himself king. The one who made fools of us before! Well, you will never make fools of us again, king!"

It bared its sharp, yellow teeth.

It is going to kill me here and now, Lief thought.

His numbed fingers tightened on the Belt at his waist. He focused his mind on it, and with all his strength, called on the power of the gems.

Help me!

The Granous jerked back as if it had been stung. It glared at Lief for a moment, then its eyes narrowed.

"Now I know how you escaped us the first time," it hissed. "You cheated! You are carrying powerful magic. But you will not escape again. This time you are alone, and it is twelve against one. No talisman can save you."

Only then did Lief think again of Jasmine and Barda. Were they safe? Were they even now watching from the trees, trying to think of a way to rescue him?

Stay back, he begged them silently. *There are still too many of them. I insisted on coming here. Now I must pay the penalty. But while you live there is a chance that the Belt of Deltora at least can be saved.*

The other Granous shuffled. "Four of the pack went into the trees and did not come back," one growled nervously. "If this king has enchanted them . . ."

Their leader looked up with a snarl. "His sorcery does not frighten me," it snapped. "Watch me tear out his throat!"

Then, abruptly, its eyes widened in alarm. "Beware!" it roared. "Enemies behind you!"

But already two of the shaggy beasts, the two that held the Capricon, were falling to their knees, mortally wounded.

Dark blood dripping from their weapons, Jasmine and Barda leaped back and faced the rest.

"Kill them!" roared the Granous leader.

Save them! Help me!

The Belt grew hot under Lief's hands.

There was a tearing crash in the distance, and suddenly the sky overhead was filled with birds, tens of thousands of birds. The hills echoed with their panicking cries and the sound of their frantically beating wings.

The other Granous howled and covered their faces, but their leader did not falter.

"Die, sorcerer!" it hissed. It bared its dripping teeth again, its lips drawn back so far that Lief could see its black gums.

The birds scattered. The sky darkened. There was a thundering roar. Something huge plunged downward.

The Granous leader looked up and screamed.

Lief caught a terrifying glimpse of vast golden claws, heard the beating of mighty wings.

And the Granous was plucked, shrieking, up into the sky.

9 - The Golden Eye

Lief crawled to his feet. Terrified and leaderless, the Granous pack had fled. The Capricon lay motionless in the dust. Only Barda and Jasmine remained standing in the clearing.

They staggered over to Lief, and the three clung together for a moment, deeply shaken.

"The dragon," whispered Jasmine at last. "It broke through the forest canopy, and came . . ."

"It was the Belt," Lief said. His voice sounded hollow and strange to his ears. "The Belt called to it."

As he spoke, he looked up. The topaz dragon was perched on the top of the next hill, like a bird on a tree. It was eating.

Lief shuddered.

"Do you think it will come back?" Barda muttered. "Perhaps we should — "

On the ground at their feet, the Capricon stirred and moaned. Jasmine knelt down beside him.

"We can do nothing until I have bandaged his wound," she said. "He has already lost much blood. It would be a pity if he died, since we nearly killed ourselves to save him."

Calmly she inspected the injured hand. The little finger was just a ragged stump, now once again bleeding freely. She pulled out her water flask and began to clean the wound.

Lief felt queasy, and turned away.

"He is a strange-looking being. What is he?" Jasmine asked in a low voice.

"A Capricon," said Barda. "The first I have seen with my own eyes, though I have met travelers who told of sighting small groups of them in the mountains of the east."

"Are they wanderers, then?" Jasmine asked.

Lief wondered if she was trying to keep her mind from her gruesome task with these questions.

Probably not. Jasmine was never squeamish. More likely she was trying not to think of the dragon still feasting on the next hill.

Determinedly, he turned back to face her. He, too, preferred not to think of the dragon.

"The Capricons are wanderers now," Barda said. "Those who are left. But it is said that once they lived in a rose-pink city called Capra, the most beautiful city in the east. The people of Broome claim that their city is built on Capra's ruins, but I do not know if that is true."

"I wonder why the Capricons left their home," Jasmine said as she smeared ointment on the ghastly wound and quickly began to bandage it.

"Perhaps they were driven out by servants of the Shadow Lord, as the people of the City of the Rats were," murmured Lief.

"For what purpose?" Jasmine tied the bandage firmly and sat back on her heels with a sigh.

"Who knows?" Lief said, his eyes on the dragon. "We might as well ask why the Shadow Lord wanted the City of the Rats to be abandoned. He could just as well have enslaved the people there as anywhere else."

Barda shrugged. "In any case, it is ancient history. It is said that Capra was in ruins before Adin made the Belt of Deltora, and Capricons have always held themselves apart. Little is known of them."

"Dragons," mumbled the Capricon. "Dragons took Capra from us."

His eyes fluttered open. They were a deep, violet blue, glazed with shock and confusion.

"Once the Capricons were many," he said thickly. "Once we were a great people, with a great city. But the dragons envied us. They wanted Capra for their own, because it was rich and beautiful. So they attacked again and again, killing and destroying, till at last the Capricons were driven out, and Capra was in ruins . . ."

His voice trailed off. He lifted his bandaged hand and stared at it dazedly. "I . . . I am hurt," he stammered. "How have I . . . ?"

Then his face changed as memory slowly returned. He began to tremble.

"I came from the mountains of the east, to seek help from the king," he murmured. "Help for my people . . ."

Kree landed on Jasmine's arm with a warning squawk. She looked up.

Lief glanced up, too, and his heart pounded as he saw that the dragon, its meal finished, had turned in their direction, and was spreading its wings.

"Barda," he said urgently. "You and Jasmine move into the trees. Take our friend — "

"I am Rolf," the Capricon broke in. "Rolf, eldest son of the clan Dowyn, heir to the lordship of Capra. I — "

Without ceremony, Barda hauled him up and began dragging him out of the clearing, his hoofs trailing in the dust.

Jasmine remained where she was, her eyes fixed to the sky. Filli, too, was looking up, chattering fearfully. Jasmine murmured to him, and he crept beneath her collar. But Kree stayed on her arm, still as a statue.

"Jasmine — " Lief began.

She shook her head. "I am not leaving you, Lief,"

she said. "Do not waste energy arguing with me. Be ready!"

Lief looked up again, and for a wild moment could see nothing but empty sky.

Yet the dragon was coming. He knew it. He could hear the beating of its wings. He could see the treetops thrashing and the leaves flying, as if tossed by a gale.

The clearing darkened as something blocked the sun. Lief's eyes strained as he searched for the shape he knew he must find.

Then, with a thrill of awe and terror, he saw it.

The golden dragon was hovering directly above the clearing, huge and menacing. Its whole underside was pale blue, blending perfectly with the afternoon sky, so that from below it was almost invisible.

As Lief watched, it began to sink lower, lower, its wings beating lazily, its terrible talons spread.

The Belt of Deltora seemed to throb in time to the wingbeats. Lief tore his eyes from the dragon and looked down. The topaz was gleaming like the sun.

His head was spinning. Dimly he realized that he had been holding his breath. He forced himself to breathe out, take in more air.

Dust was swirling around him. He felt Jasmine grip his arm, heard her shouting over the roaring of the wind, but he could not understand what she wanted of him.

There was a blur of black in front of him. It

was Kree screeching, wings beating on his face. And now Jasmine was in front of him, too, pushing him, screaming at him. Confused, he stumbled back, back to the edge of the clearing.

And only when he found himself pressed against the tree to which the Capricon had been bound did he realize why Jasmine had wanted him to move. Only then did he raise his head, just in time to see the vast beast land, settling onto the dust, curling its tail around its huge body, completely filling the clearing with a blinding shimmer of gold.

The dragon turned its massive head and fixed him with a golden eye. Lief felt himself captured, held. He could not look away.

"You wear the Belt of the ancients," the dragon said. "The great topaz shines for you. I feel its power flowing into me, like new blood in my veins. You are the king who was promised."

The words vibrated in Lief's ears, hollow and echoing as if rising from a deep well. He could see his own reflection in the dragon's eye, drifting there like a small, lonely creature drowning in an ancient sea.

In his mind there was no thought. Everything he had planned to say had vanished from his mind.

The dragon blinked, and the spell was broken. Suddenly freed, Lief gasped and staggered.

"I have slept long, and in my sleep I dreamed," the dragon said. "My dreams were good dreams of times as they once were, when the skies were free and the air of my domain was sweet. Now you have awoken me — to this!"

Its black, forked tongue flickered out, tasting the air. "The land is not well. I feel an evil presence, poison leaking into the earth from some dark center. Who has done this, while I slept?"

"The Enemy from the Shadowlands," Lief said huskily. "The Enemy whose creatures destroyed your race, long ago."

The flat, golden eye regarded him coldly. "My race was not destroyed," the dragon said. "Am I not here? Do you think *I* am a dream?"

Lief stared, not knowing what to say.

Thoughtfully the dragon raised a claw and picked a small piece of bone from between its sharp, white teeth.

"The topaz you wear has given me new life, but my long sleep has left my body weak," it said. "One Granous has done little to satisfy my hunger. But when I have fed well and gathered strength, I will search out this evil thing that lies in my land like a worm in a bud, and I will destroy it, if I can."

Lief's heart leaped.

"There is more than one," he said eagerly. "There are four — called the Four Sisters by the Enemy. And we already know where one of them lies. It is on the east coast, in a place called Dragon's Nest."

The dragon's eyes seemed to glaze. "The east

coast is the territory of the ruby, and not my concern," it said.

The blood rushed to Lief's face. "But surely the whole of Deltora is your concern!" he exclaimed. "As it is mine!"

The dragon's terrible jaws gaped wide. Jasmine cried out in warning and reached for her dagger. But then it became clear that the beast was only yawning.

"The territory of the ruby is not my concern," it repeated at last. "Even if I wished to enter it, I could not do so without breaking the oath I swore before I slept. And I cannot break my oath, for I swore it by my blood, and by my teeth, and by my young as yet unborn, to the man called Dragonfriend."

Hearing Lief's cry of astonishment, it seemed to smile. "Do you know of Dragonfriend?" it asked. "The one your people called the Dragonlover?"

"Of — of course!" Lief stammered. "But — "

"Seven savage enemies prowled our skies in those days," the dragon said. "Together they hunted us. They killed and killed again till at last it came to pass that I was the only one left of all my tribe. Dragonfriend came to me in my loneliness. He said that each of the other dragon tribes had suffered the same fate."

"You mean — only one dragon remained from each of the seven tribes?" Lief burst out.

The dragon moved restlessly. "So Dragonfriend

told me, and so I believed, for I had known him of old, and he had never lied to me."

The golden eye flicked in Lief's direction. Lief swallowed and nodded.

"Dragonfriend had made a plan to preserve our lives," the dragon went on. "He was wise in our ways. He knew that dragons can sleep for centuries, if they must. He said that I and the other six should hide ourselves from the Enemy and let sleep embrace us until it was safe to wake."

"But how — how would you know when it was safe?" Jasmine asked. "What was to stop you sleeping forever?"

The dragon turned its cold gaze upon her. Lief saw the flat, golden eye dwelling with interest on her flowing hair, and wished she had not spoken.

"Dragonfriend said that one day each of us would be called by the great gem of our own territory," the dragon said. "He said the call would only come when the heir of the ancient king Adin was near us, wearing the Belt of Power. For that would mean that the Shadow Lord had been defeated and his creatures banished from our skies."

"So the seven of you slept," Lief breathed. "And — you each swore not to take advantage of another's sleep to invade its land."

"That is so," said the dragon. "And I will not break my oath. If you wish to seek the evil at Dragon's

Nest, you must rouse the dragon of the ruby to help you."

"But what if the ruby dragon cannot be found?" Lief asked desperately. "What if it is unwilling? Or dead? Will you come to me then?"

The dragon closed its eyes. After a long moment it opened them again. "If it cannot be found, or if it is unwilling, the oath to Dragonfriend must stand. If it is dead . . . then we shall see."

10 ~ A Change of Plans

Night was falling by the time Lief, Jasmine, and Barda half-carried Rolf the Capricon out of the Os-Mine foothills and back to their camp.

Even on the plain, the howls of Granous being hunted by the ravenous dragon drifted on the air. The companions were not surprised to find the horses snorting and restless and the guards huddled together over a huge fire, weapons and torches at the ready.

From the shelter of the trees around the clearing, Rolf had caught a glimpse of the dragon. From that moment he had retreated into shocked silence. The pain from his wounded hand and the ghastly cries that had rung in their ears on their downward trek had made matters worse.

Now his eyes were glassy, he trembled continually, and his legs seemed to have lost the power to support him. He paid no attention at all to the curious stares of the guards as he was helped into the camp.

"Put him by the fire," Jasmine said in a low voice. "I will make a brew to ease his pain."

"If it will make him sleep, too, all the better," Barda muttered. "I do not want him babbling of dragons to the men. They are nervous enough as it is."

The guards, mightily relieved to have their chief and their king back safely, and satisfied with Barda's mutterings of noisy wolves in the Hills, settled to preparing their meal.

The Capricon drank half a cup of the herbal tea Jasmine held to his lips, and fell into an exhausted sleep. At last, the sounds from the Hills died away.

"Our scaly friend seems to have decided it has eaten enough for one day," Barda said, slumping down in front of the fire with his companions.

"It is just too dark for it to see its prey," Jasmine said. "That beast did not look to me as if it would ever have enough of feasting."

"What will happen, then, when it has eaten all the Granous in the Hills?" growled Barda.

Lief felt a chill, but shook his head determinedly. "There are many Granous," he said. "They bred to plague proportions while the dragon slept."

"Perhaps. But who is to say it does not like to vary its diet sometimes?" said Jasmine. "Remember the story of Capra. And I did not like the way it looked at me in the clearing. If you had not been present with the Belt, I am sure it would have made short work of me."

"I think it only wanted your hair to line its nest," Lief murmured. "What a strange story it told. I can still hardly believe it."

"I would be pleased at least to have the chance to try," Barda said drily. "I was in the trees minding a trembling Capricon while you spoke to the beast, and I heard nothing. But as we are here, and it is still up there, I gather it has refused to help us."

"It is more complicated than that," Lief said.

He told the dragon's story, and Barda listened carefully, all the while playing with the little locked box he had picked up before leaving the clearing.

"So Doran persuaded the last dragons to sleep," he said when Lief had finished. "Then, traveling back to Del, perhaps, he began hearing whispers of the Four Sisters. But by then it was too late. The dragons would not wake, even for him."

He sighed, turning the carved box over in his hands, pressing it here and there, trying to find the hidden lock that would open it.

"No wonder Doran's last note in the *Annals* was so desperate," he said. "He must have felt that he actually helped the Enemy by removing the last barriers to his plan."

Jasmine shrugged. "If he thought that, he was wrong. There was only one dragon left in each territory. They would have been killed by the Ak-Baba, one by one, if they had tried to interfere."

"Unless the Belt was with them," Lief said slowly.

He was remembering words he had seen in the *Deltora Annals* — words scrawled in desperation, long ago, by Doran's hand:

Whoever reads my words, show them to the King if you can. The King, wearing the Belt of Deltora, is Deltora's only salvation now.

Lief looked down at the Belt — at the great topaz gleaming with strange new depth and life. The golden dragon had added to its power. And the topaz had added to the dragon's power. He was certain that it would be the same with the ruby — if they could find the ruby dragon.

If . . .

He felt inside his jacket for the Dragon Territories map Josef had given him. Carefully he unfolded it and spread it out so his friends could see it.

"We had planned to move back south after this, then travel east to Dragon's Nest by the coast road," he said, rapidly tracing the path with his finger. "But if we take that way we will not cross into the territory of the ruby until we have almost reached our goal."

"Does that matter?" asked Jasmine.

"I think so," Lief said. "We do not know where

the ruby dragon sleeps, but surely the less of its land we cover, the less are our chances of finding it."

Barda nodded slowly. "You think, then, that we should move northeast," he said. "That will take us into ruby territory almost at once. But it is a longer way. Unless you plan to lead this parade of ours through the Forests of Silence — which would surely be madness!"

"The Forests are not so bad, if you keep to the trees and stay alert," Jasmine said stoutly.

"With you as our guide, Jasmine, the three of us alone could try it," Lief agreed. "But Barda is right. Our present party is far too large to risk such a dangerous shortcut."

He put the map away and stretched, suddenly aware of how weary he was. "We had better eat now, and get some sleep," he said. "Barda, will you tell Brid we leave at dawn?"

"A little before dawn, I think," said Barda, giving up on the locked box and thrusting it into his pocket in annoyance. "Whatever you say, Lief, I want to be well away from here by the time that dragon begins hunting again."

❋

The next two days were long and filled with frustration. The weakness of Rolf the Capricon, who was mounted unsteadily on a spare horse led by Barda, slowed their pace to a walk. Also, once the Os-Mine

Hills were behind them, the travelers began to encounter farms and villages.

Seeing the string of riders approaching, people ran out to greet them, overjoyed at this unexpected visit from their king, thrilled to see the heroes Jasmine and Barda, impressed by the guards, and fascinated by the Capricon.

The people were tired and worn, exhausted by the effort of toiling in barren fields while at the same time trying to rebuild houses destroyed in the time of the Shadow Lord. Many had been prisoners in the Shadowlands, and had only recently been restored to their homes.

It was impossible to disappoint them. Impossible to refuse their pleas to stay a while, to share what food and drink they could provide, in the way of the country.

But even as his heart bled for them, Lief fretted over the hours that slipped by as he inspected the work they had managed to complete, and sympathized over failed crops and scrawny herds.

What was worse, as he and his party ate the stringy chicken, wizened apples, and hard bread put before them, he was uneasily aware that the food could not really be spared.

The travelers always left a parting gift of food from their own supplies when at last they were allowed to leave, but Lief knew it could not make up for the feast they had been served. He knew that the villagers would be even hungrier as a result of the royal visit.

"If only we did not have the guards with us," he murmured as they rode away from yet another cheering crowd on the third day. "They make our group so large that we cannot go anywhere unnoticed."

"They are our official escort," said Barda, turning in his saddle to wave at a pair of skinny, redheaded children who were running after them, trying to keep up with the horses. "We cannot send them home without raising suspicion in Del that our reason for this journey is not what we claimed. Rumors will start. People will panic. And that is exactly what we do not want."

He glanced at Lief's dismal face. "Do not despair," he said. "By my calculation we are about to enter the territory of the ruby. Keep your eyes on the Belt. We must not risk passing the ruby dragon by."

Lief nodded and straightened his back, ashamed of his gray mood. He glanced down at the Belt. The topaz still glowed, but the ruby was dull pink instead of the shining red it should be.

Danger. Danger here or approaching.

He looked warily from side to side, and then behind him, but could see nothing. The road was deserted. Even the red-haired twins had disappeared. He guessed they had grown tired of the chase, and had run back to the village.

"Another road crosses this one not far ahead," exclaimed Jasmine, standing up on her stirrups and shading her eyes. "But there is a signpost."

They reached the signpost not long afterwards. It was battered and faded, and bent forward a little as though exhausted by its long years of service.

"Ah, good, Ringle!" Barda said with satisfaction. "It is on our way. I thought it would be marked. It is quite a large town, or used to be."

"Another town! At this rate, we will never reach Dragon's Nest," Jasmine muttered as they turned their horses' heads to the right and plodded on. "Of course, all these stops would not matter so much if only we could move faster when we were actually on the road."

Lief glanced back at Rolf, who was already slumped forward. "Rolf slows us sadly, I know, but we cannot leave him to be cared for by the farmers here," he said in a low voice. "They do not have enough to feed themselves! And he is still far too weak to be left alone."

"He could be strong if he wished!" snapped Jasmine, taking no trouble to keep her voice down. "He eats and sleeps well enough, and his wound is healing. He puts all his energy into pitying himself."

"He has lost his nerve," Barda said. "I have seen it happen to soldiers who have suffered sorely in battle. The sight of the dragon was too much for him."

"*Everything* is too much for him!" Jasmine retorted. "I doubt he had any nerve to lose."

"Do not argue," Lief begged, feeling that his own nerves could take no more. "At present we have no choice but to go on as we are. We may as well make the best of it, and hope that something happens to change things soon."

Not long after that something *did* happen. But not at all the sort of thing he expected.

11 ~ Signs of Trouble

The road quickly narrowed to a rough, winding path. After more than an hour there was still no sign of Ringle or its outlying farms.

The ground on the left of the path began to fall away steeply. At last, the travelers found themselves being forced to ride in single file, with a steep, rocky hill on one side and a jagged chasm on the other.

Lief reined in Honey and called a halt. "I think someone must have tampered with that signpost at the crossroads," he called, looking down at the fearsome drop on his left. "This is surely not the way to Ringle."

"I agree," Barda rumbled from behind him. "I fear we have been led to End Wood Gap. The post was leaning badly. No doubt it was loosened when it was turned around."

"But who would do such a thing?" exclaimed Jasmine in irritation.

Barda shrugged. "Some lout with a tiny brain, who thought it amusing to mislead travelers."

But Lief was not sure it was as simple as that. The ruby and the emerald in the Belt of Deltora were still as dull as river stones. His skin prickled with the awareness of danger, with the feeling that someone or something was wishing him ill.

On an impulse, he lowered his hand and pressed his fingers against the ruby. He shut his eyes and with all his strength thought of the ruby dragon.

"Wherever you are sleeping, dragon, awake!" he whispered. "I summon you! The Belt of Deltora summons you!"

He opened his eyes. Nothing had changed. Nothing moved on the rocky hill, or in the chasm. The sky was blank and empty.

"We will go back," he muttered. Impatiently he tried to turn Honey around, but the horse reared and snorted in terror as the earth at the edge of the narrow path crumbled under her hoofs.

Jasmine, Barda, Rolf, and the guards shouted with one voice. Dirt and stones showered to the depths below.

Lief held on grimly, turning Honey's head to face the front once more, urging her on till she found sure footing and at last stood trembling but safe on firm ground.

Sick with relief he patted her, speaking to her softly, cursing his own foolishness.

"It is not safe to turn the horses here," said Barda unnecessarily. Lief turned in the saddle to glance at him. The big man's face was beaded with sweat.

At a word from Jasmine, Kree took flight. He soared upward, made a great circle above their heads, and moments later was back, squawking harshly.

"Kree says that ahead there is a bridge over the Gap," Jasmine said, ignoring the fascinated stares of the guards.

The straggling group moved on again. Sure enough, just around the next bend, where the gap narrowed a little, a rickety wooden bridge straddled the sickening drop. A roughly painted sign stood beside it.

The companions looked at the sign in silence, then glanced at one another. Barda raised his eyebrows. Lief and Jasmine nodded.

"So that is how it is," said Barda grimly.

Lief bit his lip. "Yes," he said. "I have feared it for some time. This is the proof."

By now the guards at the head of the troop had seen the sign, and the dreaded words "Forests of Silence" were passing in whispers down the line. Rolf had shrunk down in his saddle, his eyes wide and fearful.

"We will have to lead the horses across, sir," Brid called to Barda. "They will need coaxing. Will I tell the men to dismount?"

"No," Barda growled, without turning around. "I do not think we will be crossing this bridge. I think we will be going on."

Brid sat rigidly, eyes straight ahead. He was plainly dismayed, but was too well trained to complain about his chief's order.

Rolf, however, gave a high, strangled cry. "We *cannot* go on!" he squealed. "You cannot lead us into the Forests of Silence to die!"

Barda swung down from his horse. He strode to the sign and ran his fingers over it thoughtfully.

As his men watched intently he pulled his large hunting knife from his belt. Then, gently but firmly, he began to scrape the face of the sign.

Curls of gleaming white paint fell to the ground

as he worked. And when he stood aside, the guards gasped.

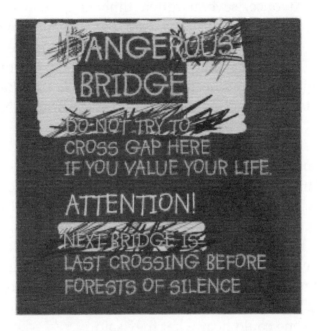

"So," Barda said, rubbing his knife on his leggings to remove the shreds of paint still clinging to the blade. "It is as we thought. Not content with leading us astray, someone painted over the bridge sign to try to put an end to us. It is fortunate that this was done so recently, and so clumsily, that we saw through the trick at once. Otherwise . . ."

Frowning, he sheathed his knife and picked up a large rock. He threw the rock onto the first few planks of the bridge. The bridge groaned, but held firm.

Barda lifted another rock. This time he threw it further, so that it landed towards the bridge's center.

At once, several rotten timbers gave way, the bridge jolted and sagged, and the rock plummeted down, smashing into pieces on the ground far below.

There were muffled groans as everyone present imagined what would have happened if Lief, Barda, and Jasmine had led the way across the bridge. Nothing was said as Barda remounted his horse.

The party plodded on, this time with the companions in the lead. Rolf and the guards turned often, looking back at the ruined bridge until it was out of sight. But Lief, Barda, and Jasmine did not look back at all. They were talking together in low voices.

If any were curious about their conversation, that curiosity remained unsatisfied. Barda had let the lead rein on Rolf's horse out as far as it would go, creating a gap between the three and all their followers, so no one could hear what they said.

✳

Gradually the Gap became narrower, and in time, as the sign had promised, the travelers reached another bridge.

Here the path ended, and not far ahead the Gap was swallowed up by a forbidding mass of trees. All guessed that this was End Wood, the last of the three Forests of Silence.

On the other side of the bridge a narrow road wound away into the distance. The bridge itself looked sturdy and almost new. A carved stone stood proudly beside it.

NEW
END WOOD
BRIDGE

←——— To Ringle

"Now listen carefully," said Barda, raising his voice so everyone could hear. "Twice, signs on our path have been altered. We believe these were deliberate attempts to injure us. We have decided, therefore, that our party should separate, for the safety of all."

Rolf made a small sound of protest, then clapped his hand over his mouth. The guards stared.

"Under Brid's command, you are to go to the outskirts of Ringle," Barda went on. "There, without troubling the citizens, you will make camp for the night. Then you will move on to Broome. Is that understood?"

Brid cleared his throat. "What of you, sir?" he

asked. "You, and the lady Jasmine, and the king?"

"We will also go to Broome," Barda said evenly. "But we will go on foot, and by another way."

Every man's eyes turned to the forest ahead. Every face filled with dread. Rolf clutched his heart and began to wail.

"But what of me?" he howled. "What of me?"

"You will go with the guards," said Lief quickly, hearing Jasmine draw breath for a sharp retort. "You will be perfectly safe, Rolf, I promise. Is that not so, Brid?"

Brid nodded, his scarred face wooden.

"Then let us waste no more time." Barda clapped Brid on the shoulder. "Keep safe," he said.

"And you, sir," muttered Brid. A nerve high on his cheek twitched, but he pressed his lips together and said no more. He turned to his men and began to give orders.

In moments, the guards were moving across the bridge. Brid, leading Rolf's horse, was at their head. Honey, Bella, and Swift, on lead ropes, trailed at the rear.

Lief sighed with relief as the whole party reached the other side in safety. He saw the men turn and wave in farewell, and raised his own arm in response.

"I hope we are doing the right thing," Barda muttered. "Brid clearly thinks we are mad."

Jasmine snorted. "Brid thinks anything out of the ordinary is mad," she said. "He is so dull!"

"Brid survived ten years as a slave in the Shadowlands," Barda said quietly. "No doubt this made him thoughtful."

Jasmine bit her lip. "I did not mean to insult him," she said. "But you should not let his disapproval shake you, Barda. This is our best chance of losing our enemy and reaching Broome without endless delays."

She sighed. "It is a pity we had to let the horses go, but we had no choice. Horses cannot sleep in trees as we can."

Filli chattered agreement, delighted to be rid of the large creatures that had jolted him about so painfully.

Barda groaned. The idea of sleeping in the fork of a tree did not appeal to him at all.

Lief said nothing. He was startled to find that, despite everything, he was feeling extremely happy.

Am I as mad as Brid thinks? he wondered. *There is nothing to be happy about!*

But he *was* happy. Yes, he was worried by what had passed. Yes, he knew that danger lay ahead. But as for the present — why, he felt like singing as he stood with Jasmine and Barda, watching the guards move away.

Watching the guards move away . . .

And that, he thought suddenly, *must be the answer*.

The guards were always very respectful to him. They regarded him with awe. But this did not please him. Instead, it made him feel like a fraud. It made him terribly aware of just how young he was, in comparison to them. And it made him feel that he had to act like a king at all times, so he wouldn't shock or disappoint them.

Now, however, with only Jasmine and Barda for company, he could be himself. He was free.

He felt as if his blood was fizzing in his veins. As if the air was sweeter and the colors in the world brighter than they had been before.

"Come on!" he shouted. And began running towards the Forest.

12 - End Wood

After several hours of walking, Lief's bubbling happiness had settled to a feeling of quiet contentment. The twisted, weed-choked trees of the Forest fringe had been left behind. End Wood was now a beautiful place, filled with birdsong. Golden pools of sunlight dappled the soft earth, and ferns clustered at the roots of the mighty trees.

All the companions knew, however, that the evil reputation of the Forests of Silence was well deserved. They knew, too, that within the greatest beauty terror could be lying in wait. So they walked in silence, one behind the other, alert for signs of danger.

Just before sunset, Jasmine chose a tree for them, and they climbed up to high branches where they could eat and sleep in some safety.

It was not a restful night. They dozed fitfully in turns as unseen creatures slid and prowled below them. In the darkest hours, when the moon had set, a faint, chilling chorus of howls and screams began. It lasted only a few minutes, but after it had died away, the companions slept no more.

They welcomed the dawn gratefully, but forced themselves to wait until sunlight fell on the forest floor before venturing down from their hiding place and moving on.

As before, Jasmine led them, threading her way almost silently through the trees, brushing the smooth bark of each one lightly with the tips of her fingers as she passed. Kree fluttered ahead of her, a black shadow against a background of green and gold.

After a time, Jasmine began to move faster. Lief and Barda, their muscles stiff and aching after their night in the tree, found themselves struggling to keep her in view.

"Jasmine, slow down!" Lief called in a low voice. But Jasmine only turned with a frown, her finger to her lips, beckoned impatiently, and set off again, even faster than before.

At last Lief became aware that a new sound had begun to mingle with the birdsong. It was the sound of trickling water — a stream, somewhere near.

It made him realize how thirsty he was, but he did not dare to stop and drink from his water flask. Jasmine was almost running now, and all he could do was follow.

The gurgling, rippling sound grew louder, and at last Jasmine stopped.

Lief saw that she had reached the stream he had been listening to for so long. Broad and shallow, the stream ran directly across their path, sunbeams dancing on the clear water that gurgled over its pebbled bed.

On the other side of the stream there were no trees, only a mass of giant ferns, rising like a feathery barrier that completely hid whatever was beyond.

Kree fluttered down to the water's edge. Jasmine waited while he drank. Only when he had finished, and had flown up to perch on a branch high above her head, did she kneel to drink herself.

Filli scuttled down from her shoulder and began to drink also. His tiny pink tongue lapped busily, but all the time his dark eyes darted from side to side, so he could not be taken by surprise.

"Did you have to go so fast?" Barda muttered as he and Lief at last reached the stream and crouched beside Jasmine to quench their raging thirsts.

"The trees say we are being followed," Jasmine said shortly. "Someone has been tracking us since dawn, from the direction of End Wood Gap."

As she spoke she glanced up to where Kree kept watch. He was so still that he looked part of the tree itself. Only his yellow eye was moving, fierce and bright.

Lief had lifted a handful of water to his lips. Now he felt as if the icy liquid was trickling down his spine.

He glanced down at the Belt. The topaz still gleamed brightly, but the ruby had paled once more.

"Who?" he murmured.

Jasmine lifted Filli to her shoulder, wiped her mouth with the back of her hand, and stood up.

"The same enemy, I imagine, who tried to make us fall to our deaths at End Wood Gap," she said. "All the trees can tell me is that he is tall and fierce, and moving much faster than we are. Where we have traveled above ground, he does also, swinging from tree to tree. Where we have gone on foot, he runs bent double, sniffing the ground like a beast."

The words painted a disturbing picture. Lief's scalp crawled.

"How close is he now?" Barda asked. Once, the big man had scoffed at the idea that Jasmine could understand the language of trees, but those days were long past.

"Already he has almost reached the place where we spent the night," Jasmine said. "We must throw him off the scent. That is why I made haste to reach the stream. If we wade through the water he will not be able to smell our tracks. He will not know if we have gone left or right, and so we may escape him."

"Why should we try to escape?" Barda growled. "Why not stand and face him? I would like to give him proper thanks for all he has done for us." Scowling, he touched his sword.

"We took this way to save time, Barda," Jasmine pointed out coldly. "The forest edge cannot be far away now. Do we want to waste energy fighting a beast-man who has a grudge against us? Or do we want to reach Dragon's Nest with all speed?"

"We want to reach Dragon's Nest," Lief said reluctantly. "Let us use the stream, as Jasmine says."

He felt as Barda did, but he knew that Jasmine's plan was more practical. To Jasmine, all that mattered was the task at hand. Pride, revenge, curiosity . . . to her, such things were not important, and could wait.

And they can *wait — of course they can,* Lief told himself. But secretly he sympathized as Barda grumbled in annoyance.

Jasmine stepped into the stream and waded a little way along it to the right. She touched the violets often with her hands and let her hair tangle with the ferns that overhung the water's edge. Then she turned, tucked her hair beneath her collar, flattened herself in the water, and crawled back, being careful to touch nothing.

"That should lead him astray very well," she grinned. "Now follow me. Keep in the center of the stream and very low, so that the ferns do not brush your backs."

She set off towards the left, following her own advice. Lief and Barda crawled after her.

They moved through the cold water for what seemed like a very long time. Lief's hands were numb and his teeth were chattering when Jasmine at last called a halt.

"I think we have gone far enough now," she whispered, getting to her feet. "And see here!"

She pointed at the bank beside her. There, to his amazement, Lief saw a pathway of large, rounded stones winding away through the ferns.

"It must be the bed of another stream that once joined this one," Jasmine said. "If our luck holds, it will at least lead us through the ferns — and perhaps all the way to the forest edge."

"Anything to get off our knees and out of this cursed water!" muttered Barda, crawling to his feet.

Shivering, the companions waded out of the stream and began following the mossy path.

Soon it was as if they were moving through a soft green tunnel. Great, arching fronds met over their heads so they could not see the sky.

The air was thick with the smell of damp earth and rotting leaves. There was not a breath of wind, and no birds sang. They walked with their hands on the hilts of their weapons, not speaking, barely breathing.

Lief glanced down. He could not rid himself of the idea that there was something very odd about the path.

He tried to convince himself that Jasmine was right, and it was an old stream bed. Yet the stones were so large and so evenly placed — almost as if someone had gathered them and put them on the path, one by one.

But who would have done such a thing? And for what purpose, in this wilderness?

"Oh!"

Lief's head jerked up as Jasmine gasped, and his sword was in his hand before he realized that she was not in danger.

She was standing stock-still, holding a feathery veil of ferns apart, staring at something ahead.

"Look!" she breathed.

Lief and Barda crowded in behind her and peered over her shoulder . . . at something that was like a picture in a book of fairy tales.

Beyond the ferns, countless small trees loaded with golden fruits grew in a broad pool of still, shallow water. They were perfectly reflected in the water's mirror-like surface, their graceful trunks rising, their broad green leaves spreading, their fruits glowing like tiny, floating suns.

Jasmine moved forward.

"Wait, Jasmine!" Barda called urgently. "Wait! We do not know . . ."

But Jasmine had already stepped into the water. It barely reached her ankles. She turned her head, smiling.

"It is warm," she said. "Oh, and see the fruit! Can you smell it?"

111

Lief could indeed smell the fruit. It was a glorious, rich, sweet scent. His mouth began to water.

Kree flew from Jasmine's shoulder and perched on a bough of the nearest tree. Greedily he dug his beak into one of the golden fruits.

Juice dripped into the water, making circles of ripples where it fell. The delicious fragrance grew stronger.

Filli began to whimper and chatter. Jasmine splashed to the tree and let the little creature leap up beside Kree.

The golden fruits were as big as Filli himself, but that did not dismay him. He clutched one with his paws and began nibbling it eagerly.

This was too much for Lief. He stepped into the water and moved to Jasmine's side.

"Do the trees say the fruit is safe to eat?" he murmured.

Jasmine shrugged. "These trees speak only to one another, and keep their secrets," she said. "But Filli and Kree seem sure that all is well."

Lief stretched out his hand and picked one of the fruits. It was shaped a little like a pear, but much larger and heavier. In places its smooth golden skin was slightly flushed with pink.

He lifted it to his nose and breathed in the delicious fragrance.

Then, almost without intending to do it, he took a bite.

13 - Sweet and Sour

A glorious taste filled Lief's mouth. Sweet, golden juice ran down his chin. Then suddenly he realized that something very bitter was mingling with the sweetness.

Quickly he spat what remained of the chewed skin into his hand, grimacing.

"The skin is bitter," he said, wrinkling his nose. "Oh! It is disgusting! How can Filli and Kree bear it?"

Jasmine grinned and pulled out her knife. "They are not as fussy about food as we are," she said. "I am glad you made the experiment before me."

She took a fruit from the tree and began to peel it. In moments she was sinking her teeth into sweet, gleaming golden flesh, murmuring with pleasure.

Lief followed her example. And after a few moments of watching suspiciously, Barda did the same.

Soon each one of them was silently absorbed in

the blissful enjoyment of a rare feast. The water around their feet was littered with fruit skins and the long, flat seeds they found in the fruits' centers.

Time passed. The sun was high in the sky. Lief, warm and full, crouched to rest his pleasantly aching legs.

He closed his eyes and began daydreaming of telling the hungry people in the villages about this rich supply of food growing at their very doorstep.

Once they know about it, they can come and gather the fruit each year, he thought lazily. *Perhaps they can even flood a field or two, and grow their own trees from the seed. How wonderful that would be! How wonderful . . .*

He became aware that Kree had begun squawking, and Filli was chattering shrilly. His brow creased in annoyance. Why were they disturbing him with their noise?

He opened his eyes, and it was then that he realized, with mild surprise, that he was not crouching any longer, but lying on his back in the water.

How strange, he thought. But he smiled, and did not try to move. The water was warm. There were a few large stones buried in the soft mud on which he lay, but they were pleasantly round and smooth.

Like the ones on the path, he thought dreamily, pushing his hand through the mud to touch a stone with his fingers.

As he stroked its warm smoothness, it came into his mind that the stones on the path could have been taken from beneath this soft, warm water. They could have been taken and used by someone who wanted to mark a trail to this place, so that creatures great and small would come here, see the beauty, taste the fruit.

Someone. Or something . . .

The thought drifted into the golden haze of Lief's mind like a small dark cloud.

He wanted to brush it away. He was so sleepy, so very comfortable . . .

But Filli was shrieking now. And he could hear Kree's cries, and the beating of his wings.

Making an enormous effort to rouse himself, Lief turned his head towards the sound. He saw Jasmine and Barda lying motionless not far away. Their hair floated like weed in the water. Their eyes were closed, their faces peaceful. Their chests were gently rising and falling.

They were deeply asleep. But how was that possible? For Kree was flapping wildly around Jasmine's head, screeching, his wing tips brushing her face.

He is trying to wake her, Lief thought dreamily. *Poor Kree.*

Then he lifted his eyes and saw something moving through the trees towards them.

It was a giant bird, as tall as the trees, with a snowy white chest, neck, and head, and black wings.

Silently, unhurriedly, the bird stalked through

the water on long orange legs, delicately lifting one foot then the other, barely stirring the mirror-like surface.

Its fixed, glassy eyes looked as if they had been painted on to its head. Its neck was like a smooth, white snake. Its orange beak was like a sword.

Lief tried to shout. But his tongue was thick and heavy, and his throat seemed swollen. The only sound he could make was a rasping groan.

And he could not move. His limbs felt as if they were fixed in the mud of the lake bed.

The Belt. The diamond . . . for strength.

Sweat broke out on his brow as he forced his left hand up to his waist. His fingers moved with agonizing slowness to the diamond beside the clasp as his terrified eyes watched the bird reach Jasmine's side.

Kree flew at the giant, screeching and pecking, but it took no more notice of him than Kree would have taken of a sparrow.

It put its head on one side and regarded the helpless girl with cold interest. Then, without haste, it dipped its sword-like beak into the water and began sharpening it on a stone.

Lief felt a thrill of fear. His fingertips touched the diamond. A tingling rose up his arm, spread through his body. It was as if strength was battling weakness in his veins.

A stone. Throw a stone.

Lief forced his sluggish fingers to curl around the stone they had been caressing. He pulled, and the stone eased out of the mud with a wet, sucking sound.

It came to the surface, mud-streaked and streaming with water. And then he saw what it was.

It was a human skull. Mud clogged its grinning jaws. Long, thin worms dangled from its eye sockets and fell squirming back into the water.

Instinctively Lief recoiled, dropping the hideous thing with a splash.

The next instant, his mind was flooded with terrified understanding.

They had been lured to a killing ground. Like so many before them they had eaten the glorious fruit that made them sleep.

So that at its leisure the giant bird which lived among the trees could come, with its stealthy tread, its snaking neck.

So that the bird could kill and feed, the bones of its prey sinking at last into the soft, warm mud of its domain.

Later, much later, picked clean by worms, polished by the muddy water, the skulls could be used to decorate the path. To make it even wider and more inviting.

The bird lifted its beak from the water and raised

it over Jasmine's body. One downward jerk of its head, and the dripping, razor-sharp point would plunge deep into Jasmine's heart.

With a strangled cry Lief heaved himself onto his side, picked up the skull again, and threw it wildly.

The skull bounced harmlessly against the giant bird's snowy breast and splashed into the water. The bird paused and tilted its head. Its unblinking eye stared at Lief without expression.

Perhaps it was wondering why this prey was moving. Or perhaps there was no thought in its mind at all.

As Lief scrabbled clumsily for another weapon, as Kree swooped and screeched around its head, it turned back to Jasmine and raised its beak again.

A blur of gray streaked from a branch beside it, and suddenly something was clinging to its long, white neck.

It was Filli — Filli as Lief had never seen him, fur standing up in spikes, tiny white teeth bared. The next instant, Filli had attacked, biting deeply. A bright spot of blood appeared on the white feathers.

Instantly the neck writhed, the head turned, and the long, sharp beak stabbed viciously.

Soundlessly Filli fell. He splashed into the water and struggled there, a small, feebly moving bundle of draggled gray fur.

The giant bird looked down at him, then lifted a huge, clawed foot to stamp him into the mud.

Lief's fingers closed around a long bone. He tore it from its soggy bed and threw it. The bone spun through the air and hit the raised foot.

This time the bird felt pain. It made a deep, rattling sound and its foot clenched. Again it turned its head, and again it fixed Lief with its cold gaze.

The feathers on the back of its neck rose in sharp quills. It lowered its bruised foot and began stalking towards him. Plainly it had decided that Lief had become a nuisance.

Lief struggled to rise, struggled to cry out, but his body was still heavy, so heavy, and still he could make no sound but harsh, gasping groans. He had another bone in his hand, but it was small and useless. His sword was pinned beneath him. Even with the help of the diamond, he could not find the strength to pull it free.

The bird looked down at him with blank eyes. It raised its beak to strike.

Then suddenly there was a roar from the bank of the lake and a spear flew over Lief's body, grazing the bird's black wing before plunging into the water behind it.

The bird faltered, took a step back. The quills on its neck rose further. Its beak opened.

The roar came again, and then there was the

sound of splashing as someone ran through the water towards them.

"On your way, Orchard Keeper!" boomed a voice. "These people are mine!"

Another spear hurtled through the air, this time scratching the bird's neck.

The bird decided it had had enough. It turned and began stalking rapidly away. In moments it had disappeared among the trees.

There was a peal of mocking laughter. A shadow fell across Lief's face. He looked up, dazed and squinting.

An enormous figure in a cap of fur towered over him, blocking the sun. An arm stretched out to pluck the spears from the mud.

"That was a near thing," boomed the voice. "One moment more and you would have been dead meat. I have been tracking you since first light — but what a dance you led me with that trick in the stream! If the black bird had not screeched fit to crack the heavens I would never have found you."

Lief struggled, and tried vainly to speak.

Again the booming laugh rang out. The shadow moved. Long legs bound with strips of leather stepped over Lief.

Lief watched in confusion as the giant stranger lifted Filli from the water, inspected him, sniffed his wet fur, then nodded and placed him gently on Jasmine's chest.

"Who . . . are . . . you?" Lief rasped.

"Why, has your sight grown as feeble as your voice, Lief of Del? Do you not know me?" roared the stranger, tearing off the fur cap.

Relief and amazement swept over Lief as he focused on the long, narrow black eyes, the straight black brows, and, most unmistakable of all, the shaved head painted with swirling red designs.

"Lindal!" he rasped. "Lindal of Broome! But how . . . ? Why . . . ? . . . Oh, it is so good to see you!"

"You will not think so when you hear the news I bring," Lindal said grimly. "But that will have to wait. First I must get you and your foolish friends on your feet. We must leave here, and I cannot carry you all."

She splashed to the nearest tree and picked a golden fruit. Then she returned to Lief and squatted beside him.

"Eat this!" she ordered, tearing off some of the fruit's skin and pressing it into Lief's mouth.

He choked and tried to spit the bitter stuff out.

"No!" Lindal shouted, pressing her hand to his lips. "Chew and swallow! Do you want to lie in this boneyard croaking like a frog forever? The skin is the antidote to Sleeper Fruit flesh. You must have eaten some before, or you would be as helpless as your friends."

When she saw that Lief had understood, she removed her hand and stood up.

"Now for the others," she said, grinning at the faces he made as he chewed the vile-tasting peel. "I will have to feed them the antidote little by little — at least until they begin to stir. When you can stand, come and help me. The bird may return in a danger-ous mood, and I do not want to have to fight it to the death. It is bad luck, they say, to kill an Orchard Keeper."

14 - A Message in Blood

By the time Jasmine and Barda had been revived, the sun was low in the sky. All three of the companions were weak, and Filli was dazed and helpless, but Lindal insisted they move on.

"It is not far to the forest edge from here," she said. "When we are in the open, you can rest in safety."

Refusing to say another word, she set off at a brisk pace.

Lief, Barda, and Jasmine had no choice but to follow her. With Kree flying ahead and Filli lying limp beneath Jasmine's shirt, they beat their way through a tangle of ferns, then through thickets of brush and brambles, their legs trembling, their heads spinning.

At last, at sunset, they burst into open ground. Ahead was a vast plain. The sky was streaked red and orange. A fresh breeze cooled their faces.

They stood, exhausted and staring.

"This is my country," Lindal said with satisfaction. "Sit! Rest! I will build a fire and hunt for some food."

And so tired were Lief, Barda, and Jasmine that they crumpled to the ground where they stood.

When they woke, the sky above them was like black velvet sprinkled with diamonds. The fire had died down to a mass of glowing coals, and the air was filled with the smell of cooking.

Lindal was already eating, sitting cross-legged and chewing on a bone with relish.

When she saw that her companions had awoken, she tossed the bone aside. She licked her fingers, then seized a wicked-looking knife and began sawing at the joint of meat still sizzling on the coals.

"Here," she said, passing hot, dripping chunks to each of them. "Pig rat — a fine, plump one, too, for once."

Even Jasmine, who rarely ate meat, fell upon the food, which was rich and savory, despite its doubtful name. There was warm, flat bread, too, baked in the ashes of the fire, and some fresh, curly green leaves Lief had never seen before. They tasted slightly peppery, but were crisp and strangely refreshing.

"Traveler's Weed. Good for the belly!" said Lindal, cramming a handful of leaves into her mouth with one hand and slapping her flat stomach with the other. "I was lucky to find it. There is little around these days, though once, the old folk say, it grew in every ditch."

Her heartiness sounded a little forced, and Lief suddenly remembered what she had said about having bad news. He realized she was delaying the moment when she would have to tell it.

He leaned forward, but before he could say anything, Barda spoke.

"What a meal, Lindal!" the big man said. "How our guards would envy us! No doubt they are making a miserable dinner of traveler's biscuit and dried fish tonight."

Lindal looked stricken.

Here it comes, Lief thought, with sudden dread. *It is something about the guards.*

The smile faded from Barda's face. "What is it?" he demanded. "Why do you look like that?"

"There is something I must tell you," Lindal muttered. "Something bad. Your men . . . "

She bent her head and rubbed her hand over her painted skull. Then she looked up and met Barda's eyes.

"Your men are all dead," she said.

Jasmine gasped with shock. Barda's face looked as if it had been turned to stone.

"How?" Lief heard himself asking, and wondered how his voice could sound so calm when his mind was roaring with grief and horror.

"Their camp on the outskirts of Ringle was attacked last night," Lindal said, staring into the fire. "Everyone in the town heard their cries and woke."

"As did we," Lief whispered, remembering the distant screams he had heard in the darkness of the night.

"Many people in Ringle snatched up weapons and hurried to the camp," Lindal said. "But by the time we reached it, the guards were dead — dead and burning."

"Burning!" whispered Jasmine. She glanced at Lief, and a wave of heat swept over him.

It cannot be! he told himself. *No! It cannot . . .*

Barda wet his lips. "They must have been taken by surprise," he said with difficulty. "Attacked by someone they would never suspect. Treachery . . ."

Suddenly, he looked suspiciously at Lindal. "And how did you just happen to be in Ringle last night of all nights, Lindal of Broome?" he asked, his hand moving to the hilt of his sword.

Lindal lifted her chin. "I do not have to answer to you, you bumbling ox," she sneered. "Any more than you have to tell me why you are traveling inland instead of by the coast road, as planned."

Her lip curled. "Or why you chose to play the hero in the Forests of Silence while your men went on to Ringle, and their deaths," she added.

With a roar Barda sprang to his feet, drawing his sword, scattering the remains of his meal into the fire.

But Lindal was up just as quickly, a spear already in her hand.

Glowering, the two giants faced each other over the fire, their weapons gleaming, their bodies dyed scarlet by the light of the glowing coals.

"Barda!" thundered Lief. "Lindal! Stop!"

But neither Lindal nor Barda moved a muscle.

"You are fools, both of you," cried Jasmine in disgust. "You are shocked and grieved, so to relieve your feelings you turn on each other. Oh, very good!"

Lindal's eyes slid in her direction. The hand holding the spear tightened. For a terrifying moment Lief thought that Jasmine had spoken her mind once too often.

Then the hand relaxed, and the spear was lowered so it pointed to the ground.

"I was staying the night in Ringle because Ringle is on the way to the Os-Mine Hills," Lindal said, looking straight at Barda. "I had heard reports of a disturbance in the Hills. Screams and bursts of fire."

The Dragon hunting the Granous, Lief thought numbly. *Of course.*

"I have traveled the Hills many times," Lindal went on coldly. "I thought I would do my king a service by investigating the disturbance, so I could report when I met him in Broome. I am a loyal Deltoran — whatever others may think."

Barda put down his sword and bent his head.

"I beg pardon for doubting you," he muttered. "I just — cannot take this in. We thought *we* were the ones in danger. An enemy had been setting traps for us. That is why we entered the Forests. We never dreamed our escort would be attacked."

He shook his lowered head, his face grief-stricken. "Those guards were handpicked men — fine fighters, fine soldiers! How could they have been destroyed?"

"They had no chance," Lindal said grimly. "No chance without the Belt of Deltora to protect them."

The words stung Lief like a lash. His eyes blurred as Lindal dropped her spear and bent to the leather bag that lay beside her, pulling out a roll of what looked like stiff, brown parchment.

"It must have been a sudden, terrible attack," Lindal said, straightening slowly with the roll in her hand. "The whole camp was blackened, smoking, blasted by flame. The horses were running wild in the fields, mad with fear. The men — had been torn to pieces. The shreds of their bodies were in a heap, and the heap was burning."

Lief's throat tightened. He knew the truth now. His childish wish to be free had killed twelve brave men.

And Rolf, the Capricon.

You will be perfectly safe, Rolf, I promise.

His own words came back to haunt him. Had Rolf remembered them as he died — died, as long ago

the people of Capra had died? Torn, burning, screaming . . .

Lindal's mouth twisted. "It was a terrible sight,"
she said softly. "Even in the time of the Shadow Lord,
I saw nothing like it. I wish I could forget it."

Barda groaned softly.

"Somehow, one man had escaped the fire," said
Lindal, glancing at him. "A man with the Shadow
Lord's brand on his cheek."

"Brid," Jasmine murmured. "Brid . . ."

"He was terribly burned," Lindal said. "There
was a great wound in his chest, and his leg had been
torn off at the knee. But he was valiant. Still he managed to crawl to a tree and write — write a message in
his own blood."

She held out the stiff brown roll. "I peeled off the
bark with my knife. I thought it best that the people of
Ringle did not see it."

Lief took the bark from her hand and unrolled it.

Lief stared at the scrawled words in horror.

"It — it is impossible," he said haltingly. "Brid must have been seeing visions, because of loss of blood. Perhaps bandits . . ."

"No bandits could do what I saw," said Lindal. "And some of the people hurrying with me to the camp said they had seen a huge shadow in the sky, flying east. It looked like a dragon of old, they said."

She shrugged. "I told them they were dreaming — that there had been no dragons in Deltora for hundreds of years. Then I reached the place, and found the message on the tree. And now I do not know what to think."

"I do," muttered Barda. "I know very well what to think."

Lindal's face did not change, but she watched him closely.

Barda swung around to Lief, his fists clenched.

"Lindal of Broome may as well know the truth, Lief, for soon everyone will," he said bitterly. "We have roused something we cannot control. The golden dragon lied to you. It deceived you utterly, with its talk of borders and oaths. As soon as it had regained its strength, it came after us, hungry for blood."

Lief's heart was pounding. Lindal's words as she described what the people of Ringle had seen were still ringing in his ears.

. . . a huge shadow in the sky, flying east.

Why would the topaz dragon fly east? Why, its hunger satisfied, would it not return to its lair in the Os-Mine Hills?

He forced his stiff lips to move.

"I may indeed have roused something I cannot control, Barda," he said. "But I do not think it is the topaz dragon. I think . . . I fear . . . it is something worse."

15 - Fears and Visions

The next few days, trudging across the barren plain with Lindal, were among the worst Lief had ever spent.

That first night, he had told his companions of his fear. He had seen the lines deepen on their faces as they listened and understood. He had sat and talked with them for many hours, making decisions, forming plans.

At dawn the next day, Kree had set out for Del with a message for Doom. The companions knew that news of the tragedy at Ringle would spread quickly, and that Doom would soon hear of it. A description of Brid would alert him to the fact that the dead men were the royal escort, far from the coast road where they were supposed to be.

And unless he heard otherwise, he would certainly think that Lief, Barda, and Jasmine had shared the guards' fate.

Lief had written the note with a heavy heart, using a simple code that he and Doom had used several times before.

EPPN -
XIBUFWFS 2PV NBZ
IFBS, XF BSF TBGF BOE
NPWJOH PO. MJOE BM PG
CSPPNF JT XJUI VT.
m

It was strange to be walking without Kree wheeling ahead of them. Jasmine was very quiet. She was concerned about Filli, who was bruised and listless, and Lief knew she also feared for Kree, because the skies were no longer safe.

Bitterly he regretted that his actions had brought them to this.

All the talk, all the planning, had not relieved his guilt, or his anger with himself.

Jasmine, Barda, and Lindal had not breathed a word of blame, but he knew he had failed them. As he had failed the guards, and Rolf, and all the people of the east, who now faced terror as well as famine.

133

Time and again, trudging over the rough, bare ground by day, lying beneath the canopy of stars by night, he remembered riding on the narrow path beside End Wood Gap, his fingers pressed to the great ruby.

He had tried to summon the ruby dragon. He had been quite sure that he had failed.

But what if he had not failed?

What if the ruby dragon had stirred indeed? What if it had woken in some dank hiding place nearby and lain still for a time, gathering strength?

What if it had remained hidden until Lief and the Belt were long gone into the Forests of Silence, and only then crawled into the light, its belly gnawed by the hunger of centuries?

Never had Lief considered, when he called to the ruby dragon, that it might not come to him at once, as the topaz dragon had.

Never had he dreamed that it might simply take to the skies with nothing on its mind except filling its belly.

But he feared there was no other way to explain what had happened in the camp near Ringle.

The topaz dragon had no grudge against the guards or Rolf — it had never even seen them. If it was just in search of food, surely it would have raided one of the villages closer to the Hills. And if it was seeking the Belt of Deltora, it would have followed Lief into the Forests of Silence.

It would have had no reason to attack the guards.

But the ruby dragon, ravenous after its long sleep, drawn to the camp by the scent of the Capricon, its ancient prey, would have had every reason.

Just as it would have had good reason to fly east, when its terrible feast was done — to fly east to Broome, where once stood Capra, its conquest of long ago.

Or to fly even farther, perhaps, to the place called Dragon's Nest.

✳

They reached the end of the plain and began climbing through a range of low hills. Very near them, to the north, the rugged mountains that marked the Shadowlands border rose dark and sinister against the sky.

Lief, Barda, and Jasmine knew from the map that on the other side of the hills lay that narrow, isolated part of Deltora that stretched like a bony finger into the wild eastern sea. They knew that when they reached the hills' highest point, they would look down on the coast, and the lonely city of Broome.

But even if they had not known, Lindal's behavior would have told them. She had begun to walk faster. Often she lifted her head and sniffed the air.

Lief knew that she was checking for the smell of fire. She was dreading what she might see when at last she looked down at her home.

She feared as he did, as Barda and Jasmine

feared also, that history might have repeated itself, and that nothing would be left by the sea but smoking ruins.

But when at last they peered down at the city of Broome, they saw at once that all was well.

The city was solid and untouched, the bright flags on its square white towers whipping in the crisp breeze.

Carts trundled along its roads. Fishing boats with red and yellow sails bobbed in its sparkling harbor.

"The dragon has not been here," Lindal said.

She turned to Lief, relief shining in her eyes.

"Do you see?" she said. "Every flag has been raised. Broome is preparing for your visit. But if we go quietly past, we will not be noticed. You are not expected so soon, and the guards will pay no attention to four dusty travelers."

Lief gazed down at the bright, welcoming city. Grimly he wondered how many flags would be flying if the people of Broome knew of the menace he had unleashed in their territory.

At least I do not have to face them now, he thought as Lindal began leading the way downward.

They had made their plan the night Lief confessed his fears of the ruby dragon and, throwing all caution aside, told Lindal of the quest to find the Sister of the East.

They had decided that if they found Broome safe, they would go straight on to Dragon's Nest, to face whatever was awaiting them there.

Lindal was to guide them. That had been decided, too — or, rather, Lindal had announced it, and refused to listen to any argument.

"Of course I must take you," she cried. "I have known the way to Dragon's Nest since my earliest years. It was forbidden to me then. My mother threatened me with a beating if ever I was to go near it. And so, of course, I went as near to it as I dared, whenever I could. As a child I was foolish and willful, and had no sense."

"And what has changed?" Barda demanded.

Lindal roared with laughter. "Why, now I am big enough to do as I please without fear of a beating," she said. "Unless you wish to fight me yourself, old bear?"

"No," Barda growled. "I might lose, and that would not be good for the pride of chief of the guards."

But he grinned as he said it. It had been clear to all that he would be very glad of Lindal's company.

Lief looked along the coast to the left of Broome's harbor, along the line of foaming white where waves crashed against the jagged rocks.

Gradually the mountains of the Shadowlands border closed in on the white line as if marching towards the sea. And at last, at Deltora's most eastern point, the rocks of coast and mountains met and mingled in a tumble of gray stone.

Somewhere in that grim confusion was the place called Dragon's Nest. There, Lief was sure now, they would find the ruby dragon.

The memory of Doran's hasty scrawl in the *Deltora Annals* was clear in his mind.

> I now know why the Enemy wanted the Dragons destroyed. He had a plan that the Dragons would not have tolerated.

Lief was sure that once its first, terrible hunger had been satisfied, the ruby dragon had sensed the intruder in its territory, and sped to Dragon's Nest to destroy it.

Perhaps even now it is doing our work for us, he thought, plodding doggedly after Lindal.

But the flicker of hope was small, and battered by the chill winds of fear. The ruby dragon was out of control. And it was only one.

Without the Belt to aid it, it might fail to destroy the evil thing hidden in Dragon's Nest. Then its rage would be terrible indeed. It would lash out at anything that crossed its path.

And soon it would be hungry again.

✳

The shadows were lengthening by the time they reached the bottom of the hills, and, as Lindal had promised, they slipped by Broome unnoticed.

When they were well past and the sun had begun to set, Lief turned to look back.

What he saw made him gasp. He stood, staring, unable to believe his eyes.

The city was bathed in pink light — and its whole shape had changed. It had become a dreaming, magical place of tall, delicate spires and shining glass domes.

Its sturdy outer walls had gone. In their place were groves of slender trees hung with glowing red globes that clinked softly together in the breeze making sweet, chiming music.

So beautiful . . .

His eyes filled with tears.

"Lief, what is the matter?" exclaimed Jasmine. She, too, spun around to look at the city, but clearly she could see nothing unusual.

"Ah — he can see Capra," said Lindal quietly. "The topaz in the Belt makes him sensitive, no doubt — and sunset is the dangerous time, they say."

She took Lief's arm and shook it.

"It is not real, Lief," she whispered. "It is a dream of something that is dead and gone. Turn away from it."

Lief did not move.

Lindal tugged his arm more roughly, almost pulling him off his feet, then began to walk briskly again, dragging him after her.

He stumbled at her heels, shaking his head as if waking from a dream.

"So beautiful . . ." he mumbled.

"Beautiful, but dangerous," Lindal said, striding on. "Keep walking! I should have warned you, but I had forgotten the old tales. Few ordinary mortals ever see Capra. No one from Broome has seen it in my lifetime."

She felt Lief dragging his feet and tightened her grip on his arm.

"Do not turn around again," she warned him. "You are fortunate you were not alone when you saw the illusion. There are tales of lone travelers who have died of thirst, so long did they stand with their eyes fixed on Capra. Once you have seen it, it captures your mind and holds you. Or so the old folk say."

"A ghost city!" muttered Barda, fascinated.

"Yes. They say that is why the last of the Capricons still haunt the mountains, instead of moving into Broome or building a new city of their own," Lindal said, keeping up her fast pace. "They watch for Capra at sunset. The old ones teach the young ones to love it, and to mourn what they have lost."

"But Capra was destroyed before the time of Adin!" Jasmine cried. "How long ago was that?"

Lindal shrugged. "If the Capricons would rather grieve over what is lost than live in the present, that is their own affair," she said carelessly. "They cannot be persuaded differently. The few that are left keep to themselves, and look down on everyone else."

"Rolf was not like that," Lief said, finding his voice. "He left the mountains and journeyed towards Del, to seek help for his people."

And so was killed by his worst nightmare.

The thought pierced him like a dart.

"Your friend would have found help in plenty if he had simply gone into Broome," said Lindal curtly. "He would also have learned that you were on your way there, and he had only to wait. But he would not enter Broome, oh, no!"

She shook her head, striding on, her eyes fixed on the horizon. "He would not lower himself to speak to ordinary mortals. Only the king himself was good enough to deserve the notice of a Capricon!"

"He had been brought up to think so," Lief murmured. "His ancestors — "

Lindal bared her teeth. "*My* ancestors were great warriors, who ate the brains of their slaughtered enemies," she said. "Do you suggest I do the same?"

"Lindal is perfectly right," snapped Jasmine.

"Rolf was cowardly, vain, and foolish. Why deny it, just because he is dead? I think — "

"I think we should stop arguing and light some torches," Barda put in calmly. "I can barely see my hand in front of my face, but there is something written on a stone ahead, and I suspect it is a warning."

16 - Dragon's Nest

The stone was very old, and looked unpleasantly like a tombstone. The very sight of it filled Lief with dread. He had to force himself to approach it, and lift his torch to read the words engraved upon it.

STRANGERS, DO NOT PASS THIS WAY!
ALL ARE DOOMED WHO DISOBEY
TURN YOUR FACES TO THE WEST
DEATH AWAITS IN DRAGON'S NEST

Jasmine shivered. "This stone gives me a bad feeling," she said. "Who made it?"

"No one knows," said Lindal. "It has always been here — and it has kept most people well away from Dragon's Nest."

"But not you," Barda said gruffly.

"Not me," Lindal admitted. "As I told you, I was a willful, disobedient child. Still, I hated to pass this stone. I always shut my eyes so I could not see it. I do not quite know why — or why I used to have nightmares about it afterwards. The verse is ominous, but . . ."

"It is not just the verse," Lief said slowly.

It had become extremely cold. Waves were crashing on the rocks, very near. He realized that without noticing it they had almost reached the tumble of rocks they had seen from the hills. A sickening trembling had begun deep within his body. His arm felt unbearably heavy as he held his torch flame closer to the stone.

"It is not just the verse," he repeated. "It is the carving in the background. Do you see? Those marks are the Sister signs, repeated endlessly. And the border . . ."

Barda leaned forward, peered at the border, then looked up, shaken. "Despair and die . . ." he muttered.

Filli whimpered beneath Jasmine's collar. She put up her hand to soothe him.

"The whole stone is a curse," she said softly. "It is an evil thing — full of hate."

"Come away from it," Lindal said abruptly, taking a step back.

Barda forced a grin, his white teeth gleaming in the darkness. "It seems you were braver as a child than you are now, Lindal!" he said.

"Only more foolish," Lindal retorted. "But still I never passed by the stone in darkness. The way to Dragon's Nest is fearful, even in daylight. At night — "

Lief backed away from the stone, gripping the Belt of Deltora with both hands. With relief he felt his mind begin to clear and the deep trembling to ease.

"We must stop in any case," he managed to say. "We need food and sleep. We will move on in the morning. Everything seems better in the light."

Lindal chose a camping spot well away from the evil stone. They lit a small fire for warmth and comfort. They ate, and at last they slept, keeping watch in turns.

But their sleep was far from peaceful. The sound of the crashing waves was cold and lonely. Dark, formless shadows haunted their dreams.

✳

They set off at first light the following day. One by one they passed the standing stone, their eyes turned away from it, fixed on the churning sea.

Beyond the stone there was no path to follow —

only a wilderness of huge rocks piled one upon the other.

Lindal led the way, scrambling through the maze, more often crawling than walking upright. Lief, Barda, and Jasmine soon realized that without her they would have become hopelessly lost.

Kree had still not returned. No one spoke of it, but fear for him hung over them like a cloud.

On they went, and on. They could see nothing but cold stone, the looming mountains, and the sky. They could hear nothing but the booming of the waves, beating like a great drum.

There was no sign of life at all. Everything was cold and dead.

Their fingers grew numb and clumsy. A feeling of dread was growing within them, weighing them down.

Despair and die . . .

Lief shook his head, trying to rid himself of the memory of the message on the stone. But it clung in his mind like an evil tick, draining his strength, spreading its poison.

The mountains of the Shadowlands border grew larger, closer. The sound of the waves grew louder. They could feel the tingling of sea spray on their faces, and taste salt on their chilled lips, but still they could see nothing.

And then, at last, Lindal stopped at the foot of a great slab of rock that slanted upward.

She waited until they caught up with her, then crawled with them to the top of the slab.

"There," she said in a low voice.

Straight ahead of them the stones fell away into a vast, bowl-shaped hollow squeezed between the mountains and the sea. The hollow was so deep that from where the companions lay, clutching the edge of the slanting rock, they could not see the bottom.

The mountains brooded over the hollow, glowering and secret. Waves crashed against its far edge, spattering the rocks with foam.

Lief guessed that at high tide the hollow was flooded with swirling water, for the stones that formed its sides were rounded and polished smooth, and strands of parched seaweed trailed over them like long, tangled hair.

Dragon's Nest . . .

Lief did not need to look at the emerald in the Belt of Deltora. He knew it would be as gray as the rock on which he lay. He could feel the evil crawling about him like a clammy mist, raising the hair on his arms and the back of his neck.

His mind swirled with shadows. His body was covered with freezing sweat, and the terrible, deep trembling had begun again.

Feebly he felt for the Belt, willing its magic to work for him as it had done so often before.

The topaz to clear his mind. The amethyst to soothe and calm. The diamond for strength . . .

"This was my lookout. I never went closer to the Nest than this," Lindal shouted over the sound of the pounding waves. "I was reckless as a child, but not quite mad."

She hunched her shoulders. "Ah — I had almost forgotten this feeling! It is as if some vile, invisible vapor rises from that hollow. It makes my skin crawl."

"It is the Sister of the East," Lief murmured through stiff lips. "The dragon has not been here — or has not been able to destroy it."

A great wave thundered onto the rocks with such force that the spray flew high into the air, raining down into the hollow, and spattering the companions with icy drops.

Gasping, they half slid, half clambered back down to the foot of the slanting rock.

"The tide is rising," Lindal said, shaking water from her painted head like a dog. "It took longer to get here than I remembered. We must move quickly — before the Nest begins to flood. Otherwise we will have to wait in this accursed place for hours until the tide turns again."

Together they moved forward. The sound of the waves was deafening. The cruel wind whistled around them, and every now and again they were sprayed with freezing foam.

By the time they reached the hollow they were crawling on their bellies, shivering and breathless.

They hauled themselves to the very edge. And as

they looked down, they all caught their breath in shock.

Whatever they had expected to see, it was not this.

The vast, stony bowl of the Nest was completely empty, except for a small, piteous figure lying huddled in the center.

Lief stared at the dark, curly head, the slender arms, the sprawled, furred legs tipped with delicate hoofs.

"Rolf!" he whispered. "It is Rolf! The dragon must have carried him off — brought him here. But why?"

"Any creature finds it useful to have a little of its favorite food put aside for later," Lindal pointed out, gazing down at the Capricon with interest.

At that moment, Rolf's crumpled body moved feebly.

"He is still alive," breathed Jasmine.

Lief's stomach knotted.

"Do not call to him! Do not make a sound!" Barda warned sharply, his eyes scanning the looming mountains. "The beast must be around somewhere. We do not want to alert it."

Impulsively Lief moved to hurl himself down the sloping sides of the Nest. Barda caught him and held him back.

"No, Lief!" Barda whispered. "Think! Once we are down there, we will be helpless if the dragon attacks. And I am not sure that Lindal is right. To me, the Capricon looks unpleasantly like bait."

"*Bait?*" hissed Lief. "Bait for what?"

Barda shrugged. "Possibly for other Capricons who roam the mountains. But I suspect — I fear — bait for us."

"Are you mad?" Lief struggled to tear himself free. "What does the ruby dragon know of us?"

"Have you forgotten the enemy who tricked us into going to End Wood Gap?" Barda demanded, tightening his grip. "What did that enemy do after we went into the Forests of Silence?"

Lief grew still. His mind was whirling.

"What if when the ruby dragon arose, our enemy's face was the first thing it saw, and our enemy's voice was the first sound it heard?" Barda demanded. "What if they formed some sort of alliance? To trap us, kill us, and defend the Sister of the East?"

Lief wet his lips. "That is impossible," he whispered.

"It does not seem likely," Lindal agreed. "From what the old folk say, dragons do not form alliances — even with one another. And surely your enemy hoped you would die in End Wood? As you nearly did, in fact."

"He might have hoped for it, but he would not have depended upon it," said Barda. "The Shadow Lord does not tolerate mistakes by his servants."

Lief shook his head stubbornly.

"The dragon would not harm me," he said. "Not while I wear the Belt of Deltora. And it would never agree to defend the Sister. No dragon would tolerate such a thing in its territory. Doran said — "

"Forget what Doran said!" Barda broke in. "Who knows what might have happened to the body and brain of a beast that has slept for centuries?"

He clenched his fists. "You cannot argue with the proof, Lief! The dragon has been here, but it has made no attempt to find the Sister and destroy it. The Nest has not been disturbed. Not a stone is out of place."

A giant wave smashed against the rocks beyond the Nest. Icy spray rained down. Far below them, the Capricon writhed and wailed.

"You are all wasting time," Jasmine snapped. "This argument is pointless! We are here to destroy the Sister of the East. We know that it is somewhere in Dragon's Nest — somewhere down there, hidden under the stones. So we must go into the Nest and dig for it. It is all very simple."

"Simple!" Barda growled. "With a dragon lurking and Rolf moaning and squirming around our feet?"

"Oh, we will have to get Rolf out first, I suppose," Jasmine said impatiently. "Otherwise he will get in our way."

"Lief will have to go down for him," said Lindal,

peering down at the wailing Capricon. "It would be too much to hope that he would cooperate with anyone else, even to save his own life."

Jasmine nodded and turned to Lief, pulling the coil of rope she carried from her belt.

"Barda must lower you down, Lief," she said. "The stones on the sides of the Nest look far too loose to support you. Take my rope for Rolf. Then Barda and Lindal can pull you both up together."

Lindal grinned broadly. "Why, how this little mouse is ordering us about, old bear!" she jeered, digging Barda in the ribs. "Are you going to take that?"

"It seems I am," Barda muttered as Lief began tying his own rope around his waist. "I fear I have no choice."

17 - Fire and Water

As Jasmine had feared, there were no safe footholds on the sloping sides of the Nest. The stones slid downward the moment they were touched, setting Lief swinging at the end of the rope like a puppet. And the lower he dropped, the colder it grew, and the more he was gripped by dread.

It is the Sister, he told himself, struggling to keep his mind clear. But his teeth had begun to chatter and his heart was pounding in his chest as though it would burst.

He landed awkwardly on the floor of the Nest, sinking almost to his knees in the bed of smooth stones. Stones slipped beneath his feet, and dried weed tangled around his ankles as he stumbled towards Rolf, the end of Jasmine's rope clutched in his hand.

The stones are deep, he thought numbly. *Very, very*

deep. How far down is the Sister of the East? How long will it take to find it? It may not even be below the floor of the Nest. It may be in one of the sides. What then?

Waves of sickness threatened to engulf him. Every step was an effort. He realized that he had begun to stagger.

This place will defeat us, he thought suddenly. *Its evil is too strong. No one could dig in these stones for more than a few minutes at a time. We are going to fail.*

Fighting despair, he reached Rolf's crumpled body and knelt down beside him.

"Rolf!" he croaked, the word sticking in his throat.

With a choking cry the Capricon sat up. He snatched at Lief and clung to him, his huge violet eyes swimming with terrified tears.

"Oh, why did you abandon me?" he moaned. "The guards did not protect me! You said they would protect me, but they did not! Oh, the screams — the blood — the fire! Never will I forget it!"

"I know, Rolf," Lief muttered. "Be still now."

"The dragon seized me . . . carried me — " Suddenly, Rolf broke off and looked around in bewilderment. "But where are your friends?" he squeaked. "Did they not come with you?"

"They are waiting at the top," said Lief briefly. With difficulty he freed his arms and began looping Jasmine's rope around Rolf's waist.

"Oh!" Rolf covered his face with his hands and

rocked from side to side. "Oh, soon the dragon will return! We must get away!"

"Stay still then!" begged Lief. He pulled at the rope to make sure it was secure, then hauled Rolf to his feet and, with the last of his strength, half carried him to the side of the Nest.

Jasmine was standing up above, keeping watch. Barda and Lindal were kneeling, peering over the edge of the Nest, the ropes gripped ready in their hands.

Lief signaled to them and at once they began to pull the ropes up, hand over hand.

Rolf looked up as the rope tightened around his waist and his feet left the floor of the Nest. When he saw Lindal's grim face and straining arms above him, he shrieked.

"Be quiet!" Lief whispered.

"But the woman of Broome is lifting me!" cried Rolf in horror. "How could you let *her* lift me? She and her kind are demons who dance on the bones of Capra! She is not worthy to — "

"Shut your mouth, Rolf!" hissed Lief.

But Lindal had heard. "I am happy to drop you if you wish, Capricon," she called.

Rolf whimpered and pressed his lips together. He clung to the rope, a dead weight, as slowly he and Lief were dragged upward over the loose and sliding stones.

But the moment he reached the top, he scrambled away from Lindal, avoiding her hand.

"Do not touch me, foul woman of Broome!" he gabbled, tearing the rope from his waist and casting it aside as though it were poisoned. "Keep away from me!"

"It would be a pleasure," said Lindal scornfully.

Barda gripped the hilt of his sword "How do you dare to insult Lindal, who has risked her life to save you?" he growled, looking at Rolf with contempt.

Eyeing the sword warily, Rolf crawled to his feet.

"My king," he cried in a trembling voice. "Your man is menacing me!"

But Lief, still slumped on the ground where Barda had left him, knew he could not interfere, even if he wanted to. He felt sick and desperately weak, as though stricken with a grave illness. He could only wonder how Rolf could move.

Barda took a threatening step towards the cowering Capricon.

"Lindal has more strength in her little finger than you have in your whole body," he growled. "She has a better brain than you will ever possess, and a bigger heart than a hundred of you put together!"

"Why, thank you, Barda," murmured Lindal, raising her eyebrows. "Though, now I come to think of it, it is not so great a compliment."

Barda ignored her. "Get out of my sight!" he spat at Rolf. "Go and hide your miserable self from the dragon, and trouble us no more!"

With a gulp and a last, beseeching glance at Lief, Rolf scuttled away. Soon he had disappeared among the giant stones.

"Good riddance," said Jasmine calmly. "Now we can get down to work. How should we begin?"

Feeling her eyes upon him, Lief made an effort to sit up. A wave of dizziness overcame him, and he fell back with a groan.

He heard Barda and Jasmine exclaim, and felt them kneel beside him. He tried to focus on their anxious faces, looming above him amid a spinning haze.

"I — I do not know where to begin," he mumbled. "I do not know what to do. The Belt does not help me. In the Nest, there is evil everywhere. It batters you from all sides. It is . . ."

Despair and die.

Another giant wave smashed on the rocks. Freezing water rained down on them and ran in streams into the Nest.

"We have to get him away from here," Lief heard Barda mutter.

"No!" Lief managed to say. "The feeling is passing. Just give me a moment to — "

"BEWARE!"

Lindal's cry rose high and urgent over the sound of the waves. A freezing gale suddenly pounded down upon the rocks. A dark shadow swept overhead, blocking the sun.

Jasmine and Barda cried out, sprang to their feet.

And as they moved, Lief saw a horror above him — a vast, bloated thing of glittering scarlet.

The beast's spiked wings sliced through the air like knives. The stunted mass of lumps and spines that was its tail twisted and thrashed. Its tiny red eyes, almost hidden amid puffy folds of scaly skin, were the mad eyes of a killer.

Who knows what might have happened to the body and brain of a beast that has slept for centuries?

Barda's words roared in Lief's mind.

Desperately he struggled to get to his feet, fighting the dizziness, the weakness. Desperately he fumbled for his sword.

Curved black talons, impossibly long, struck viciously downward. Lief rolled, and a claw missed him by a hair, scraping on the rock.

The creature roared in fury — a harsh, high sound like shattering glass. Fire belched from its gaping jaws. Boiling red slime dripped from its fangs and fell, sizzling, onto the streaming rocks. Steam billowed upward.

Lost in the steam, blind and helpless, Lief gripped the Belt of Deltora.

He fixed his mind upon the great ruby. With all his strength he willed the dragon to feel the power of the great gem, to hear him and understand.

But the beast bellowed in rage and madness and came for him again, a monstrous glistening fury, red as blood.

Lief felt Jasmine and Barda seize his arms and haul him back. He heard the razor-sharp claws scrape the rock again, felt the hot blast of fire on his face.

A wave thundered onto the tall rocks behind them. Cold spray drenched them, instantly turning to steam in the monster's fire.

Barda was bellowing over the sound of the waves.

". . . get as close to the water as we can!" Barda was shouting. "Our only chance . . ."

But the dragon was above them, striking at them, sending them sprawling on the greasy stone, rolling and scrabbling away from its clawing feet, its bursts of fire.

And then, through the swirling veil of steam, Lief saw the tall figure of Lindal standing her ground, her spear arm raised.

"Lindal!" Barda bellowed, scrambling to his feet. "Get down!"

A spear flew through the air. It struck the dragon's thrashing tail, bounced away, and clattered uselessly to the ground.

Lindal did not falter. Another spear was already in her hand. She hurled it, and this time it reached its mark — its point piercing the softer, paler flesh of the monster's belly.

The monster screeched, clawed the waving spear from its body, and wheeled to face its attacker.

They all saw Lindal's teeth flash in a savage grin of triumph. "Now! Go!" she shouted.

Barda hesitated.

"Barda!" shrieked Jasmine, pulling at his arm.

"Do not make this all for nothing, you bumbling ox!" roared Lindal, reaching for her last spear. "Get to the water!"

And with a groan Barda obeyed her. He turned his back on her, seized Lief with his free arm, and leaped for the tall rocks where the sea pounded upon the land, where spray now rained down unceasingly, and water ran in streams.

They squeezed into a gap between the rocks and turned, in terror, just in time to see Lindal fall — fall, crumpled and bleeding, beneath the monster's beating wing.

The beast's ghastly head turned on its swollen neck. It glared at its fallen enemy. It roared, and a plume of fire belched downward.

Lindal's clothes burst into flames. The puddles on the stones around her hissed and steamed.

Lief and Jasmine cried out in grief and horror. But Barda stood rigid and silent as the rock.

A giant wave thundered behind them, and this time the water frothed over them in a flood, streaming over the smooth stones, running down into Dragon's Nest.

The beast snarled. It shook its head as if to clear its eyes. And then, suddenly, its neck twisted again —

twisted away from Lindal. Suddenly, it was looking up — up into the swirling steam above its head.

It gave a broken cry, its crooked mouth gaping, its forked tongue darting. Its leathery wings began to flap wildly. Its ungainly body jerked, turning this way and that as if in panic. Its spiked, stubby tail thrashed on the steaming rock.

Then abruptly the billowing steam was swept away — swept away as if by a great wind. And Lief's heart leaped as he saw, plunging down from the sky, a vast, glittering creature red as the setting sun, with eyes like glowing coals, wings like scarlet sails, and a tail sleek and slender as a stream of fire.

"Another dragon!" Jasmine gasped. "Another ruby dragon!"

But Lief was looking down at the Belt of Deltora, at the glowing, scarlet star that the great ruby had become, and was wondering how ever he could have been deceived.

"No," he shouted. "Not another ruby dragon. *The* ruby dragon. The true ruby dragon has risen at last."

18 - Fight to the Death

Snarling, the monster on the ground rose to defend itself. It clawed the air, and fire spurted from his jaws. But then its enemy was upon it, and in moments the battle was over.

Indeed, it was no battle at all, for the rage-filled beast that had answered Lief's desperate call had a dragon's heart, mind, and will, and the nightmare copy on the ground did not.

The copy could tear frail humans apart, and its fire could burn their flesh to blackened cinders, but it was no match for the most ancient and mysterious of Deltora's beasts.

In seconds it was on its back, its throat torn and bleeding, its body heaving as its life drained away.

The ruby dragon raised its head, spread its wings, and roared its savage triumph as waves thundered on the rocks and spray flew upward to fall like rain.

It licked its lips, as if tasting the salt. Its great head turned towards the sea.

And as the echo of its roar still growled like thunder in the Mountains, it launched itself into the air and was gone.

Lief, Barda, and Jasmine crawled shakily out of hiding. They were drenched, and very cold. Shivering, they turned towards the crashing waves and looked up.

The ruby dragon was a vivid splash of scarlet against the blue sky. Water streamed from its scales. In its mouth was the flashing silver of a wriggling fish. The fish disappeared. The dragon wheeled and dived again.

"It will be back," Barda muttered. He began to move across the stones, towards the place where Lindal fell.

The scarlet beast lay across their path. Its scales had darkened to the color of dried blood, but all of them could see that it still lived.

As they cautiously approached it, its tiny eyes opened and fixed them with a look of dull hatred.

"Keep back," Jasmine muttered. "It would strike at us, even now, if it could."

The beast hissed, as if with loathing, and suddenly the bulbous folds of its misshapen body began to heave and roll like the waves on the sea, the scales shimmering like dark water.

The companions jumped back, staring in disbelief as the rippling mound of flesh collapsed in on itself and melted away.

Then it had gone, and all that was left lying on the stones was the sprawled, torn body of Rolf the Capricon.

"Rolf!" Lief whispered. And, all at once, a long line of things that had puzzled him made perfect sense.

Rolf's reckless exposure of him to the Granous. The dimming of the ruby when no enemy could be seen. The lightening of his heart as the guards, with Rolf, moved away. The guard troop, taken by surprise despite the night watch. The sparing of the horses. Rolf's lack of surprise on seeing that Lindal was with them. Rolf's strength after being in the Nest . . .

And most of all, the false dragon, ugly as a nightmare in a fevered brain.

Rolf's pale lips stretched into a malicious smile.

"You fools!" he said. "How easily I deceived you! A finger was a small price to pay for your trust. The sacrifice of my pride was not."

His head rolled from side to side. "Do you think I did not know how you despised me?" he hissed. "Me! — the one who could have transformed and torn you limb from limb in a moment — if it had not been for that accursed Belt."

He paused, panting, licking his foam-flecked lips.

"I knew I had to wait — wait until you reached the home of the Sister, the heart of my power, where even the Belt could not save you. So I watched and stayed my hand, even when the loathsome woman of Broome joined you and I longed to attack."

His hands twitched, clutching at the air. His hatred was almost visible. It was as if it oozed from the pores of his skin, and hung about him like a poisonous cloud.

"I had hoped you would all come into the pit, but you cheated me and did not," he rasped. "So again I waited, until you were all together once more, for I had sworn a mighty oath that not one of you would escape my wrath, as you escaped it at End Wood Gap."

He smiled crookedly, "Not for a moment did you suspect me," he breathed. "I was too clever for you."

"You do not look so clever now," snarled Barda, staring down at him.

Rolf sneered. "Your evil beast has been the death of me, but there are others — other servants of the Master — who lie in wait for you. This is your last battle, scum of the land. And it is a battle you will never win."

"What did the Shadow Lord promise you, that you would betray your king?" asked Lief dully.

"You are not my king, Lief of Del," Rolf spat.

"What did you know of me, before I threw myself in your way in the Os-Mine Hills? What did you know of Rolf, eldest son of the clan Dowyn, heir to the lordship of Capra?"

"I knew nothing," Lief said quietly. "But how could I have known, Rolf? You kept yourself secret and apart, even from the people of Broome."

"Do not argue with him, Lief," murmured Jasmine. "Truth does not matter to him. His mind feeds on pride and anger, nothing more."

"You cared nothing for me, king," Rolf said. "But the Master knew me, and knew my worth. The Master's voice came to me one night at sunset, as I huddled alone in the Mountains, looking down at Capra. The Master understood my greatness. He gave me precious gifts, in return for my service. And much more will follow . . . so much more . . ."

His breath was coming in shallow gasps now. His beautiful violet eyes were glazed.

"I serve the Master," he whispered. "For the Master, I will protect the Sister of the East. And in return he has made me a great sorcerer. I can do things of which my ancestors never dreamed. I can change shape. I can fly through the air. I can tear and burn my enemies, and hear them scream, as they deserve."

Barda cursed under his breath. His fists were clenched. But he said nothing aloud and made no move.

"When the Master triumphs, I will be the ruler of the East, as is my birthright," Rolf rasped. "Capra will rise again, and the vile strangers in my land will be dust and ashes beneath my feet."

Again he smiled. And then his gaze grew fixed, and the restless twitching of his hands stilled. He was dead.

The companions turned away, sickened.

A wave pounded on the rocks. Spray pelted down. Water foamed between the stones.

And in the brief quiet before another wave struck, they all distinctly heard a low groan.

They scrambled towards the sound.

Lindal had rolled into a deep cleft between two rocks. The left side of her face bore the raised scarlet mark of the dragon's pounding wing. Her clothes were blackened and her left arm was blistered. Her eyes were glazed and blinking. She was drenched to the skin.

But she was alive!

"Help me out of this accursed hole," she slurred, holding up her uninjured arm. "Every time a wave breaks, water flows over me like a stream. I am freezing!"

"Stop complaining," shouted Barda, joyfully hauling her upright. "The last we saw of you, you were burning like a torch! The wave must have put the fire out."

Lindal stood swaying and shivering, looking around her blankly. Plainly she could not understand what had happened.

She saw Rolf's body lying on the stones and frowned in puzzlement. Then she looked up and her face twisted in alarm.

"The dragon is returning!" she shouted. "It is coming straight for us!"

And the dragon was coming, indeed — flying back from the sea, its scarlet body wet and gleaming, brilliant against the sky.

Filli began chattering frantically. He had had quite enough of dragons.

Lindal felt for her spears, remembered they were gone, and lurched forward, her eyes desperately searching the ground.

"My spears!" she mumbled. "I must find — "

Barda took her arm and gently drew her back. "Be still, Lindal," he said. "We will explain everything later. Just be still now, and wait."

They backed against the nearest rock. There was nowhere else to go.

A huge shadow swept over them. They bent beneath the wind of mighty wings. And then the wind abruptly ceased and they looked up.

The dragon had landed at the edge of the Nest. It was watching them calmly.

Speak to it, Lief told himself. *It is waiting.*

But his mouth was dry, and he felt as though his

back had become part of the rock. He summoned up his courage and forced himself to step forward.

The ruby dragon looked down at him and seemed to smile.

"So!" it said, its voice soft and whispering. "So you have come, king of Deltora, wearing the great ruby of my territory. It is just as Doran promised."

"Yes," Lief said. "I searched for you, and at last I found you."

"Or *I* found *you*," said the dragon. Its eyes flashed and its forked tail twitched.

"There is evil here," it said. "Evil and poison. You allowed an intruder to enter my land while I slept."

Lief felt a chill of fear, but forced himself to hold the dragon's blood-red gaze.

"Not I," he said. "It happened long, long ago. Can you destroy the evil? As you have destroyed its guardian?"

He glanced at the limp form of Rolf, lying on the stones.

"We will see," said the ruby dragon. "Come closer. You alone."

Lief did as he was bid, though his knees were trembling so that he could hardly stand.

"And closer still," the dragon said.

Lief moved so close that if he had stretched out his hand he could have touched the glittering red scales of the beast's neck. The scent of the dragon filled his nose. It was like the smell of hot metal mixed with burning leaves.

The ruby on the Belt of Deltora blazed like fire.

The dragon spread its wings and closed its eyes.

For a long moment it seemed to bask in the ruby's radiance. And when its eyes opened once more, it seemed to Lief that they were deeper and darker than they had been before.

"Now," the dragon said.

Its wings still spread, it plunged into the hollow called Dragon's Nest. With its mighty claws it began to rake away the stones in the center, scooping them out by the hundreds, by the thousands, flinging them up and away.

19 - The Sister of the East

S tones pelted the companions like giant hail. Covering their heads with their arms, they stumbled away from the edge of the Nest.

From a safe distance they stood and watched in awe as stones showered from the hollow to pile in great drifts around its rim. But gradually their excitement died, and a feeling of foreboding took its place.

As the dragon dug deeper into the pit, as the heaps of stones grew larger, the air was becoming thicker and harder to breathe. The light was dimming. And a strange, low ringing sound was growing louder.

Giant waves pounded on the shore, now sometimes foaming over the tops of the tall rocks and streaming down like a waterfall to run in rivulets between the stones.

But even the waves could not drown out the terrible song of the Sister of the East floating up from the hollow.

It was a song of barren despair, of ruin and misery, of dullness and death. One low note, haunting, penetrating, relentless.

And worst of all, strangely familiar.

Filli was whimpering beneath Jasmine's collar. Jasmine herself was hunched and frowning as if in pain. Lindal sat slumped on the stones, her head bowed, her hands pressed to her ears.

"I did not know," Barda murmured. Lief glanced at him. The big man's face was gleaming with sweat.

"I have been hearing this sound all my life," Barda muttered, his lips scarcely moving. "Not like this. Not so that I was aware of it. But now I realize that faintly it has always been there, like the sun on my face, or the air I breathe. I did not even think of it as sound. I thought it was the sound of silence."

"Yes," said Lief.

And then they both realized that the stones had stopped falling, and they could hear no movement inside the hollow.

"Where are you? Come to me!"

Lief did not know if the dragon had called in his mind or aloud.

It does not matter, he told himself slowly. *All that matters is that I must go.*

He forced himself to move forward, pushing

through the dull, thick air, scrambling up a towering heap of stones. He crawled to the very edge of the heap, and peered down into Dragon's Nest.

The broad, flat surface of the Nest had become a yawning pit at the base of a vast, stony funnel.

The dragon had dug down to the bare rock. Now it crouched on the rock, in the center of the pit, staring at the thing it had uncovered.

The thing was like a glowing, pulsating egg. It was a poisonous, flaring yellow, so bright that it seemed to hurt the eyes.

Its low, continuous song drilled into Lief's ears. And from it radiated evil so intense that his throat closed and his skin burned.

"Come to me, or I am lost."

The dragon's voice was very faint. Lief saw with terror that the rich scarlet of its scales was slowly dimming.

Without hesitation, without a thought, not even hearing Barda's shout of alarm, he flung himself over the edge.

Tumbling and gasping, he slid down through the piled stones, down into the pit where the dragon crouched.

He landed heavily near the beast's hind feet. A mass of stones came with him, beating on the dragon's folded wings, half covering its tail.

The dragon did not speak, did not move. There

was not a quiver of its skin or a twitch of a claw. Its great body was utterly motionless.

Lief tried to stand, and found he could not. The sinister song of the Sister of the East filled his ears and his mind. Its evil power battered him, beat him to the ground.

He could not stand. He could not walk. But the dragon lay rigid, fading as he watched. And the Sister of the East sang on, spreading its terror and its poison.

Lief began to crawl, being careful not to touch the dragon's body as he passed it.

His breath coming in sobbing gasps, he pushed himself towards the poisonous yellow thing that radiated horror and despair. He knew only that the thing must be destroyed — that if it could not be destroyed, all was lost.

But moment by moment, his strength was draining away. His arms and legs were trembling as if he was in the grip of a terrible fever, yet he was chilled to the bone. He feared that soon he would be unable to move at all.

Hardly knowing what he did, he pressed his hands to the great ruby in the Belt of Deltora.

Warmth stole through his fingers, rushed into his arms. And he became aware of a new sound mingling with the low song of the Sister.

It was a slow, heavy thumping sound, like the beating of a great drum. And slowly Lief realized that it was the dragon's heart.

The Belt . . . we are linked by the power of the Belt, he thought dimly.

Words flashed into his mind. Doran's words:

The king, wearing the Belt of Deltora, is Deltora's only salvation now.

Following an impulse he did not understand, but did not question, Lief lifted one hand from the Belt and placed it on the dragon's cool, dry skin.

Instantly his fingers tingled, and his own heart swelled in his chest as he felt power surge through him, rush through his body like a raging torrent from the great ruby to the beast.

The dragon stirred. The dull scales beneath Lief's hand brightened, deepened to rich scarlet. And Lief saw with wonder the patch of color spread from beneath his hand, spread surely and rapidly until the whole mighty body was glowing like the ruby itself.

The dragon raised its head. Its red eyes flashed. Its heartbeats crashed like thunder.

And still the power of the ruby streamed through Lief, and he could not have lifted his hand from the glowing scales even if he had wanted to.

He could not move or speak, but he knew it did not matter.

He was doing all he had to do. He was the link. He was the connection between the dragon and the ruby, the ancient talisman dug from deep within the dragon's earth.

The dragon fixed its red eyes on the pulsating

yellow egg before it. It roared, and a narrow jet of flame gushed from its mouth, wrapping the egg in fire.

Again the dragon roared, and again. Bathed in fire, the egg glowed red, then white. White-hot, it shimmered, burning like an evil star.

There was a sharp cracking sound as its surface split. Its low song rose to a shriek. For a long moment, it seemed that time stood still.

Then the dragon hissed like a giant snake. And beneath a fresh blast of heat so intense that Lief felt in terror that his own flesh must melt, the Sister of the East flashed with white flame, then simply withered and fell into dust.

Lief closed his burning eyes. As if suddenly released, his hand slipped from the dragon's side. He lay still, facedown on the rock, his mind empty of thought, aware of nothing but the crashing of the waves above and, beside him, the slow, steady beating of the dragon's heart.

✳

When Lief opened his eyes again, he found that he was no longer in the hollow with the ruby dragon. Or even at the edge of Dragon's Nest.

He could hear the waves, but they were some distance away. He was lying on a sleeping blanket, in front of a brightly burning fire.

On the other side of the fire, Barda, Jasmine, and Lindal were murmuring together. Firelight flickered on their faces, but their bodies were shadowy and behind them the light was dim and strangely stained with pink.

At first Lief feared that his sight had been damaged by the heat of the dragon's fire. Then he looked up.

The first thing he saw was Kree, perched on the tip of a jagged rock. Kree had returned at last!

Relief washed over him like cool water. Then he realized that Kree was silhouetted against a sky that was a riot of red and orange streaks, and he sighed with gratitude.

There was nothing wrong with his sight. The sun was going down!

Gingerly he sat up, feeling bruised all over.

"You have certainly taken your time to wake," Jasmine said. "We brought you out of that pit and carried you away from the spray hours ago!" Her voice was just as usual, but her face shone with relief.

"The dragon — " Lief broke off, wincing. His throat felt raw and scorched. He took the flask Jasmine passed to him, and drank gratefully.

"The dragon is at sea, hunting for more fish," said Barda, putting aside the little locked box he had been playing with. "I doubt we will see it again before morning."

"And I am glad of that," Jasmine said. "The beast makes me nervous. It seems to like the look of my hair even more than the other dragon did."

Lindal laughed, smoothing her smooth skull.

"It likes mine not at all!" she crowed. "Because it cannot see it! Which is exactly why it is a tradition for the women of my people to shave their heads clean."

Then her face sobered. "In the old days there were many scarlet dragons in the east. I have heard dread tales of them from the cradle. Now one, at least, has returned."

"Without it, the Sister of the East could not have been destroyed," Lief reminded her.

Lindal nodded. "I know," she said ruefully. "And I know that because the Sister has gone, the fields of the east will be fruitful again, and the fisherfolk will no longer come to shore with empty nets three days out of five. It is a cause for great rejoicing."

She sighed. "But still, it has come at a price. The dragon respects you, Lief, for you wear the Belt of Deltora. But I fear what may happen to the people of Broome when you move on. The mountains of the north are very far from — "

Jasmine gave an exclamation of annoyance, and Barda dug Lindal in the ribs. She clapped her hand over her mouth.

Lief's heart lurched. "The mountains of the north?" he exclaimed. "What — ?"

Avoiding his eyes, Barda picked up the little box and began turning it over in his hands again.

"No!" rasped Lief. "You must tell me! What do you know that I do not?"

"We had intended to wait until you were stronger before we told you," Jasmine murmured. "We wanted you to rest, just for tonight, and not to think about — "

"Not to think about what?" Lief roared, then groaned and grasped his aching throat.

Jasmine glanced at Barda. He shrugged reluctantly.

"While you slept, we buried Rolf, as is proper," he said. "But before that . . ."

"Before that, I searched the body," Jasmine said calmly, taking a yellowed, folded paper from one of her many pockets. "Which is *not* proper, according to Barda. But stitched into the hem of the Capricon's cloak, I found this."

She handed the paper to Lief. Eagerly he unfolded it. As he had hoped, it was the second part of Doran's map.

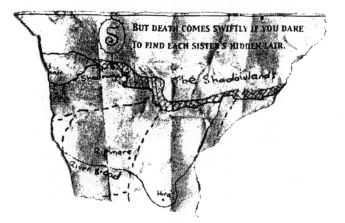

Jasmine leaned over to tap a finger on the Sister symbol. "There," she said. "That is why we will be going to the mountains of the north."

"Shadowgate," Lief muttered, reading the name beside the symbol. "I have never heard of it, or seen it on a map before!"

"Nor I," said Barda grimly, frowning at the box in his hands. "It does not sound an appealing place."

"Neither did Dragon's Nest," said Jasmine. "But at Dragon's Nest we made a lie of the verse printed here. We not only found the first Sister, but we destroyed it. And we survived! *That* is what we should be thinking of tonight, Lief."

She took the map fragment from Lief and put it away once more. "Tonight, we must rest and be glad," she said firmly. "What is the point of worrying about the future? It will come soon enough."

"Indeed!" Lindal agreed heartily. "This is a time to celebrate, not moan and worry about things that cannot be changed."

She sprang to her feet. "Let us go to Broome at once!" she cried. "We will take them by surprise, but all the better! I hate speeches and parades. Hot baths, fish stew, good ale, loud music, and friends to clap us on the back — what more could anyone ask?"

"Nothing at all," said Barda with satisfaction.

There was a tiny click and he gave a shout of surprise. Somehow his blunt fingers had found a hidden catch in the carving of the box. A small rod of polished wood now protruded from the cube, very near to the top.

He pulled eagerly at the box's lid, but it remained firmly closed. He looked up in comical dismay.

"There is more than one lock!" he exclaimed. "Curse this foolish toy!"

Lindal laughed uproariously. "Throw it away, old bear!" she cried. "You will never solve the puzzle."

"I will," Barda grunted, shoving the box back into his pocket. "I will solve it, if it is the last thing I ever do."

Cold fingers seemed to run down Lief's spine. He shivered, and wondered why.

I am cold, he told himself. *I am cold and tired, that is all.*

"Lief!" shouted Jasmine, jumping up and kicking at the fire to put it out. "Lief, are you ready?"

Her face was turned to him, full of love and laughter. Barda and Lindal towered behind her, scuffling with one another like children.

Lief's heart warmed.

What is the point of worrying about the future? It will come soon enough.

"Yes," he said, grinning and climbing to his feet. "Lead on! I am ready."

181

SHADOWGATE

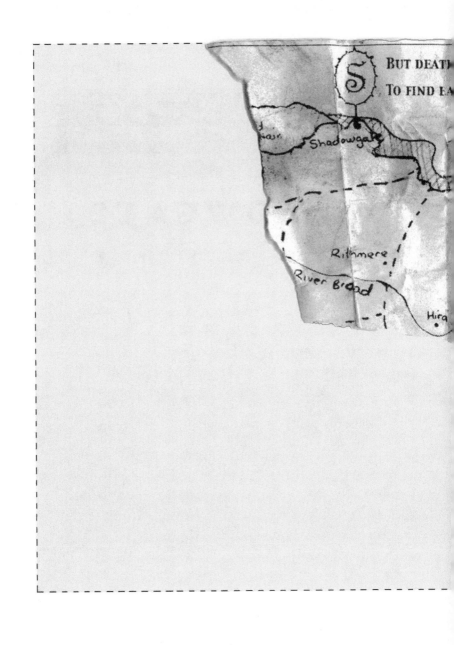

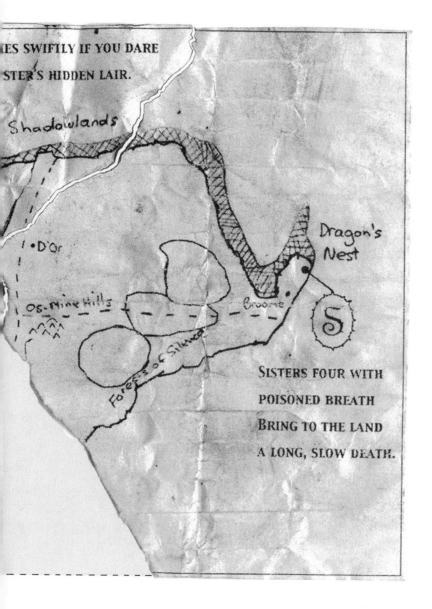

IES SWIFTLY IF YOU DARE

STER'S HIDDEN LAIR.

Shadowlands

•D'Or

Os-Mine Hills

Forests of Silence

Dragon's Nest

Broome

S

SISTERS FOUR WITH
POISONED BREATH
BRING TO THE LAND
A LONG, SLOW DEATH.

Contents

The story so far . . .

Lief, Barda, and Jasmine have begun a secret quest to find and destroy the Four Sisters, evil creations of the Shadow Lord which are poisoning Deltora. To succeed, they must wake Deltora's last seven dragons, which have been deep in enchanted sleep for centuries.

Deltora's dragons were hunted almost to extinction by the Shadow Lord's creatures, the seven Ak-baba. In the end, only one dragon from each gem territory remained. To save them, Deltora's most famous explorer, Doran the Dragonlover (known to the dragons as Dragonfriend), persuaded the seven to sleep until a king, wearing the magic Belt of Deltora, called them to wake. He made each dragon swear that it would not take advantage of another's sleep to invade its territory.

The disappearance of the dragons allowed the Shadow Lord to put the Four Sisters in place. Only when the power of a dragon joins with the power of the gems in the Belt of Deltora can the Sisters be destroyed.

The dragon of the topaz has been woken. With the help of a fragment of an ancient map and the dragon of the ruby, the companions found and destroyed the Sister of the East, in Dragon's Nest, near the coastal city of Broome.

In doing so, they found another map fragment, telling them that the second Sister is hidden in the far north, at a place called Shadowgate.

Now read on . . .

1 - Warning

The people of Broome were dancing. The music was loud. The floorboards of the great hall shook beneath the pounding of hundreds of feet.

Outside, it was dark. Cold wind moaned around the city walls, and waves crashed on the shore. But inside the great hall, all was warmth and light.

The people had much to celebrate.

King Lief, with his companions, Jasmine and Barda, had been in Broome for ten full days. That was a joy in itself. But there was something even better. During their stay, like a miracle, the barren land and the empty sea had come alive.

The fishing boats had begun hauling in fat fish. The hunters were bringing home meat almost every day. The crops were at last showing strong new shoots.

Suddenly, the long time of hunger was over. There was new life everywhere. It was even said that a scarlet dragon had been sighted in the sea above Dragon's Nest!

The people of Broome did not know how or why this wonder had occurred. They simply rejoiced. And their rejoicing was at its height on this, the last night of their young king's visit.

Part of a spinning circle of dancers in the center of the hall, Lief looked as carefree as all the rest. But, in truth, his mind was on other things.

Only he, Barda, Jasmine, and their friend Lindal knew that the land was healing because the evil thing called the Sister of the East had been destroyed.

Only they knew that the journey the companions would begin at dawn was to end in Shadowgate. There the Sister of the North lay hidden, spreading its poison and singing its song of death and despair.

The music ended with a mighty clash of cymbals. At the same moment, Lief caught sight of Jasmine beckoning urgently from the door. Filli was perched on her shoulder, almost hidden by her tangled black hair.

Lief hurried towards them.

"We went out to get some air," Jasmine whispered as he reached her. "See what we found!"

They slipped outside. Perched on the veranda rail outside the hall, golden eyes gleaming in the light of a hanging lantern, were two black birds.

Lief stared, startled. One of the birds was Kree, who was never far from Jasmine's side. But the other . . .

"Ebony!" he muttered.

Ebony was the most trusted of all the messenger birds Jasmine had trained. On their second day in Broome, Ebony had arrived with a message from Doom, demanding news. She had flown back to Del, bearing tidings as glad as Doom could wish.

Why had she returned so soon?

Jasmine held out the parchment she had taken from Ebony's leg. Lief recognized Doom's writing at once.

HIDDEN FLOCKS TRAVEL SINGING.

SPARROW FRIENDS FEATHER OLD NESTS ONLY DUCKS TRUST CAGES.

BEAKS STOPPED CHIRPING BE TO CHICKS ARE YOU TWITTERING WHISPERS WINGS ARE THERE.

YET AS TREES KNOWN MORE BRANCHES NOTHING HOOTS.

HERE FLUTTERING THINGS WITH EGGS PEAL PECKING WILL I FLY.

SEED FORTUNE PERCHES GOOD EAGLE.

"Doom has gone mad," said Jasmine. "Or . . . is he trying to write poetry? If so, he has no talent for it. This does not even rhyme."

Lief grinned at the thought of Doom as a poet. "Poems do not have to rhyme," he said. "But they do have to make a kind of sense. Doom has used a new code."

"Well, I cannot make head nor tail of it," Jasmine said flatly. "It seems just a lot of nonsense about birds."

Lief frowned over the note. "Perhaps it is a warning to us to keep Kree safe," he muttered. "Doom thinks someone drugged Kree's water, the night he returned to Del. And he must be right. Kree remembers nothing of that night, or the following day."

"I do not need a warning," Jasmine snapped. "I do not need a drawing of birds being freed to remind me how lucky Kree was to escape death."

An idea flashed into Lief's mind. He scanned the message rapidly.

"Why, of course!" he exclaimed. "The picture is the clue. We must free the birds!"

He took the stub of a pencil from his pocket and crossed out some of the words in the message:

HIDDEN ~~FLOCKS~~
TRAVEL ~~SINGING~~

~~SPARROW~~ FRIENDS
~~TWITTER~~ OLD ~~NEST~~ ONLY ~~PERCH~~
TRUST ~~CLAWS~~ .

~~BEAKS~~ STOPPED ~~CHIRPING~~ BE TO
~~CHICKS~~ ARE YOU ~~FLUTTERING~~
WHISPERS ~~WINGS~~ ARE THERE .

YET AS ~~EAGLE~~ KNOWN MORE
~~BRANCHES~~ NOTHING ~~HOOTS~~ .

HERE ~~FLUTTERING~~ THINGS WITH
~~EGGS~~ REAL ~~PECKING~~ WILL I ~~FLY~~.

~~SEED~~ FORTUNE ~~PERCHES~~ GOOD ~~EAGLE~~

"You see?" he said. "That is what the picture means. All the words that have anything to do with birds — 'flocks,' 'singing,' 'sparrow,' and so on — have to be taken out of the message before it can be read."

Jasmine began reading the new note. " 'Hidden . . . travel. Friends . . . old . . . only . . . trust . . .' — it still does not make sense!"

Then she saw the second small trick, and smiled. "Unless you read each sentence backwards!" she added.

Lief could not return her smile. Grimly, he spoke the words of the message aloud.

" 'Travel hidden. Trust only old friends. There are whispers you are to be stopped. Nothing more known as yet. I will deal with things here. Good fortune.' "

Jasmine did not spend time wondering what had made her father send such a message. She concentrated on practical matters.

"It will not be easy to travel hidden," she said. "Everyone knows we are touring the kingdom. Everywhere people will be watching, in case we come their way."

"Indeed." Lief was still staring at Doom's note. "And the guardian of the Sister of the North among them, it seems. The Shadow Lord must have sensed that the Sister of the East is no more. He cannot know if we found the map fragment directing us to Shadowgate. But he is taking no chances."

Jasmine slowly nodded agreement. "And plainly the guardian of the north has allies," she said. "Doom has heard rumors . . . surely there could *be* no rumors if only one person was involved."

Lief looked down at the magic Belt of Deltora. The seven great gems gleamed, the topaz and the ruby brighter than all the rest.

The Belt's power keeps the Shadow Lord back for now, but his hand still stretches into Deltora, he thought bitterly. *We cannot trust smiling faces or loyal words. Even here in Broome . . .*

He felt a small, strong hand grip his own. He lifted his head and met Jasmine's bright eyes.

"I doubt we have an enemy in Broome, but we will take no risks," she said, as though she had read his mind. "We will leave here now — tonight. Then . . . we will disappear. We will disguise ourselves and take new names. We have done that before. Remember?"

"Yes," Lief muttered. "But I did not think we would ever have to do it again. In those days, I was not king and the Belt of Deltora had not been restored. In those days, I thought that if we succeeded in our quest we would all live happily ever after. I did not dream the nightmare would go on and on — "

He and Jasmine spun around as the door to the hall swung open in a blast of sound. Barda and Lindal of Broome strode out onto the veranda.

"Lindal saw you through the window," Barda said. "What — ?"

He broke off as his eyes fell on the parchment in Lief's hand. His face sobered, and he glanced at Lindal.

"You will be wanting privacy," Lindal said quickly. She turned to go back into the hall.

Trust only old friends.

"No, Lindal, please stay," begged Lief. "We need your help."

❋

Less than an hour later, four figures slipped silently out of the city gates. The dance was still in full swing, and no one saw them go.

Even if they had been seen, it was unlikely that the first three would have been recognized.

Only the woman turning to close the gates behind them would have been familiar. Lindal looked as she always did — tall and straight in leather jacket, leggings, and boots, her shaved skull painted with swirling red patterns.

Her friends, however, now looked very different.

All were dressed in the drab, close-fitting woolen caps and long oiled coats of Broome fisherfolk, and their most famous features had been disguised.

Lief no longer wore his cloak, and the Belt of Deltora was concealed beneath his clothes. Jasmine's hair was hidden under her cap and her face was streaked with grime so that she looked like a grubby young boy. Barda's dark beard had been cut back to rough stubble.

"It was bad enough playing the part of a beggar, in the old days," he grumbled. "But at least I still had my beard then. And I did not stink of fish that died before I was born!"

Lindal laughed. "Your garments smell very strong, I must admit. I suspect that no one will want to keep company with the rough-looking man Berry and his two young nephews, Lewin and Jay, for long."

"That will suit Berry, Lewin, and Jay very well," Jasmine answered, though Filli, crouched on her shoulder and rubbing his nose, plainly disagreed.

"Filli will have to stay hidden, Jasmine," Lindal warned. "And Kree will have to keep his distance."

"I know," sighed Jasmine, glancing at the black bird perched on her arm. "And the journey to Shadowgate will be very long. I only wish Honey, Bella, and Swift were still with us."

"The horses are back in Del by now, no doubt," said Barda. "But we may be able to buy others in the north."

Lindal shook her head in wonder. Horses were unknown in Broome, where people used their own legs to carry them from place to place, whatever the distance.

"Thank you for all you have done for us, Lindal," Lief said, anxious to be gone. "Send Ebony back to Del in the morning. And remember, the ruby dragon has promised me that it will do the people of Broome no harm — as long as they leave it in peace."

"Time will tell," Lindal said darkly. "I do not place great value on a dragon's promise. Perhaps the ruby beast kept faith with Doran the Dragonlover. But that does not mean it will keep faith with you."

And at that very moment, Kree screeched a warning, and the stars above them were blotted out.

The ruby dragon swept above them. Its red scales glittered in the moonlight. Its wing beats were louder than the wind.

"Why, the beast has already broken its vow!" cried Lindal furiously, reaching for a spear. "It thinks to take advantage of the celebration, to plunder the city!"

"Wait!" shouted Lief, throwing himself in front of her. "Lindal! Let me speak to it!"

Lindal tightened her lips, but pointed her spear to the ground.

The dragon landed in front of them and settled itself comfortably.

"Greetings, King of Deltora," it said to Lief. "You are leaving Broome a little earlier than you planned."

"Yes," Lief said uncomfortably. "It became . . . necessary."

The dragon nodded. "I approve," it said. "In darkness, we can fly unseen."

"*What?*" exclaimed Barda.

The dragon turned its flat red eyes in his direction. "Sadly, I cannot take you all the way to the second Sister," it said. "My oath to Dragonfriend prevents me from crossing my border. But I will take you as far as I am able."

It bared its terrible fangs in what it no doubt intended as a smile.

"Do you like my surprise?" it asked. "Are you not pleased? Dragonfriend always said it was the greatest happiness, to ride upon a dragon."

2 – North

It was like hurtling through a tunnel of darkness. Below them the lights of villages flashed into view and disappeared again. Above them gleamed the silent stars. But where the ruby dragon flew, there was only blackness and cold and the sound of the wind.

Bound with ropes to the dragon's neck, the companions felt as battered as shellfish clinging to the wave-beaten rocks of Dragon's Nest. Kree and Filli huddled motionless beneath Jasmine's jacket, making not a sound.

They had flown for hours. Lief had lost all track of time. Then, suddenly, his stomach gave a sickening lurch.

They were falling. They were plummeting down, down, and the thick blackness of the land was rising to meet them.

Lief screwed his streaming eyes shut.

Abruptly, the downward plunge ceased. The roaring of the wind died. Now there was only a slow, rhythmic sound — the sound of the dragon's wings, steadily beating.

Slowly, Lief opened his eyes.

They were hovering just above a field which was bordered by a massive hedge. On three sides the hedge was studded with white flowers that fluttered in the breeze. The remaining side was dark.

Beyond this dark side was a forest. Behind the trees towered the great mountains of Deltora's northern border, snow glimmering on their peaks.

The dragon sank to earth and folded its wings.

"This is the place where I must leave you," it said. "I feel it."

The ropes loosened as Barda cut through the knots. Lief slid down onto the ground and sprawled there, trying to gather his wits. The earth was rough, and the patchy grass was mingled with some sort of herb that smelled unpleasantly like overripe fruit.

"Ah, it is freezing, and as dark as pitch!" he heard Barda say.

There was the sound of scraping flint. Light began dancing on the grass as a lantern flamed into life.

Lief crawled to his knees, feeling as stiff as an old, old man and as weak as a baby. He was ashamed to see Jasmine already standing up, with Kree perched on her arm and Filli chattering on her shoulder.

"Where are we, dragon?" Jasmine was asking. "Can you show us on our map?"

"I know nothing of maps," the dragon said. "I know only that this is the far north of my territory, and very near to the land of the opal."

It turned its great head towards the forest. "As I landed I saw lights there, and heard music," it added helpfully. "Humans are camped not far away. No doubt they can tell you what you wish to know."

Lief found his voice. "Thank you for carrying us," he said. "You have saved us weeks of travelling."

The dragon bowed. "It is the least I could do for the king who roused me to life again," it said, its red eyes gleaming. "Dreams are all very fine, but not as fine as the splash of sparkling water or the warmth of the sun."

The breeze blew, bringing with it the oversweet, slightly rotten smell of the field, and the faint sound of music. The dragon moved restlessly.

"I must go," it murmured. "I do not like the smell of this place. I know that our tie will not be broken now, wherever you may go, but partings make me sad. Farewell. I will think of you."

Without waiting for an answer, it launched itself into the air. In moments it was gone.

Barda looked around. "It would be best to stay away from the forest for tonight, I think," he said. "Let us see what is behind the hedge on the other side."

They shouldered their packs and walked across the field. When they reached the hedge, they received their first surprise. It was not covered with flowers at all, but with huge white moths.

The moths were big as small birds, and all exactly alike. There were thousands of them. A few were on the outer leaves of the hedge. Most were clinging to twigs deep inside it. All were slowly opening and closing their wings, which bore odd red markings.

"There is something strange about them," Jasmine said, peering at them. "They hardly look real!"

Impulsively, Lief stretched out a finger and gently touched the tip of a moth's wing.

At once, the red markings lit up like tiny beacons.

Exclaiming in shock, Lief jumped back. The next instant the moth spat — a thin jet of liquid that sizzled as it hit the ground.

Filli squealed. Kree screeched and took flight.

"Lief, you fool!" Barda thundered. "Did it hit you?"

"No," gasped Lief, very shaken. "But it was a near thing!"

"Beware!" Jasmine said urgently. "Get back!"

All the moths around the first one were now lighting up and spitting their poison. The hedge blazed with tiny red lights. But none of the creatures moved from their places, and after a few moments the spitting stopped and the red markings began to fade.

"What *are* these creatures?" Jasmine cried, as Kree landed on her arm once more, very ruffled. "It is as if they are alive, yet not alive. As if — "

Lief gasped. He had suddenly seen something astounding.

The strange red markings on the moths' wings made words.

"The moths make a warning line!" he exclaimed. He moved a little closer to one of the moths and, careful not to touch it, pointed to the letters one by one.

"Keep Out," Jasmine said. "So it is forbidden to pass through this hedge. But who has forbidden it? And why? What is on the other side?"

"I do not give a fig!" Barda growled irritably. "There seem to be no moths in the hedge on the forest side of the field. Come on!"

They trudged wearily to the other side of the field. They found that the dark hedge was thin and full of gaps. Plainly, people had been pushing through it very recently, moving in and out of the field.

Jasmine lifted her arm to place Kree on her shoulder. As she settled him there, her hand brushed the back of his neck, and he squawked. Puzzled, she lifted her hand to the light. It was streaked with blood.

She clicked her tongue in annoyance, pulled Kree to her, and examined his neck. He clucked uneasily.

"The Orchard Keeper's beak must have jabbed you here, Kree," she murmured, dabbing his neck with creamy green ointment from the small jar she carried with her everywhere. "I had not noticed. It is a small wound, but deep. No doubt it pulled open when you were startled just now. We must — "

Abruptly, she broke off, listening intently.

"What is it?" Lief hissed.

"Someone is coming," Jasmine breathed.

Instantly, Barda blew out the lantern. They pressed into the hedge, and peered through the sparse leaves.

As their eyes adjusted to the darkness, they saw that the hedge was separated from the forest by a deep, gaping ditch. They could see little else.

Kree squawked softly.

"Go, then," Jasmine whispered reluctantly.

Kree hopped out of the hedge, flew over the ditch, and disappeared into the darkness.

In breathless silence, they waited. In a few moments, Lief and Barda heard what Jasmine's sharper ears had heard before them — the cracking of twigs, the thudding of feet, a stream of grunts and panted curses.

Kree screeched from the trees.

"An enemy," Jasmine breathed. "Angry, and armed. Kree is sure of that. But he is not sure of anything else. He is puzzled — "

She fell silent as the bobbing, flickering light of a torch became visible through the trees.

The sounds came closer. The torchlight grew brighter. And suddenly a giant of a man burst through the last of the trees and stood at the edge of the ditch, breathing heavily.

He was vast, with legs like tree trunks, a huge belly, and enormous, beefy shoulders. He held a club in one hand and a flaming torch in the other. His massive arms were adorned with beaten metal bands. Every one of his sausage-like fingers shone with rings. Animal skins, lashed in place by leather cords, covered his body.

And then he lifted the torch and they saw his face.

They saw tiny, fierce eyes blazing over a snuffling, fleshy snout. They saw ears flopping amid bristly brown hair. They saw a snarling mouth and razor-sharp tusks.

The man had the head of a wild pig.

The pig-man growled ferociously, his small eyes darting left and right, searching the darkness.

"I know you are here, spies," he roared. "I heard your voices. I saw your light!"

There was a rustle in the tree above him and he looked up, snarling. But when he saw only a black bird silently watching him, he grunted in disgust and looked down again.

"How did you cross the line, spies?" he roared. "What trick did you use to break into the secret field? Are you going to tell me you fell out of the sky?"

Lief, Barda, and Jasmine looked at one another, all realizing the truth at the same moment. They had assumed that the moths in the hedge were to stop people moving from the field to whatever was on the other side.

But it had been the other way around. The moths were to keep intruders *out* of the field, and out of this part of the forest.

How could they have known? They really *had* dropped into the field from the sky. But they could not tell the pig-man that. And, even if they did, he plainly would not believe it.

"Show yourselves!" the pig-man bellowed.

The companions remained utterly still. There was a chance that if they remained hidden, he would grow tired of the dark and the cold and go back to his den.

Though together they could no doubt overpower him at last, none of them wanted to be forced to try. They still had far to go. Their quest was too important for them to risk needless injury. The pig-man was powerful and filled with fury.

But that is not all, Lief thought, his skin crawling as he stared at the ugly figure stamping on the other side of the ditch. *There is malice here. Something terrible, that none of us understand.*

He realized that he was shivering, as if chilled to the bone.

Evil was near, very near. He could feel it, coming closer. He could almost see it, rushing, shapeless, through the shadows of the ditch. He had an absurd urge to shout — to jump up and shriek a warning.

"You are hiding in the ditch, or behind the hedge!" bawled the pig-man. "Come out, or I will come and get you!"

He waited a moment, then lumbered forward and began sliding clumsily into the ditch. Mud squelched as his feet hit the bottom.

A black shadow soared past his head, and a beak snapped, just missing his ear. He staggered, slipped, and pitched over, disappearing from sight.

"No, Kree!" breathed Jasmine, clenching her fists anxiously as Kree returned to the attack.

The pig-man crawled to his feet, cursing. He was wet and smeared with slimy filth, but the torch was still alight. Roaring with anger, he wallowed in the mud, swinging the torch above his head to keep off the swooping bird.

The torch flame blazed as it swung wildly from side to side. Light danced in the muddy ditch, banishing shadows where it fell. Suddenly, Kree gave a screech and seemed to stop dead in midair. Then he soared upwards, disappearing into the blackness of the sky.

The pig-man grunted with satisfaction, but as he lowered the torch he gave a slight start. He leaned over a little, pushing his hideous, bristly head forward to peer into the gloom further along the ditch.

Then he chuckled. "Peek-a-boo, I see you!" he growled.

A chill ran down Lief's spine.

The pig-man raised his club, took a step forward . . .

Then he screamed — a shrill, terrified squeal that raised the hair on the back of Lief's neck. And out of the shadows of the ditch rose a thing of nightmare — a vast thing, black and hooded.

3 - The Masked Ones

The black thing loomed above the pig-man, darker than the night. He screamed again and staggered backwards. The thing did not move. Thin white hands crept out of its billowing blackness — hands with long, grasping fingers that had no marks, no lines, no nails.

The fingers twitched. Then smoothly, impossibly, they began to lengthen, snaking forward to fasten around the pig-man's neck.

The next moment he was jerked off his feet, choking and gurgling, his boots kicking at the sides of the ditch, the torch still clutched in his hand.

The thing shook him, like a dog shaking a rat. The terrible gurgling sounds stopped abruptly, and the pig-man went limp.

The thing tossed him aside. His huge body sailed through the air like a floppy, broken doll and fell heavily into the mud. With a hiss the torch went out, and the ditch was plunged into darkness.

It had all happened in the blink of an eye. Shocked, not daring to move, Lief, Barda, and Jasmine crouched in their hiding place. Then, high above them, Kree screeched.

"Kree says the thing has vanished," Jasmine said in a low voice.

And Lief knew that it was so. He was no longer shivering. But cold dread still gripped him like icy white fingers.

"It may return at any moment," he muttered. "We must get into the forest."

In feverish haste, they pushed forward to the edge of the ditch. Kree flew down to them. He perched on Jasmine's shoulder and made a low sound.

"Kree saw the thing in the shadows before the pig-man did," Jasmine said. "That was why he flew away. He says the shadow thing was not alive. Not alive as we are."

"It was alive enough to kill," Barda said grimly.

The breeze was still blowing gently. The only sound was the rustling of the leaves.

Something nagged at the edge of Lief's mind, but he could not quite catch hold of it. His brain was telling him that something had changed. But he was too tired and shocked to think about what it was.

Barda lit the lantern again, and the companions

slid down into the ditch. It was very deep. Standing at the bottom was like being buried under the earth. Sound was muffled and the air smelled of damp and slime.

The body of the pig-man lay nearby, facedown in the mud. Jasmine darted over to it.

"Jasmine!" Barda hissed angrily.

Jasmine ignored him. She bent over the mud-smeared body for a long moment. Then, rapidly, she patted the animal skins that swathed it. Something rustled, and she drew out a bundle of green papers.

Barda lowered the lantern. By its glow they read the words on the paper at the top of the bundle.

OTTO THE GREAT
thrills you with
FANTASTIC FEATS OF STRENGTH!

OTTO THE GREAT
challenges you to
MATCH HIS MIGHTY POWER!

DO YOU DARE TO FACE

OTTO THE GREAT???

entry: 1 gold coin. Children under 5 years free.

Jasmine flicked through the other papers. They were all the same.

"So now we know his name, and how he earned his living," she said. "But how he died, I cannot tell. His neck does not seem to be broken. It is as though his heart just — stopped."

Lief's scalp was crawling. "Let us get away from here!" he said hoarsely.

"It is too late for that!" a sharp voice barked.

Very startled, Lief, Barda, and Jasmine looked up.

And there, standing looking down at them from the edge of the ditch, stood two grotesque figures.

A man with the head of an eagle. A woman with the head of a fox.

And behind them was a crowd — a crowd of beings that were all half-human, half-beast.

The music has stopped! Lief thought wildly. That *is what I noticed at the edge of the ditch. The pig-man must have come from the camp in the forest. They heard his screams. And now they think —*

"*Madaras!*" cried the fox-woman shrilly.

Instantly, all the animal people behind her leaped into the ditch. Kree took flight. Lief, Barda, and Jasmine fell beneath the press of a dozen struggling bodies.

They fought valiantly. But against so many, they had no chance.

✳

In minutes, the companions were being dragged through the forest. Their weapons had been taken. Dozens of hands held them fast. Their captors jostled all around them, talking angrily in a strange language. The only words Lief could make out were two names — "Otto" and, repeated over and over again, "Bess."

"You are making a mistake!" Lief shouted. "We did not kill Otto. He — "

"Save your lies, bareface spy!" snarled the eagle-man from behind him. "You will rue the day you crossed the line of the Masked Ones."

"The Masked Ones!" Lief heard Barda exclaim.

"Ah, yes! Pretend you did not know!" the eagle-man jeered.

Masks! Lief thought with a shock. He looked around at his captors.

Their heads looked so real! But now he could see what should have been obvious to him all along.

These people were all wearing *masks*! Amazing masks, that covered their heads closely, fitting like a second skin.

"*Lat as kall tam na, Quill!*" growled a short woman with the head of a frog.

"*Na! Bess mast say tam,*" the eagle-man muttered.

Lights became visible through the trees, and moments later the companions were being dragged into a crowded clearing. A great fire blazed in the center. There was the smell of cooking and a confused roar of sound.

A huge banner had been stretched between two trees. It flapped lightly in the breeze.

THE MASKED ONES!
COME ONE, COME ALL!
You Will Not Believe Your Eyes!

Everywhere, masked people were shaking their fists, shouting, and wailing. Lief glimpsed a wolf face, a rat face, the face of a ginger cat, and several bird heads.

A grinning, hairy mask with small black eyes twitched into view. It belonged to a ragged boy who had wormed his way through the legs of the crowd to stare at the prisoners.

The face was full of cunning. Lief knew that he had seen something like it before, but could not think where. He only knew that he distrusted it.

Among the trees that surrounded the clearing stood many wooden wagons. Washing lines strung with clothes sagged between them. Big gray horses with plaited manes gazed curiously at the shouting people.

216

Suddenly, the crowd parted to reveal a wagon standing all by itself in a bright circle of light created by dozens of lanterns.

In front of the wagon, seated in a huge chair with gold-painted arms, was an enormous woman.

Somehow Lief knew that this was Bess.

She was vast — at least twice as large as the pig-man. Her billowing purple skirts were like silken tents. Her fringed, embroidered shawls were as large as bedsheets. Her great arms jangled with bracelets as big as the wheels of a small cart.

And her head was the head of a vast brown owl.

Lief only had time for a single, startled glance before he was thrown forward. He fell heavily, face-down, in the dust at the owl-woman's feet. Jasmine and Barda thudded to the ground beside him.

"*Whar as Otto?*" he heard a deep voice demand hoarsely.

"*Otto as dad, Bess!*" Lief heard the fox-woman cry out. "*Tay kalled am!*"

Why, they are not really speaking a different language at all! Lief thought. *It just* sounds *different. They use an* "a" *sound in place of* "e," "i," "o," *and* "u" *in all words except names. And they use* "t" *instead of* "th." The owl-woman said, "Where is Otto?" The fox-woman answered, "Otto is dead, Bess! They killed him!"

The stretcher bearing the lifeless body of the pig-man was carried into the circle of light. The panting bearers put the stretcher down and backed away.

Bess looked down at the body. Her great fists clenched.

"*Gat tam ap!*" she growled. "*Lat may say tayar aglay fasas!*" She drew a long, narrow knife from the silken folds of her skirt.

"Lief! She is going to cut our throats!" Barda muttered as the crowd's noise rose. "Tell her who you are. Show her the Belt. It is our only chance . . ."

His voice trailed off as he was hauled to his feet. At the same moment, Lief himself was jerked upwards.

His legs would not hold him. Head bowed, he sagged between his captors.

Tell her who you are. Show her the Belt . . . it is our only chance.

Slowly, Lief looked up.

The owl-woman gasped, and her hand flew to her heart.

"*Bede!*" she shrieked. "*Bede, ma san!*" She threw the knife aside and began struggling to rise from her chair.

Dead silence had fallen in the clearing. Lief stood gaping. What had she said?

Bede, my son!

Tears pouring from her eyes, Bess held out her arms to him.

Someone pushed him from behind and he stumbled forward. The owl-woman seized him. Suddenly, he was being crushed in her powerful arms, pressed to her heaving chest.

Gold bracelets dug hard into his spine. He was suffocating in a tangle of silken shawls that smelled strongly of spices, smoke, and overripe fruit. In panic, he struggled to free himself, but the mighty arms clasping him were like steel bands.

"*Bess!*" The harsh voice of the eagle-man seemed to be coming from far away. "*Stap! Ha as nat Bede! Ha cannat ba Bede!*"

Lief felt the huge arms quiver. Then, slowly, they began to loosen. Gasping for breath, he threw himself backwards and tumbled to the ground.

When at last he looked up, Bess was lying back in her chair, panting. Her eyes were closed. The eagle-man stood beside her, his hand on her shoulder.

"Confess!" he shouted at Lief, Barda, and Jasmine. "Confess to our leader that you have been sent here to spy upon us and destroy us! Confess that you are servants of the evil tyrant, King Lief of Del!"

Lief's heart lurched.

"We are travellers from Broome!" Jasmine's clear voice cried out. "My uncle's name is Berry. My brother and I are Lewin and Jay. We have done nothing wrong!"

"Lies!" the eagle-man roared. "You broke into our secret field. Then you killed the one who went to find you. We caught you in the act!"

"No!" shouted Jasmine. "A thing of darkness killed your friend. We saw it!"

The eagle-man laughed scornfully.

Bess's eyes opened. But she did not look at the eagle-man or at Jasmine. Instead, she looked at Lief.

"Is this true?" she asked, almost gently.

Lief met her gaze squarely. He knew that he had to make the most of her softened mood. He had to convince her.

"It is true," he said. "The thing was hiding in the ditch. It caught hold of Otto around the neck, and he died. We did not harm him, I swear it!"

"*Ha lays, Bess!*" hissed the eagle-man. "*Tay ar spays!*"

"We are *not* spies!" Lief exclaimed furiously, without thinking.

There was a murmur in the crowd. The eagle-man drew back with a hiss.

"Then how do you know our tongue, bareface?" he spat.

Cursing himself for his foolishness, Lief spoke directly to Bess, forcing himself to keep his voice level.

"I used my ears," he said. "Your tongue sounded strange to me at first, but soon I found I could understand it."

And perhaps the great topaz I wear beneath my clothes helped me, he added to himself. *The topaz that sharpens the mind. The topaz that has been so powerful ever since the golden dragon came back to life.*

But Bess had leaned forward, her eyes shining.

"Of course!" she breathed. "It comes naturally to you. Now I see — "

She broke off, and shook her head. *"Ay mast nat bay hastay,"* she murmured to herself. *"Ay mast bay shar . . ."*

She raised her voice. "Lock them in Otto's wagon," she ordered, gesturing at the prisoners. "I will examine his body. Then I will decide what is to be done."

4 ~ A Surprising Offer

The companions were thrown into a nearby wagon, locked in, and left in thick darkness which smelled strongly of sweat and damp fur.

As soon as their captors' footsteps had died away, there was a cautious squawk from outside. Keeping out of sight, Kree had followed them.

"He says they took the key," Jasmine whispered. "He cannot help us."

Quickly, they began feeling around, looking for a weapon or a way of escape. They found nothing but a wooden trunk full of animal skins and a mattress covered with a stinking fur rug. They could discover no gaps or loose boards anywhere.

At last they gave up. None of them felt like sitting on the mattress. They sat on the floor, resting their backs against the wall.

"Bess may well decide that we are innocent," said Jasmine, stroking Filli to comfort him. "She wants Lief, at least, to live."

Lief squirmed, remembering Bess's crushing embrace.

"Bess may want us to live, but that fellow in the eagle mask is thirsting for our blood," Barda said.

"If they knew who we really are, things would be even worse," Lief muttered. "It sounded as if they would be only too glad to kill Lief the tyrant."

He had tried to keep his voice level, but the bitterness he felt as he said the last words was very clear.

"They must be mad to call you a tyrant!" Jasmine exclaimed. "Or . . . perhaps they are allies of the guardian of the north! Clearly they are sorcerers. The moths prove that — and so does the thing in the ditch."

"The thing in the ditch killed one of their own people," said Barda, shaking his head. "It cannot have been their creature. Besides, nothing I know of the Masked Ones leads me to think they would serve the Shadow Lord — or anyone else."

"What do you know?" asked Lief.

"Only what I have heard from travellers," Barda said. "Masked Ones have been roaming the far-flung parts of Deltora for centuries. They are entertainers — acrobats and singers and such. The troupe is like a large family. It keeps to itself, passing its secrets on from generation to generation — "

Outside, Kree screeched warningly.

"They are coming back," Jasmine whispered.

Hastily, the three scrambled to their feet.

A key turned in the lock. The door of the wagon creaked open. The shape of the fox-woman loomed in the gap.

"There are no marks upon Otto's body, except what seem to be burns around the neck," the fox-woman snapped. "Therefore, Bess has chosen to believe your story. She wishes to see you."

✳

A small round table draped with a purple cloth had been placed in front of Bess's chair, and three stools had been set out for Lief, Barda, and Jasmine. In moments they found themselves drinking vegetable soup, eating strips of warm, flat bread, and being treated as honored guests.

The fox-woman, whose name was Rust, stood behind Bess's chair, her sharp eyes watching everything they did. Otto's body had been removed. The eagle-man was nowhere to be seen.

All the other Masked Ones had gone back to dancing and playing music. But Lief saw them staring curiously at the companions whenever they thought they could do so without being noticed.

"They keep their masks on even when they eat!" Jasmine whispered in Lief's ear.

And it was true. Even the children ate, drank, and played with their masks firmly in place. It was fascinating, yet it made Lief uneasy. With faces so well hidden, it was impossible to tell what people were thinking. Only the eyes and hands provided clues.

Now that he was calmer, he could see that some of the masks were better than others. The frog-woman's mask, for example, was a glistening green masterpiece. Rust's fox mask, too, and Bess's owl's head looked so real that it was hard to believe they had been made by human hands.

But many of the masks worn by others in the troupe were far more ordinary. They were just false heads of fur or feathers with holes for eyes, mouth, and nose.

Bess was gobbling her food, filling her vast soup bowl again and again from a pot simmering on a fire beside her. She seemed tense, as if with excitement.

"What has brought you to this part of the country, may I ask?" she said abruptly, at last.

"My nephews and I left Broome to find work," Barda said, telling their planned story. "Food is scarce at home."

"It is the same everywhere," Bess nodded. "But, just lately, things have begun growing again! That is why we came to this place, which we have not visited for many years. We have been here five days, for we were delighted to find that — "

She broke off as Rust's hand tightened on her shoulder.

Lief wondered what she had been going to say.

Plainly, it was something that Rust did not think the visitors should know. Something about why the Masked Ones were camped in the forest.

And why are they here? he thought suddenly. *There is no space in the forest for staging a performance. And clearly they want people to stay out of the field.*

He met the fox-woman's suspicious eyes.

She, at least, thinks Bess is wrong to trust us, he thought. *She thinks we are lying. And she is right, of course. We will have to be very careful.*

He concentrated on keeping his face expressionless, wishing heartily that he had a mask himself.

Bess cleared her throat. "Tomorrow we will be moving west along the mountains, to a place called Happy Vale," she said. "See here!"

She pulled a pink leaflet from the folds of her skirt and held it out to Barda.

THE MASKED ONES!

★Jugglers ★Acrobats ★Magic
★Fortune-telling ★Mind reading
★Games of skill ★Feats of strength
★Prizes to be won!!

COME ONE, COME ALL!
You Will Not Believe Your Eyes!

NEXT PERFORMANCE HAPPY VALE

"We have not performed in Happy Vale for a long time," said Bess, watching intently as Lief, Barda, and Jasmine read the notice. "It will be a grand night. And it could be just the first of many grand nights for you. If you accept my offer."

The companions looked up at her in surprise.

Bess leaned forward. "You are looking for work," she said. "Well, I am offering you not only work, but a home as well. I am inviting you to join us — to join the Masked Ones!"

Stunned, Barda glanced at Lief and Jasmine, then turned back to Bess.

"We are most honored," he said carefully. "But the Masked Ones are entertainers — fine ones, too, I hear. We are only humble fishermen."

"Ah! But we can train you for greater things," cried Bess eagerly. "Many here were not born Masked Ones."

She nodded as Barda looked surprised. "It has always been our habit to adopt bareface infants and small children — orphans, with no family to care for them," she said. "But a year or two ago, I began taking in older children — and adults as well."

The fox-woman sniffed disapprovingly.

"It was necessary if the troupe was to survive," Bess said, raising her voice slightly. "Our old families have dwindled sadly. So — will you join us, Berry? If you do, you will be set for life! The Masked Ones look after their own."

"Do not try to persuade them, Bess," snapped Rust. "Surely we have enough bareface hangers-on already!"

Bess's huge fists clenched. "These would not be hangers-on!" she growled. "Have you forgotten who we lost tonight?"

"We lost a friend and brother — one of the inner circle," Rust said resentfully.

"We also lost our strong man," said Bess. "How can we perform at Happy Vale or anywhere else without one of our most popular acts? Otto would have been the first to say it is impossible!"

She pointed at Barda. "Look at this fellow! Powerful as an ox! Dressed for the part, he would make an excellent strong man."

"And what of his nephews?" Rust enquired icily, turning her fox head to look at Lief and Jasmine. "How will they earn their keep?"

"Oh, I am sure they can be trained for something," Bess said, with false casualness. "Lewin, for example, has the look of one who can sing like a bird."

"Bess, you say that only because he reminds you of Bede!" Rust exploded. "Think what you are doing!"

"How dare you question me?" thundered Bess. "Leave us!"

Without a word, the fox-woman backed away and disappeared into the shadows.

"Truly, I am not sure that I would make a good singer, Bess," Lief murmured. "My voice is not — "

"Nonsense, Lewin!" Jasmine broke in, to his great surprise. "Your voice is very sweet."

While Lief was still gaping at her, she turned to Barda.

"I think we should accept this generous offer, Uncle," she said firmly. "After all, the Masked Ones are moving west, as we always intended to do. Why should we not join them — at least for a time? There is safety in numbers."

Plainly, she was giving Lief and Barda a message. She was telling them that joining the Masked Ones would be the best possible disguise.

"Oh," Barda said blankly. "Well, perhaps . . . for a time . . ."

"Excellent!" cried Bess, rubbing her hands. "Then it is agreed. You can have Otto's wagon. Tomorrow we will move on — and your training will begin!"

✳

The companions spent that night huddled beneath the tree that shaded Otto's wagon, with Kree keeping watch above them.

The ground was cold and hard, but they preferred it to sleeping inside. Someone had taken away the mattress, the fur rug, and the trunk of clothes. But, even empty, the wagon seemed haunted by memories of the pig-man and his horrible death.

Gradually, the lights around the camp were put out as people went to their rest. But just when all seemed quiet, the great central fire began to burn more brightly, and low voices began chanting and singing.

The sounds went on and on. The fire blazed higher.

Several times Lief sat up. Several times he peered at the figures chanting around the roaring fire, and wondered what they were doing.

In the darkest hours of the night, the voices rose a little. For the first time, Lief heard some words clearly.

Farwall, Otto. Farwall, ald frand. Yar mask as ashas. Yar bady as dast. Naw ya dwall an ta grayt layt. Wan day way wall jayan ya. Wayt far as. Wayt far as . . .

Then, at last, he understood.

Farewell, Otto. Farewell, old friend. Your mask is ashes. Your body is dust. Now you dwell in the great light. One day we will join you. Wait for us. Wait for us . . .

Otto's body and all his possessions were being burned. The inner circle of the Masked Ones was farewelling one of its own.

Lief lay down again and pulled his blanket close around his chin. He closed his eyes. He willed himself to sleep. But when at last sleep came, leaping flames and a shapeless black figure with long white fingers haunted his dreams.

5 - Happy Vale

Just before dawn, Lief was woken by a clamor of shouting, banging, and clattering. Horses were snorting. Harness was jingling.

"What is it?" he asked sleepily.

"They are preparing to leave," groaned Barda, throwing aside his blanket and sitting up.

"Indeed we are," said a sharp voice. "And if you intend to come with us, you had better rouse yourselves."

Rust emerged from the shadows. "Bess sent you these," she snapped, throwing a cloth bag on the ground. "Put them on and keep them on. The sight of your naked faces offends us as much as your smell."

She turned on her heel and left them.

"I do not think she is very fond of us," Barda said, upending the bag. Three masks tumbled out.

The first was a massive animal head, striped in

black and yellow. The second was smaller and older, but far more exquisitely made. It was a blue-feathered bird head with a yellow beak. The third, the smallest of all, was a shapeless mass of gray fur, with a black nose and bent whiskers.

Barda put on the striped mask and was instantly transformed into a glaring stranger.

He threw the bird mask to Lief. "This is yours, I suspect, young Lewin, since you are to be Bess's songbird," he said.

Reluctantly, Lief pulled the blue-feathered mask over his head. To his surprise, he could hear, see, and breathe far better than he had expected.

All the same, he felt uneasy. He touched his feathered face and a chill ran down his spine.

Jasmine put on the gray mask. Kree screeched and flew to a higher branch. Filli chittered anxiously.

"They do not like it," Jasmine said sadly. "They do not know me."

Barda burst out laughing. "I am not surprised!" he said. "No one would know you. No one would know any of us! Why, we could travel the length and breadth of Deltora and never be recognized! This is a fine plan!"

He jumped to his feet and strode off to hitch Otto's horse to the wagon.

"I am not so sure," Jasmine muttered. "But — "

She broke off as an eerie, high-pitched screech floated from the direction of the field.

"What was that?" Lief gasped.

"I do not know," Jasmine said, puzzled. Then she shrugged, dismissing the problem from her mind.

"But in any case, we made Bess no promises," she continued. "We will stay with the Masked Ones only as long as it suits us."

Lief nodded unhappily. He could not rid himself of the feeling that somehow he had lost control of his own destiny.

✳

Dawn was breaking as the wagons moved out of the forest and turned onto a rough road that ran beside the mountains.

Only the drivers rode. Everyone else walked beside the wagons or trailed in a straggling line behind.

Barda drove Otto's wagon. Lief and Jasmine trudged beside it. Kree flew above, keeping them in view but never venturing close enough to be noticed.

The road became smoother and broader, and the wagons picked up speed. In another hour they passed a new sign. The Masked Ones pointed and jeered.

Lief sighed. Plainly Mad Keeth Nose, whoever he was, believed that the king chose to build bridges and roads instead of ordering more food to be grown.

If only I could *order the crops to grow strong and the trees to bear fruit,* he thought. *If only it were that simple!*

Now and again the wagons passed a tiny village. People always came running to stare and wave.

The Masked Ones would wave back. Some would juggle a few colored balls or play a tune on a pipe. But the wagons kept moving.

"Why do we not stop?" Jasmine said as they passed the fourth such ragged group.

"It is not worth their while to perform at small places," sighed a woman behind them.

They turned to look at her. She was wearing a neatly made ginger cat mask. The eyes behind the mask were dull. Plainly, she was one of the "bareface hangers-on" the fox-woman had spoken of with such contempt.

"How long have you been with the Masked Ones?" Lief asked, to keep the conversation going.

"My man and I joined them last winter," the woman said in a low voice. "He does heavy work around the camp. I mend costumes and masks. Make them, too, for once I was a fine seamstress."

Again she sighed. "At least we eat every day now, which is more than we did at home. But I am sick of travelling."

"What of the mask?" Lief asked.

"Oh, I am used to that by now," the woman said carelessly. "Most of the time I forget I am wearing it."

She raised her hand to her mask.

"Even at first, I did not mind it," she said slowly. "I have no love for what is beneath it. And neither does my man, I am sure, whatever he says. I was branded on my cheek, in the time of the Shadow Lord. Whatever beauty I had is long gone."

Lief said nothing. For once he was glad of his own mask. It hid the pity he knew his face must show — and what could helpless pity do but make this sad woman even sadder?

✳

By midafternoon, Lief knew they must be well into opal territory. But clearly they had crossed another border also.

They had left the budding hope of the east behind them. Gradually, they had moved into the desolate realm of the Sister of the North.

Thorns tangled on the roadsides. Crops were yellow and stunted. Kree was the only bird in the sky.

Lief felt Jasmine nudging him, and looked up.

The fox-woman stood just ahead. When they reached her, she fell into step beside them.

"When we arrive in Happy Vale, go straight to Bess's wagon," she said to Lief, her voice totally without expression. "Bess wishes your training to begin at once."

She stepped to the side of the road again and began walking rapidly towards the front of the procession without a backwards glance.

✳

Happy Vale turned out to be nothing like its name. The windows of its houses and shops were filmed with dust. Dead leaves blew in the deserted streets.

The wagons of the Masked Ones creaked down the main road. Eerily, the town clock chimed four.

"Where are all the people?" Jasmine whispered.

"Dead or gone, no doubt," the woman in the cat mask muttered. "Bess thought that because things had begun to grow again in the east, it would be the same everywhere. She was wrong, it seems. Now, I suppose, we will have to go back the way we have come."

Her voice was flat and listless, as if she did not care what she did.

If the Masked Ones do decide to turn back, we will have to leave them, Lief thought. *Well, I, for one, will be glad of it.*

The line had slowed to a crawl. Lief and Jasmine craned their necks to see what was happening.

"There is a noticeboard in the town square," Barda called. "People are slowing to read it."

In a few more minutes, they had reached the square. The first thing they passed was a fountain, which had been sealed with planks of wood. The tall clock tower rose behind it.

The noticeboard came next. As Lief looked at the notes pinned to it, his heart sank.

The small ones seemed to speak of a life that was now ended, and a future that was never to be. The large notice on the right dominated them all.

Dean the Smoke will trade 3 hens for a sack of grain.

FOR SALE
These are bargains!
Fine bed. Table with 2 chairs. Kate Mendshoe

Dame Henstoke can teach you to dance. Cheap ra

Hank Modestee who can follow orders needs work. Ask at tavern.

IF YOU WANT TO SEND GOODS AHEAD TO PURLEY SEE ANDOS THE MEEK

TO ALL WHO PASS THIS WAY

We, the remaining citizens of Happy Vale, have voted to leave our town and walk south-east to Purley. We have heard that there is wild food to be had in Purley, and that the spring there has begun to run clean. We heard this from Jord the knife-sharpener, who saw the wonder with his own eyes.

If you have come seeking a relative or friend from Happy Vale, you will find that person either in Purley or in the graveyard.

IMPORTANT! READ THIS!

DO NOT DRINK FROM THE FOUNTAIN! THE WATER MAKES BLISTERS ON THE TONGUE & IS FULL OF WHITE WORMS. ONLY RAINWATER IS SAFE.

Seek the Nomad! Laughing Jack your friendly travelling moneylender, is now camped at the Riverdale sign post

Lief bent his head in an agony of frustration. How many people would die, how many more towns would be abandoned, while he, Barda, and Jasmine hid behind masks and dawdled towards their goal?

Travel hidden.

He ground his teeth, but knew that he had to heed Doom's warning. Secrecy was their most powerful weapon. He had to be patient.

✳

Not long afterwards, they reached a field where wagons were being pulled up into a rough circle.

Masked children of all ages were already scurrying about, collecting sticks for the central fire under the stern eye of the frog-woman.

Rust the fox-woman was standing by the fence, shouting orders at some people who were unloading large red boxes from a covered cart.

Bess's wagon was on the far side of the field, beneath the overhanging branches of a tree.

"You had better be off, Lewin," Barda said, climbing down from the wagon seat. "We will see to things here."

Reluctantly, Lief started across the field. As he passed the growing woodpile, a small figure carrying a towering bundle of sticks darted heedlessly across his path.

There was no way of avoiding a collision. Lief staggered and the child fell. Sticks flew everywhere.

"Watch where you are going, bird-head!" the child shouted angrily.

His small black eyes were sparkling with fury through a grinning, hairy mask. He was the boy Lief had noticed the night they were captured. The boy wearing the mask of a . . .

. . . a polypan, Lief realized, remembering the strange, thieving beast he and his companions had met on the River Tor.

The polypan-boy scrambled to his feet and began gathering his fallen sticks.

"Now I will be the last of all Plug's orphans to bring fuel for the fire," he grumbled. "That means I will be last in the line for food. And it is all your fault!"

"Zerry!" the frog-woman roared. "What are you playing at, you lazy young hound?"

The boy's head jerked around. Without waiting to pick up the rest of the sticks, he shot away towards the woodpile.

"It was not me, Plug!" Lief heard him shouting as he ran. "It was *his* fault! He tripped me!"

Lief hurried on, wondering how many of the children in the camp were orphans, taken in by the Masked Ones to be trained in their ways. Quite a number, if Zerry's words made sense.

He reached Bess's wagon and moved under the tree to the back.

The door was closed. A lumpy sack was propped against the wall beside it. The sack smelled very strongly of rotten fruit. Here and there a thin white stem poked through the rough cloth.

Curious, Lief pinched off the tip of one of the stems and squinted at it. It was not a stem, he thought, but a root. Some sort of crop. And, by its smell, it was from the field beside the forest.

He remembered how rough the ground had felt when he was lying in the field. That was because the Masked Ones had been digging there, he thought. Digging there for five whole days!

He saw that a large, empty iron pot hung over a pile of wood nearby. Bess was planning to make soup from the white roots, it seemed. Lief wrinkled his nose at the thought of it.

He moved to the door and raised his hand to knock. Then, with a shock, he heard voices coming from inside the wagon. He pressed his ear against the door, and listened intently.

"*Yar hart as raling yar had, Bess!*" hissed a voice he recognized as that of Quill, the eagle-man.

"*Ta bay was lad ta as!*" Bess growled back. "*Ta sayns are all taya!*"

The boy was led to us, Lief translated to himself. *The signs are all there!*

"*Sayns!*" snarled Quill. "*Trackary, ya mayn! Can ya nat say at, Bess? Ta kang chays tas bay ta spay an as bacas ha laks layk Bede!*"

240

. . . *Trickery, you mean! Can you not see it, Bess? The king chose this boy to spy on us because he looks like Bede . . .*

Yes, that is just what a tyrant king would do, Lief thought uneasily. *He would know that Bess was more likely to accept someone who looked like her lost son.*

But why did the Masked Ones fear spies at all? What were they hiding?

"*Ya ar wrang, Quill,*" he heard Bess say coldly. "*Na, plays layv ma. Ha wal ba haya an a mamant.*"

"*Haya?*" the eagle-man thundered. "*Bat, Bess, ha wall say . . .*"

Lief's heart thumped. "See what?" he whispered. "What will I see?"

"*Ha wal nat naw wat ha as saying,*" snapped Bess.

He will not know what he is seeing . . .

The door of the wagon began to open. Swiftly, Lief jumped back, then took two rapid steps forward, as if he was just arriving. Quill stepped out of the wagon and they almost bumped into each other.

"Oh — I beg your pardon!" Lief stammered.

The eagle man stared, then brushed past him without a word and strode away. It was impossible to tell whether he had been deceived.

"Ah, Lewin!" Bess called from the dimness of the wagon. Suddenly, her voice was warm and welcoming. "Come in!"

6 - Mysteries

The wagon was richly furnished. The air was heavy with the scents of spices and perfumed candle wax.

Bess was sitting at the round table. A candle threw flickering light up onto her smooth owl face. Her hands were cupped around a glass ball in front of her.

"Sit down, Lewin," she said, nodding at the chair on the other side of the table.

Unwillingly, Lief did as she asked.

"Ah," Bess breathed. She stared, as if drinking in the sight of him.

But there is nothing to see, Lief thought. *She cannot see my face. I am wearing a mask.*

Then it struck him. The bird mask he was wearing must have once belonged to Bede. When Bess looked at him, she saw her son reborn.

He felt sick.

He looked down at the table. The glass ball was swirling with shadows. Was this what Quill had not wanted him to see? He thought of the Shadow Lord's crystal and shuddered.

Bess took her hands from the ball, and the shadows disappeared.

"Do not fear the glass, Lewin," she murmured. "With its aid I read the signs, as my mother did before me."

She pushed the ball away, revealing another object lying on the table in front of her. It was a row of eight small metal rods fastened to a wooden base. She struck the first of the metal rods with her long fingernail and a low, clear note rang out.

"Can you name that note, Lewin?" she asked.

Lief had no idea what she meant. He shook his head.

Bess sighed. "I feared as much," she said. "You have a great deal to learn."

She passed a sheet of paper to him. "Music is like another language," she said. "This is how we write it down."

"Now, I am going to play the notes on this paper," Bess said. "Listen carefully."

She struck the rods one by one. Notes rang out, going up like stairs from low to high. She played them again, this time singing their names.

Lief's fingers felt hot. He looked down and saw that the liquid that had oozed from the fragment of root was drying to gray jelly. His fingertips were stinging. Suddenly fearful, he rubbed them against his coat. The gray jelly peeled from his skin in tiny balls, which he brushed quickly onto the floor.

"Stop fidgeting and pay attention, Lewin!" snapped Bess. "You *must* learn to read and write music. How else will you be able to note down the beautiful songs you will compose for me, as Bede used to do?"

Lief's face grew hot beneath his mask.

"Bess — " he mumbled. But Bess's voice flowed on as if he had not spoken.

"Ah, Bede's songs could charm the birds from the trees," she sighed. "The words were full of feeling. The rhymes were perfect. The melodies were charming. And, of course, his voice was without compare. Wherever we went, silly village girls were drawn to him like bees to a honeypot."

She laughed. "They paid well for the chance to swoon over Bede! When we moved on, we would leave a trail of broken hearts behind us, and our purses would be heavy with bareface gold."

She reached across the table and took Lief's hand. "And you will be the same, Lewin," she said. "You will restore the fortunes of the Masked Ones!"

Lief winced, glad that the mask was hiding his face.

"Bess, I will never be like Bede," he said awkwardly. "And — I do not want to be."

He tried to free his hand, but Bess held it fast.

"Trust me, Lewin," she said. "This was fated to be."

Lief shook his head.

"Yes!" Bess insisted. "I lost Bede seven years ago. I had grown used to my grief. But lately, thoughts of him have haunted me. The glass kept showing me his face. I did not know why. I feared I was losing my reason!"

She freed Lief's hand and drew the glass ball towards her again. She bent over it, gazing hungrily.

"But then — then you came, Lewin," she murmured. "You came into our secret place, through our barriers, guarded by a phantom. A boy so like Bede. A boy who could speak our language! I saw the signs and realized what they meant. My thoughts of Bede had been preparation for the coming of his replacement. You!"

She tapped the huge gold ring on her little finger. It was the only ring that had no stone. Its broad surface was covered in carved signs.

"This ring is worn by the leader of the Masked

Ones," she said softly. "One day, it will be yours. You must work hard to be worthy, for in the hand of the leader lies the gift of life . . . and death."

Lief did not trust himself to speak.

Bess was wrong, so wrong. Her "signs" were only matters of chance. As she would realize, if only he could tell her the truth.

But he could not tell her. Not if he valued his life, and the lives of his companions.

Bess was waiting for him to speak. He blurted out the first thing that came into his head.

"Bess, what happened to Bede?"

For a moment, he thought she was not going to answer. Then she spoke.

"Seven years ago, when we were last in the northwest, Gray Guards attacked our wagons," she said. "Eight of the inner circle died defending us."

Her enormous hands were clasped on the table-top, the rings biting deep into the flesh of her straining fingers.

"The Guards were killed, but we knew that soon more would come. We fled to a village deep in the mountains. It is a lonely place, but we had visited it only the year before, and knew the way. So we went — to Bede's doom."

"What is its name, this village?" Lief asked softly. His scalp was tingling.

"You would not know it," said Bess. "It is not worth knowing. They call it Shadowgate."

Lief sat frozen. *Can* this, *too, be chance?* he thought. *Or can it be that Bess is right after all? Can it be that all this is somehow meant?*

The memory of the dragon's voice whispered in his mind. *This is the place where I must leave you . . . I feel it.*

"There are beasts, deep in the mountains," Bess muttered. "Monsters beyond imagining. Things that crawl in the shadows. Things that growl deep below the rock. Shadowgate lies among them. A dread pass is the only way to reach it. We hid our tracks, disguised our scent, so the Guards could not smell us out."

She drew a deep, shuddering breath. "We hid in Shadowgate for a full month. I wanted to make sure we were safe. And safe we were — though the villagers did not welcome us. But there was another danger I had not expected."

Lief wet his lips. "What happened?" he asked.

"Bede . . . lost his heart," said Bess. "To a silly bareface girl not worthy to tie the strings on his shoes."

The bitterness in her voice was chilling.

"I suspected nothing," she went on. "He and the scheming wench had been meeting in secret. He came to me the night before his eighteenth birthday. The mask of his adulthood was ready. The ceremony of his entry to the inner circle was planned for the morning. He said he wished to leave the Masked Ones — to become a travelling minstrel, and marry this — Mariette."

She spoke the name like a curse.

"I could not believe my ears," she hissed. "I said, 'You will quickly tire of this ignorant little bareface! Why, only last year you were dallying with her sister — that proud beauty, Kirsten, who ran off into the mountains in shame when you left her, and caused these villagers to hate us.' "

She snorted, as though Kirsten's fate was no concern of hers.

"But Bede told me that he had always preferred Mariette to her sister. He said it had begun as a fancy, but that in this past month he had learned what true love was. He said he could not live without the girl. He talked wildly, like one in a fever."

So, Lief thought grimly. *Bede was caught in the net he had so often set for others. There is justice in that.*

But Bess, lost in memories, did not seem to be aware of what he could see so clearly.

"I told him to put the girl out of his mind," she said. "I told him, 'You are a Masked One. We do not marry outsiders. Tomorrow, you will put on the mask of your adulthood, and that will be the end of it.' "

She sighed.

"He seemed to accept it. He left me gently, with a kiss. But I never saw him again. That night, he and the girl ran away into the mountains. We searched, but we could not find them."

The brown owl face showed no expression. Only the trembling voice gave a sign that Bess was reliving an old, terrible grief.

"The mountains had swallowed them up, just as they had swallowed the girl's sister the year before," she said. "And so Bede threw his life away, and we lost our greatest treasure."

And what of the parents who lost two daughters because of your son, Bess? Lief thought, as her voice trailed away. *Have you no word for them?*

The silence lengthened. Then, at last, Bess seemed to rouse herself. She straightened her shoulders.

"I have work to do," she said abruptly, pushing the little row of metal rods towards Lief. "I expect you to know all your notes by tomorrow morning."

Lief stood up, pushed the chimes and the paper into his pocket, and left the wagon. He was determined that by morning he, Barda, and Jasmine would be long gone.

Outside, the sun was setting and shadows were gathering behind the line of wagons. Lief breathed in the fresh, cool air with relief.

It was quiet where he was standing, but the center of the field was full of movement. All around the unlit wood heap, Masked Ones were practicing their skills.

The frog-woman was juggling flaming torches. Three clowns were tumbling about, blowing colored bubbles from enormous pipes. The eagle-man, Quill, was standing with Barda, who was lifting a set of enormous weights. A man with the head of a lizard was doing magic tricks, assisted by the polypan-boy, Zerry.

To one side, a group of blue-clad acrobats with dog faces were standing on one another's shoulders to form a tall pyramid. Balanced at the top of the pyramid was a small, gray-masked figure, standing on its hands.

It was Jasmine. She had put aside her clumsy coat, and her feet were bare.

Lief caught his breath as she turned a backwards somersault and landed upright on the shoulders of the man at the pyramid's tip.

"Your brother is a talented acrobat, it seems," a low voice said in Lief's ear.

Lief jumped, turned, and saw the fox-woman standing very close to him. He had not heard her approach. Perhaps she had been standing there in the shadows all along.

"Oh — yes," Lief stammered.

"It is hard to believe he has never been trained," the fox-woman went on smoothly. Her eyes were narrow with suspicion.

"Jay is self-taught," Lief answered, with perfect truth. His eyes flicked around the field. And it was then that he noticed the fluttering white patches that dotted the fences on all sides.

He turned and looked behind him. Yes, the fence there was covered with white splashes, too. Poison-spitting moths clung to the rough wood, silently opening and closing their wings.

Lief remembered the red boxes he had seen being unloaded by the fence. The moths had been in those boxes, no doubt. Now they were in place. There would be no escape from the camp tonight.

He clenched his fists. The disappointment was bitter. He heard a distant screech, as if Kree were echoing his feelings.

"Is something wrong?" Rust asked coldly.

"No," Lief managed to say. "No, I — "

His voice was drowned out by a high, wavering shriek of pure terror.

7 - Phantom

Everything seemed to stop. The figures around the woodpile froze where they stood. The music faltered and died.

The terrified scream came again, dissolving into a ghastly, rasping gurgle.

His heart pounding, Lief began to run between the wagons and the fence, following the sound.

With Rust close behind him he pounded past wagon after wagon, dodging stamping, terrified horses, leaping over boxes and piles of belongings.

Otto's wagon was ahead. The door was hanging open, swinging crazily on its hinges as if blown by a gale.

And rising against the shadow of the door, rising up, up, so that at last it was outlined against the orange sky, was a deeper shadow — something black and billowing, with long white fingers that glimmered in the dark. Where its face should have been, there was a flat gleam of green.

On the ground by the wagon's back wheels, sprawled over a half-empty pack and a tangle of clothes, lay a twisted shape.

Lief's throat closed. Behind him, the fox-woman cried out. And in that moment, the black thing writhed, thinned, and was gone.

The wagon door slammed shut with a crash. Lief ran forward and bent over the sprawled figure.

It was the woman in the cat mask — the woman he and Jasmine had spoken to on the road to Happy Vale.

One side of her mask was scorched. Smoke drifted from the blackened patch, and there was the ghastly smell of burned hair and flesh. The staring eyes seemed filled with horror, and the teeth were bared in a snarl of fear.

"It is the seamstress, Fern!" whispered Rust. She sounded horrified, but the horror was also plainly mixed with relief.

She is grateful that it was not a member of the inner circle, but only a "bareface hanger-on" who was attacked, Lief thought grimly. Gently, he slipped his fingers beneath the neck of the cat mask, feeling for a pulse.

His stomach turned over as the staring eyes focused on him, and the lips moved. The burned woman was still alive! She was trying to speak. Lief leaned closer.

253

Words came to him, faint as breath. "I . . . am . . . sorry. I . . . was . . . so . . . afraid."

"What is she saying?" cried Rust. "Is she — ?"

Angrily, Lief waved his free hand to quiet her. "Be at peace now," he whispered to the dying woman.

The pulse beneath his fingers was light and fluttering. The agonized eyes held his, filled with urgent appeal. The lips moved again. "Beware . . . the Masked One . . ." the woman breathed. "Beware . . ."

The voice died away. The eyes grew fixed. The fluttering pulse stopped.

Lief waited for a moment, then drew back.

"She is gone," he said quietly. He began to pull the cat mask from the dead woman's face.

"Don't!" Rust gasped behind him.

Lief took no notice. He uncovered a scorched neck, and then a pale face. One cheek was deeply burned. The brand of the Shadow Lord shone blood-red in the center of the blackened skin. Lief could feel the heat still rising from it.

It is as if the burning came from within, he thought. His skin crawled.

"Cover her face, for pity's sake!" hissed Rust. "The others are coming."

Lief became aware of shouting and the pounding of approaching feet. He looked around, saw a blanket lying nearby amid a jumble of clothes, and threw it over the body.

The crowd was nearly upon them. Rust ran to the front of Otto's wagon, and held up her arms.

"Go back to work!" she shouted. "There is nothing to see. There has been an accident, that is all."

She folded her arms and stood immovable till at last the crowd did her bidding and began moving back to the center of the field.

Barda and Jasmine stayed. Rust seemed to know that there was no point in trying to make them go.

✳

Bess's reaction to Fern's death shocked them all.

"The woman was stealing from your wagon, Lewin," she said, shrugging. "She paid the price."

"What do you mean?" Lief exclaimed, horrified.

"Something watches over you, Lewin," said Bess dreamily, moving her hands over the glass ball. "Anyone who tries to injure you is in danger."

The fox-woman stirred uneasily. "Bess, I do not think — " she began.

"Rust, see that Fern is buried without delay," Bess said, without looking at her. "And decently, with her mask in place, as is proper. Keep to your story of an accident. The people may turn against Lewin if they know the truth."

Lief opened his mouth to protest, but Barda gripped his arm warningly, and he remained silent.

Barda is right, he thought. *Better to say nothing. If Bess really believes that I am protected by some sort of spirit, it may help us later. If she does not — if the thing that killed Fern is some hideous secret she and the rest of the inner circle share — defying her will only put us in even greater danger.*

When Fern's body had been moved, Rust left the companions alone to repack their scattered belongings. At last they could speak freely.

Jasmine called Kree to her and began tending to the wound on the back of his neck. He squawked and clucked as she cleaned the raw place and smeared it with more of the green ointment.

"Kree says he saw it all," Jasmine said in a low voice. "Fern came and began searching our packs. He was trying to decide what to do when the phantom appeared from the shadows and attacked her."

" 'Beware the Masked One,' " Barda frowned. "Are you sure Fern did not say 'the Masked *Ones*,' Lief?"

"I am sure," Lief said slowly. "She meant only one person. If only she had given a name! Then we could have told Bess which of her people is conjuring up the phantom. Whoever it is, is growing stronger. The thing was clearer this time. It had more shape. And its face — or whatever horror was inside its hood — gleamed green."

"The sorcerer may be Bess herself," said Barda. "She said the phantom watches over you. And both its victims were intent on doing you harm."

"But when Otto was attacked, Bess did not even know I existed!" Lief objected.

"Still, both deaths were certainly connected with us," Jasmine said. The sorcerer must be someone who wants to drive us away from the troupe."

"We have a wide choice, then," growled Barda. "The whole of the inner circle, except Bess, wants us gone."

"Well, as far as I am concerned, they can have their wish," Lief said flatly. "Let us tell Bess that we wish to leave at once — and tell her in front of others. That is the best way of ensuring our safety, and the safety of everyone else here."

"It is," Jasmine agreed. "And I, for one, will be very glad to go."

"I, too," said Barda. "Though I do not relish the idea of telling Bess."

✳

By the time the village clock struck ten, it was as if the attack had never happened.

Fern the seamstress had been buried. Fern's grieving husband had been given a potion and had fallen into a drugged sleep. Life in the camp had returned to normal. And Lief, Barda, and Jasmine were again sitting at the purple-draped table outside Bess's wagon, while Kree kept silent watch in the tree above their heads.

They were eating dinner, served once again by

Rust. The meal was nearly finished, but still they had not spoken of what was most on their minds. Then, suddenly, Bess gave them their chance.

"This has been a hard day," she said, spooning the last of her soup into her mouth. "The new people — especially the orphans — are growing restless. We need a performance to lift their spirits — to make them know how fine it is to be a Masked One."

She sighed heavily. "Plainly, we must forget our plans to perform here. We must go east to Purley, I fear. I have never liked the place, but at least we know that we will have a good audience there."

Barda cleared his throat. "What a great pity!" he said. "If you are returning to the east, I fear that we must part company with you."

"What?" Bess dropped her spoon with a clatter. "But you cannot leave us! Lewin has a great future before him. You, too, Berry, from all I have heard. And even young Jay — "

"Ah, well, it cannot be helped," Barda said firmly. "As you know, my nephews and I have always planned to go to the west."

Lief glanced at Rust. Her eyes were shining with amazed relief.

You did not expect this, did you, Rust? he thought. *You were so sure we were spies, and would cling to the troupe as long as we could. Well, you were wrong. Soon you will be rid of us. And we will be rid of you!*

Bess was panting, as if she had been running. She turned to Lief.

"Surely you do not want this, do you, Lewin?" she demanded.

"I am sorry, Bess, but my first loyalty must be to my uncle," Lief said, grateful that he did not have to hurt her even further by admitting he wanted to leave. "Wherever he goes, I must go, too."

Bess bowed her head, struggling to calm herself. "Well," she mumbled. "This has been a great shock."

At last she looked up. "But perhaps it is all for the best," she said, smiling bravely. "Bring a jug of wildberry wine, if you please, Rust. Berry needs restoring. Quill worked him far too hard this afternoon. And bring some oatcakes with honey for the young ones."

The fox-woman nodded and hurried away, taking the used dishes from the table with her. Clearly, she was in high good humor.

"Lewin," Bess said, "I have a favor to ask of you."

"What is it, Bess?" asked Lief cautiously.

"I want you to go into my wagon and take the round silver box from beneath my bed," Bess said. "In the box, you will find a mask. I want you to put that mask on, Lewin, and wear it for me."

Lief's stomach turned over.

"I see by your eyes that you have guessed," Bess

said. "Yes. It is the mask of Bede's adulthood — the mask he never wore. It would have been yours one day, Lewin, if you had stayed with us."

She looked down at her folded hands. "Now that will never be," she said. "But it would give me such joy to see you wear it — just for a single hour — on this, our last night together."

Lief hesitated. He could feel Barda and Jasmine staring at him. No doubt they could see no harm in Bess's request.

And what *was* the harm?

He stood up. "If it would please you, Bess," he said.

He took a lantern from the collection around the table and moved to the back of the wagon.

The sack that had stood by the door now sagged half empty. A fire burned beneath the black iron pot, which was filled with slowly bubbling liquid that looked like porridge, but smelled strongly of rotten fruit.

Lief wrinkled his nose. Plainly, Bess was cooking some of the roots from the secret field.

I am glad we are leaving tomorrow, if that is to be the Masked Ones' dinner tomorrow night, he thought.

He entered the wagon, went quickly to the bed, and soon found the silver box.

Inside, wrapped in yellow silk, was a magnificent mask — a gleaming blue bird-head, similar to the one he was wearing, but much finer and more lifelike.

Lief reached out and touched it. It seemed to quiver beneath his fingers. For a single, horrible moment it seemed alive. Lief snatched his hand away, his heart beating wildly. He clutched at the Belt of Deltora, hidden beneath his clothes.

Gradually, his panic ebbed away. He forced himself to look down.

The mask lay in its bed of silk — a beautiful, lifeless thing of feathers, fabric, and paste.

Filled with shame, Lief took off his old mask. At the same moment, the village clock began striking eleven. The sound seemed so loud and clear!

For a few moments, he relished his freedom. Then, as the last, ringing chime died away, he gritted his teeth, picked up the new mask, and pulled it on.

8 ~ Tricks

The mask felt soft and cool against Lief's skin. It was so light that he could barely feel it. It molded itself to his face and neck as though it had been made for him. It was almost like wearing no mask at all.

Suddenly, he felt more cheerful. He let himself out of the wagon and strode back to where Bess, Barda, and Jasmine were waiting.

Bess was lying back in her chair with her eyes closed, but Barda and Jasmine turned to look at him.

Jasmine started, her eyes wide. Barda gave a muffled gasp, and half-rose from his stool.

"What is wrong?" Lief asked, confused.

Jasmine swallowed. "You look — you look as if you are half bird," she whispered. "That mask . . ."

"I have never seen anything like it," said Barda,

sinking back onto the stool again. "It made the hair rise on the back of my neck!"

Feeling quite pleased at the excitement he had caused, Lief sat down.

Bess's eyes fluttered open. They focused on him, widened, and seemed to glow.

"Ah," she breathed. "Thank you, Lewin. You have made an old woman very happy. Wear it for an hour — till midnight. That will be enough."

She rubbed her hands. "Now!" she said. "Let me entertain you!"

The companions looked at her blankly, and she laughed.

"Do you think that the Masked Ones have only acrobats, singers, and clowns to offer?" she cried, waving at the people practicing by the central fire. "Why, we can do far more than that! I, for example, can read minds!"

"Is that so?" asked Barda dryly.

"Indeed," said Bess. "But to do it I must have my trusty glass!"

Grunting with effort, she bent and lifted from the ground the glass ball Lief had last seen in her wagon. She placed the ball in the center of the table.

"Now, who is to be my subject?" she asked. "Berry? Are you willing?"

"Certainly," agreed Barda, grinning broadly. "But I warn you — no one who has ever tried it has been able to read my mind. My skull is too thick, perhaps."

"Then I will begin with something simple," Bess said calmly. "Think of a number between one and nine. Make your nephews aware of what it is, if you wish, but do not tell me."

Barda shrugged. "Very well," he said. "I have it."

Below the tabletop, where Bess could not see, he held up five fingers, telling Lief and Jasmine that the number he had chosen was five.

"Concentrate on the number, all of you," said Bess. "Try to think of nothing else."

She held her hands just above the glass ball. She closed her eyes and began to chant in a low, singsong voice.

The tabletop seemed to rise slightly. Then, slowly, it began to spin. The purple cloth shimmered as it moved, its hem whispering as it brushed the dusty grass. The glass ball turned in the center, winking in the candlelight.

Lief felt a chill run down his spine. He knew this must be a trick, but the sight was eerie. *Bess is a good actor*, he thought.

Bess's blind owl face loomed over the turning table. Her hands, with their many flashing rings, cast shadows on the winking glass ball.

No doubt she has done this a thousand times, Lief thought. *As her mother did before her. And her grandmother and great-grandmother, too.*

Suddenly, he was filled with a strange sort of

pride to be among these talented people, sharing their life. He almost regretted that he had to leave them so soon.

"The visions are hazy," Bess murmured. "I cannot see clearly. Someone's mind is wandering."

She shook her head impatiently. "That number is no good to me now. I will have to try again. Berry — double the number! Then — then multiply it by — by five! The answer is your new number."

"Very well," Barda said. He glanced at Lief and Jasmine, who nodded. The new number was fifty.

They were all concentrating hard now, but Bess shook her head again.

"I cannot understand it!" she muttered to herself. "Why can I not see it?"

She seemed really distressed. Lief began to feel sorry for her.

"Divide your new number by the number you first thought of," Bess ordered, frantically moving her hands over the glass ball.

Ten, Lief thought. *Fifty divided by five is ten.*

Bess drew a deep breath. Her hands slowed.

"Better," she said softly. "Now, take away — ah, yes! — take away seven, the number of magic! And then concentrate — concentrate hard on the number that remains."

Ten minus seven, thought Lief. *Three. Three . . . three . . . three . . .*

The table slowed, and became still.

"Ah . . . at last!" Bess breathed. "I see it! The number in your minds is . . . three!"

Lief, Barda, and Jasmine exclaimed and clapped. "Amazing!" cried Barda. "How did you do it?"

Bess shrugged and straightened her shawls. "Who am I to try to explain the mysterious power of the glass?" she said solemnly. But her eyes were twinkling behind her mask.

And suddenly thinking over what had happened, Lief realized that she had been acting all the time. Her pretended hesitation and distress had disguised a very simple trick.

If you multiply a number by two and then by five, you are really multiplying it by ten! he thought. *So if you then divide your total by the original number, ten will always be your answer. Take away seven from ten — and you are left with three.*

So that was how Bess had "read" their minds. Whichever number they started with, the end result would be three, every time!

He smiled beneath his mask.

"The spinning tabletop is not so mysterious," Jasmine said boldly. "I have seen something a little like it before. I am sure you make it move by working a pedal under the table."

Bess laughed heartily. "You are not easily impressed, young Jay," she said. "But, of course, you are right. I can make the table move and stop again with the slightest tap of my foot. It is just a little trick — to make the performance more interesting."

"It does that," said Barda. "But I still do not understand how — "

"Ah, here are our drinks at last!" Bess cried. She took the glass ball and set it carefully on the ground beside her chair.

Rust appeared carrying a loaded tray. "I fear there is no honey, Bess," she said, bending to place two small cakes, two cups, and a stone jug on the table. "The last jar has disappeared from the food wagon. That young thief, Zerry, took it, no doubt. I do not know why you put up with him!"

"Zerry has very light fingers," Bess agreed calmly, taking the cork from the jug and filling the cups with deep red wine. "After all, he has lived by thieving ever since he could walk."

She handed one of the cups to Barda. "But that is just why I wanted him, Rust. If he can take a purse from a man's coat without that man noticing, he can learn to deceive an audience with ease. He will be a great magician one day."

Rust sniffed and straightened up, tucking the empty tray under her arm.

"Perhaps," she said darkly. "Though Plug says that he neglects his lessons, preferring to spend time with the horses. Perhaps — " She broke off, and her hand flew to her mouth.

She was staring at Lief, her eyes bulging with shock.

"Ah, you have noticed Lewin's mask at last," said Bess lightly. "Does it not suit him?"

"Bess!" The fox-woman's voice was a strangled whisper. "Bess, you cannot — "

"You know better than to tell me what I can and cannot do, Rust!" Bess growled. "Leave us at once!"

The fox-woman ducked her head and stumbled away.

There was an awkward silence. Then Bess sighed.

"We must not let poor Rust spoil our pleasure," she said. "She respects our old traditions far too well, and will not see that rules must change with the times."

She lifted her cup.

"Good health!" she said, and drank deeply.

"Good health!" Barda repeated. He sipped his own wine and smacked his lips. "Very good!" he said.

From his pocket he took the little carved box that he had been trying to open ever since he came by it in the Os-Mine Hills. A small rod of polished wood protruded from one of the sides, very near the top. He passed the box to Bess.

"Here is a puzzle for you," he said. "I thought I had solved it, but there is more than one lock. Would you like to try your skill?"

Bess took the little box in her enormous hands

and turned it over with interest. Barda watched, grinning, as she pressed the carving here and there. He had spent hours working on the box in Broome. He was sure she would not be able to open it.

Lief moved restlessly, glancing over his shoulder at the activity around the central fire. He longed to go and join the crowd.

Bess glanced up. "You young ones run along and watch the entertainments for a time, if you wish," she said kindly. "Take your cakes with you. Berry and I will be cozy together here."

Lief and Jasmine stood up with relief, picked up their cakes, and left the table. From his perch in the tree, Kree silently watched them go.

"Bess is being very pleasant to Uncle Berry," Jasmine said in a low voice, breaking off part of her cake and cautiously slipping it beneath her jacket for Filli. "Do you think she hopes to change his mind about leaving?"

"Perhaps," Lief said absentmindedly. He quickened his steps. He could not wait to become part of the life around the fire.

Together he and Jasmine plunged into the crowd. Jasmine was soon claimed by the dog-faced acrobats, who were forming their pyramid again. Lief wandered on alone in a happy dream, drinking in the amazing sights and sounds around him.

Jugglers, singers, musicians, magicians . . . Here a dragon-man breathing fire. There a tall, thin man with the glistening head of a snake, tying himself in knots. Beside him, a squirrel-woman dancing with bare feet on a bed of hot coals . . .

Two girls in furry masks like Jasmine's walked by casually on stilts.

"Bess says I will be given the mask of my adult-hood very soon," Lief heard one of them say to the other. "It will be a waterbird, as I requested. At last! I have been eighteen for months!"

"You are lucky, Neelie," said the other girl enviously. "Imagine! You will not have to live with the or-phans anymore. I am sick and tired of old frog-face Plug!"

"Never mind," the first girl laughed. "You will be eighteen in summer, Lin. Then it will be your turn. Bess is very pleased by how hard we worked in the Field of Masks. She says she has enough purebond roots now to make many new adult masks. Enough for all the orphans as they come of age."

They strode on, weaving gracefully through the crowd.

So — that is one mystery solved, in any case, Lief thought, fascinated. *The roots from the field are not food. They are boiled until they dissolve, and Bess uses the mix-ture to make the inner skin of the special adulthood masks. It must be an ancient craft. No wonder its secrets are closely guarded.*

He smiled after the girls, who were still chatter-ing happily. *How good it is to be among my own people,* he found himself thinking. *How wonderful to be part of this world . . . to have this feeling of safety and belonging. How wonderful, to be a Masked One . . .*

But you are not really a Masked One, a small, clear voice said in his head. *You are not part of this world at all. And you do not want to be! Only a few hours ago you could not wait to get away from it. Remember?*

Lief tried to push the voice aside, but it would not leave him. As though it had made a gap in his mind through which a cold breeze blew, he shivered.

Suddenly, he noticed Rust, Quill, and Plug standing nearby. They were watching him, talking in low voices. When they saw him looking, they quickly turned away.

Lief felt a sudden pang of grief. Then he shook his head impatiently. Why should he care if they rejected him? Why should he long to be accepted as one of them?

Why could he not stop shivering?

The crowd surged around him. Waves of music battered him. A group of masked children playing some chasing game surrounded him, jostled him, laughed shrilly, and ran on. The little apprentice magician, Zerry, was among them.

I hope Rust did not see you, Zerry, Lief thought, looking down at his honey-smeared jacket. *You would do well to keep away from her — at least until you have washed your hands.*

The crowd parted a little, and he caught a

glimpse of Jasmine swinging on a high bar with three of the blue-clad acrobats. She seemed as far away from him as if she were on the moon. In the distance, in front of Bess's wagon, he could see the figures of Barda and Bess still sitting at the table.

Bess was passing the puzzle box back to Barda. By her actions, and Barda's laughter, Lief realized that she had managed to find and release a second lock, but the box still had not opened. He smiled, watching.

Bess fumbled, and the box fell onto the ground.

Barda bent to pick it up.

And, as quickly as a striking snake, Bess leaned across the table and tipped something into his cup.

9 ~ Terror

For a split second Lief stared, hardly able to believe his eyes. It had all happened so quickly! He had seen no bottle or jar in Bess's hand.

But he had clearly seen a stream of white powder fall into the cup. He had seen it!

A wave of horror flooded through him. Frantically, he began to fight his way through the crowd towards Bess's wagon.

Bess is a good actor . . .

Oh, yes, Bess is a good actor, he thought wildly. *Good enough to convince us that she had given in gracefully. Good enough to laugh and joke with Barda while coldly planning his death.*

He groaned aloud as he remembered what he had said to Bess.

My first loyalty must be to my uncle. Wherever he goes, I must go, too.

Those words had signed Barda's death warrant.

For Bess, it had all been very simple. Berry stood between Lewin and Bess. So Berry must die.

The crowd parted briefly and Lief saw that Barda was back in his chair again. Bess was pouring more wine into his cup and her own.

"Barda!" Lief roared. "Do not drink!"

But it was useless! His voice was drowned by the crowd's noise.

Animal and bird heads loomed all around him like things out of a nightmare. Clowns capered foolishly in front of him, barring his way. He dodged around them, and cannoned into the girls on stilts.

With a shrill scream, one of the girls toppled and fell, crashing down on a group of jugglers.

That attracted Bess and Barda's attention. Lief saw Barda turn. He saw Bess peer at the crowd, one hand shading her eyes. He saw Kree flutter down from the tree like a black shadow.

Frantically, Lief shouted and waved. But Bess and Barda were looking at the girl, who was scrambling unsteadily to her feet while the jugglers crawled around her, picking up the balls they had dropped. Kree was nowhere to be seen.

Again, the crowd closed in. Lief put his head down and pushed forward desperately, thrusting people aside, ignoring their angry protests.

"Make way!" he shouted. "Make way!"

"Make way yourself, you rude young pup!"

snarled a man in a ragged bear mask. He pushed Lief violently between the shoulder blades.

Lief lurched forward and crashed, sprawling, to the ground. All the breath was knocked from his body. Coughing and gasping, he crawled to his knees, shaking his head to clear it.

He had been thrown out of the crowd. Ahead he could see clear ground. He could see the wagon beneath the tree, and the two people sitting at the purple-covered table, ringed with lanterns.

Barda and Bess had picked up their cups and were raising them in a toast.

"No!" Lief gasped.

They both threw their heads back, and drank.

"No!" Lief croaked in agony. "No! *Barda!*"

He staggered to his feet and began to run.

It was as though everything was moving very slowly. As though he was seeing everything through a bright mist.

He reached the table, the breath wheezing in his chest. Barda turned to look at him. Bess half rose, her smooth owl face expressionless.

"What is wrong?" Barda exclaimed in alarm.

"Lewin!" Bess cried, at the same moment. "I fear your uncle is not well. His efforts today strained his heart and — "

She broke off. Her golden eyes widened and filled with what seemed like surprise. She looked down at the cup still clutched in her hand.

Her fingers jerked. The cup fell onto the table, spun, and lay still.

Then she fell back, clutching her chest.

Barda exclaimed and jumped up, the stool tipping and falling behind him.

Stunned, Lief stared down at the table — at Bess's fallen cup. From its lip, the last drops of wine trickled onto the purple tablecloth — gleaming red wine, mixed with a pale sludge of white powder.

"She drank the poison herself!" he whispered. "But how — ?"

Then he looked up — up at the tree that stretched above them. Kree was back on his perch on the lowest branch. He was very still. But his yellow eyes were gleaming.

I can make the table turn and stop again with the slightest tap of my foot.

So Bess had said. They had all heard her, including Kree. No doubt Kree had reasoned that the slightest tap of a strong beak like his would work just as well.

And so it had. Lief remembered the moment when the girl on stilts had fallen. Both Bess and Barda had looked towards the crowd. And that had been the moment Kree had been waiting for. While their attention was distracted, he had flown down from his perch, hopped under the table, and done what he had to do.

The tabletop had turned. The cups had been re-versed. Bess had drunk her own poison.

Masked Ones from the edges of the crowd were running towards them, realizing that something was wrong. They stood gaping as their leader lay back, fighting for breath.

Barda had sprung to Bess's side, and was bend-ing over her. "It must be her heart!" he shouted. "She needs air!"

He began tearing at Bess's mask.

"No!" Bess muttered, her hands moving feebly, trying to push Barda's away. "No . . ."

With a tiny click, the top of the golden ring on her little finger fell open like a lid. A few grains of white powder still clung to the sides of the cavity re-vealed within.

This ring is worn by the leader of the Masked Ones . . .

Lief stared, Bess's words echoing in his mind. Words he now truly understood.

In the hand of the leader lies the gift of life . . . and death.

"Lief! I cannot get her mask off. My fingers are too clumsy. Help me!" Barda's voice was agonized.

Lief moved stiffly to his side. He knew that it was useless. He knew that Bess was doomed. But still he grasped the feathers at the base of her mask and pulled upwards with all his strength.

Bess shrieked in agony.

Startled, Lief looked down at his fingers.

They were red with blood. Blood was streaming from beneath the torn rim of the mask's base, trickling down Bess's neck, soaking into the silk of her purple dress . . .

He met Barda's horrified eyes.

"The mask will not come off," he muttered, through chattering teeth. "It is part of her. Joined to her. It will not . . ."

He backed away, holding his bloody hands out in front of him.

A woman in the crowd screamed hysterically.

"What are you doing?" shouted the voice of the fox-woman behind them. "Get away from her! Bess! Oh, Bess!"

In seconds, the members of the Masked Ones' inner circle were pushing Lief and Barda aside, clustering around Bess, trying to hide her from the gathering crowd.

But it was too late. Everyone had seen.

"Blood! He tried to pull the mask off — and her skin tore away with it!" a high voice shrieked. "The mask has grown into her face! Oh — oh, horrible! Horrible!"

There was a chorus of shuddering groans, wails of horror.

Lief looked around him. Everywhere, terrified people were tearing off their own masks and throwing them to the ground, trampling them underfoot. Faces were revealed, strangely shocking in their nakedness — faces old and young, pretty and plain, filled with disgust, with horror, with fear.

The man who had worn the bear mask was small-eyed and red-faced. Foam had gathered at the corners of his mouth.

"It is the same with all of them!" he howled, pointing at the Masked Ones gathered around Bess. "Freaks! Sorcerers! Kill them!"

The crowd surged forward, then halted, wavering. Silence fell.

The members of the inner circle had turned. Every one of them held a long, narrow knife.

Shoulder to shoulder they faced the bareface crowd, and their eyes were filled with loathing. Proudly, they lifted their heads — their heads covered by the masks which were part of them.

The masks of their adulthood, Lief thought dazedly. *Put on at the age of eighteen. Bonded to their flesh, forever . . . forever . . .*

In the stillness, the village clock began to chime. *One . . . two . . .*

Lief looked over the heads of the Masked Ones, beyond the tree to where the clock tower stood, shining in the moonlight. The hands of the clock were pointing straight upwards.

Midnight.

The skin of his face and neck seemed to warm and prickle. The memory of Bess's voice whispered in his mind.

Wear it for one hour — till midnight. That will be enough.

He looked down again. The eagle-man, Quill, met his eyes. "You had better join us, Lewin of Broome," Quill said quietly. "Like it or not, you are one of us, now."

Yes.

Lief took a step forward. Then, suddenly, his arms were seized, and he was jerked back. Bewildered, he turned his head from one side to the other. Jasmine and Barda each held one of his arms. They were holding him, shaking him, calling to him.

Lief recoiled. Jasmine and Barda had taken off their masks. Their mouths seemed to writhe horribly as they shouted. Their naked faces were beaded with sweat, creased and twisted with horror.

They were ugly — disgusting. It made him sick to look at them.

He struggled vainly to free himself. Barda and Jasmine were still shouting, but he could not understand what they were saying. The chiming of the clock filled his mind.

Five . . . six . . .

"You see?" roared the voice of the red-faced man. "See the boy in the bird mask? Bess the witch favored him! She changed him into one of them! And so she would have changed us all, at last! Turned us into freaks, like herself!"

Shouting angrily, the crowd surged forward again. Some had armed themselves with rocks, and with flaming sticks from the fire.

"Burn them!" a woman shrieked.

The Masked Ones stood their ground.

"Rust!" Quill said.

Rust cupped her hands around her mouth. Her fox-face gleamed in the candlelight as she drew breath. Then she gave an unearthly, high-pitched screech.

It was like the weird cry Lief and Jasmine had heard in the forest camp of the Masked Ones. And now they knew its purpose.

For from the fences around the field the giant moths rose in a cloud.

Like thousands of scraps of paper whirling in a breeze, the moths swarmed towards the one who had called them in.

But there were no red boxes ready to receive them. They could not land. Confused, they swooped over the crowd, a fluttering mass of white.

The air was thick with them. Their wings brushed hands, shoulders, faces. The markings on their wings swelled and glowed scarlet. They spat, and their poison burned where it fell.

Many people staggered, screaming in pain. Others dropped their weapons, covered their heads, and began to run, heedlessly trampling the fallen ones in their panic.

Run, you ugly barefaces, Lief thought, watching in satisfaction. *Leave us to ourselves!*

With part of his mind he was aware that the clock was still striking.

Nine . . . ten . . .

Soon . . .

With a shock, he felt himself thrown to the ground, held fast. Barda pinned his shoulders down. Then, horribly, he felt Jasmine's fingers tearing at his face.

"No!" he moaned. "No — "

Jasmine loomed above him. She was breathing in great, sobbing gasps. Her brow was beaded with sweat, and tears were pouring down her cheeks. But her mouth was set in a hard, straight line.

Eleven . . .

He felt a searing pain. He heard Barda cursing. He heard himself screaming.

Then all was darkness.

10 - The Bees

L ief woke suddenly, his heart pounding with fear. There was a low ringing in his ears. Needles of pain stabbed at his face and neck.

The ringing sound slowly faded away.

I must have had a nightmare, Lief thought. He lay very still, calming himself. Shadows flitted at the edges of his mind, but he could remember no dream. What had woken him, then? Woken him in such terror?

Cautiously, he tried opening his eyes. They felt swollen and tender, and he could only open them a little. Through his eyelashes he saw blue sky, and sunlight filtering through the leaves of a tree.

It was broad daylight!

He licked his dry lips and swallowed painfully. He realized that he was very thirsty.

He turned his head to look for his water flask. Pain flashed through him, bringing tears to his eyes.

Have I been burned? he thought in confusion. He could smell the ashes of a fire. He could see the remains of a small fire near the trunk of the tree, not far from where he lay.

He could see nothing else. No pack. No water flask. Only trampled earth, deeply rutted with the marks of wagon wheels.

Gritting his teeth, closing his mind to the pain, he turned his head to the other side.

Jasmine lay there, deeply asleep. Her cheek was pillowed on her arm. In her hand was the tiny jar of green ointment. It was as though she had been using the ointment just before she fell asleep.

She was wearing the blue clothes of a Masked Ones acrobat. Her hair was covered by a woolen cap. Her face was smeared with mud and what looked like blood.

Beyond her, as far as Lief could see, the field stretched broad and empty except for the ashes of an enormous fire. The fence had been broken down in several places.

What has happened to us? he thought wildly. *Where is Barda?* His heart began to thud.

Barda is in danger . . .

The feeling was strong, but another feeling, or vague memory, was mingling with it. Something about Kree . . .

A fly buzzed close to his face, then settled on his arm. Lief wanted to brush it away, but feared that he could not lift his hand.

Another fly joined the first. Then Lief realized that they were not flies at all, but bees.

And at the same moment, as if in a dream, he heard sounds drifting on the breeze from somewhere beyond the field. The jingling of tiny bells. And singing.

Here we are in Happy Vale,
Pretty bees, busy bees.
Three long hours on the trail,
Fuzzy, buzzy bees.

Did you hear the clock strike eight?
Clever bees, tired bees.
Pray that we are not too late,
Hungry, bumbly bees.

As if the song had thrown open a window in Lief's mind, he suddenly understood several things at once.

He had been woken by the striking of the Happy Vale clock. The sound had filled him with terror, but he did not know why.

It was eight o'clock in the morning. The Masked Ones had left in the night. He and Jasmine were alone here, with no weapons, no food, no water.

And the person passing by the field, the singer of the jolly little song, was . . .

Trust only old friends . . .

Lief tried to shout, but his voice was a husky croak. He struggled to sit up. His head swam and he nearly fell back. Grimly, he propped himself up with his hands.

So it was that he saw the great black bird swooping towards him. He saw the swarm of bees stretching like a trail of smoke all the way to the field gate. And he saw a shabby caravan, drawn by a fat old horse and driven by a huge, brown-skinned, golden-haired man, turning into the gateway and following the line of bees.

On the side of the caravan was a familiar, faded sign.

"Jasmine!" Lief croaked.

Jasmine's eyes flew open in fright and widened

even further when she saw Lief sitting up and looking at her.

"Lief?" she murmured uncertainly, scrambling to her knees. "Are you — all right?"

He nodded, wincing at the pain in his neck. Why was Jasmine staring at him so strangely?

With a chill, he wondered what he looked like. He lifted his hand to his cheek.

Searing pain. Sticky cream coating his fingertips.

"Am I — burned?" he managed to croak.

Jasmine shook her head. She pulled off her cap, and her black hair tumbled around her shoulders. Her eyes were very dark. Filli was hiding beneath her jacket, only the tip of his nose visible.

"Do you not remember what happened last night?" Jasmine asked. "What — what I did?"

"No." Lief swallowed painfully.

She breathed a long sigh and closed her eyes as if in relief.

"Barda," Lief rasped. "Where is — ?"

"He went in pursuit of the Masked Ones," Jasmine whispered. "Kree is with him. Lief — "

"At last!" boomed a voice. "And both alive, by the looks of it!"

Jasmine jumped violently and swung around. She had been concentrating on Lief so intently that she had not even noticed the approaching caravan.

Kree flew to her, landing on her arm. She leaped to her feet.

287

"Steven!" she cried. "Am I dreaming?"

Steven the pedlar's face split in a broad grin. "Not unless I am dreaming as well," he roared back. "How fortunate that I was in these parts! I have been in Purley, with my mother's best hive of bees. We heard that flowers were blooming in the east, but I fear there are not yet enough to have made the journey worthwhile."

He brought the horse to a halt beside them and climbed down from the driver's seat.

"Steven, did you see some wagons on the road?" Jasmine asked feverishly. "Wagons driven by people in masks?"

Steven nodded. "Oh, yes, I met the Masked Ones," he said. "Traded with them, in fact, as I have often done before. They were far fewer than the last time we met — the inner circle only, and a few youngsters. Silent and nervous they were, too."

He grinned. "Later I met someone even more interesting — or found him, rather, thanks to Kree."

Jasmine shrieked. Steven laughed, strode to the back of the caravan, and threw open the doors.

"There he is," he said triumphantly, as Jasmine jumped eagerly into the van. "He was lying in a ditch — put to sleep by some Masked One's trickery or other, no doubt. If Kree had not been guarding him, I would have passed him by."

"Steven!" Lief rasped. "Is it — Barda?"

Steven looked around and seemed to see him properly for the first time.

"Lief!" he gasped, dismayed. "By the heavens! What happened to you?"

"I — am not quite sure," said Lief, trying to smile.

Jasmine climbed back out of the caravan, her face very grave. Lief's heart seemed to leap into his throat.

"Surely, Barda is not worse than I thought?" Steven asked anxiously.

Jasmine shook her head. "He stirred when I spoke to him," she said. "He took some water and said a few words. I daresay the spell, or whatever it was, will pass off in time."

Steven laughed with relief. "Why, I thought from your expression that we would soon be attending his funeral!" he exclaimed.

Jasmine said nothing. Still she did not look at Lief. He had groaned with relief on hearing that Barda was safe. Now the tightness in his chest came back in force.

Steven glanced at him, then back at Jasmine.

"Cheer up, girl!" he said to her loudly, raising his bushy eyebrows. "Your long face is worrying Lief half to death!"

Jasmine bit her lip, but still she did not look up or speak.

Steven frowned at her. "I did good trade with the Masked Ones, did I not?" he said, a little coldly. "They wanted some Queen Bee honey. It is in short supply, but I agreed to give them six jars when I saw the goods they offered in exchange."

"Our weapons and our packs," Jasmine murmured. "Yes — I saw them in the caravan. Our packs are still sealed, just as we left them."

Lief stared at her in amazement. She sounded as if the return of all their possessions was of very little importance.

Steven's frown deepened. No doubt he had expected joy, or at least a word of thanks.

"I think the Masked Ones had forgotten they had them," he said. "They found them in an empty wagon, when they were rummaging about looking for things to trade. Then the fox-faced woman remembered the weapons, and brought them out, too."

"You recognized them?" asked Lief.

Steven shrugged. "Of course!" he said. "No one could mistake your sword. I was astounded, and fearful, too, but I did not let the Masked Ones see. They said they had found your possessions by the side of the road. I doubted that was true, but it seemed unwise to challenge them. If they had fought me, Nevets would have killed them all."

He grimaced as he spoke Nevets' name.

How strange it must be to carry your brother within

you, Lief thought. *Especially a brother who is your opposite. Who is a savage . . . a killer!*

Steven eyed Lief and tugged his rough beard. "I did not want the Masked Ones harmed, at the time," he added. "Perhaps I was wrong."

"No," Jasmine said in a low voice. "The one who caused the trouble was already dead."

She pressed her lips together. Plainly, she was going to say no more.

Steven tugged at his beard even harder. "They had thrown open every wagon in their search, so I was sure that you were not with them," he muttered. "But the wagons were all in confusion, as if they had been packed very hurriedly, for a quick departure."

"So when they had gone, you followed their wagon tracks back along the road," Lief said. "And so found Barda — "

"And Kree, who led me on to you," Steven said.

He looked from Lief to Jasmine, and shook his head.

"How did this happen?" he burst out. "How is it that I find you in this state? Why, the last I heard, you were travelling the kingdom in fine style, on horseback and escorted by a troop of guards!"

"It is a long story," Lief said. "Steven, you must help us! We must move on. We must move on, towards the west."

His mouth felt stiff. The pain in his face and neck

stabbed at him mercilessly, and his dizziness had returned. He swayed.

Steven crouched beside him and took his arm. "We are going nowhere today, Lief," he said firmly. "Later, when you are more recovered — "

"No!" Jasmine broke in. "We must leave here now!"

Steven spun around. This time he was really scowling. His golden eyes darkened ominously, as if his savage brother, Nevets, was stirring within him.

"Are you mad, girl?" he snarled. "Lief is not fit to travel! Look at him!"

Look at him!

Filli wailed, and Jasmine buried her face in her hands. Lief felt cold. Cold to his very bones.

Jasmine lifted her head. She looked directly at Lief.

"There is much to tell you," she said in a low voice. "But one thing I should have told you at once. It was cowardly of me not to do so, but then Steven came, with Barda, and I thought . . ."

You thought they would help you tell me, Lief thought. *Tell me that, whatever it was that happened to me last night, my face will never . . .*

He held Jasmine's eyes steadily, bracing himself for what was to come.

Jasmine wet her lips. "Last night, all was confusion," she said. "There was panic, and screaming. People were running everywhere. You were in great pain, and not — not in your senses. It took Barda and me both to hold you down."

Her voice trembled. She shook her head impatiently and went on.

"The ordinary people scattered — fled in every direction. The Masked Ones threw everything into the wagons and left the field at a gallop. It was only after they had gone, and you had calmed a little, that we realized — realized that the Belt — the Belt of Deltora — "

The Belt? Lief thought in confusion. *What has this to do . . . ?*

He put his hands to his waist.

The Belt of Deltora was gone.

11 - The Trail

When the village clock struck nine, Steven, Lief, and Jasmine were still in the field. A small fire was crackling between them, and Steven was pouring hot tea into cups. He had refused to go in pursuit of the Masked Ones.

"They would not have touched the Belt," he said firmly. "To them, it is an evil thing. They learn to hate it from the cradle."

"Why?" Lief said. He swallowed. His throat had been soothed by the Queen Bee honey Steven had given him, but it still felt raw.

He now knew the reason. It was because in the night, just before midnight, he had screamed in agony. Screamed and screamed . . .

"Later, I will give you something that explains the Masked Ones a little," said Steven, pushing a steaming cup into his hands. "For now, forget them and think about the ordinary folk who were travelling with them."

Lief sipped his tea, staring at the cloud of bees swarming on the fence at the far edge of the field. He let his mind drift, knowing that it was best not to force his memory.

Gradually, much of what had happened the night before came back to him. But he remembered nothing from the moment the clock began to strike midnight. He knew only what Jasmine had told him.

It was horrifying, almost unbelievable, but he knew it was true. In the mirror Steven had brought from the caravan, he had seen the proof — the raw patches on his cheekbones, chin, and neck, gleaming scarlet beneath their layers of sticky green cream.

He shuddered, thinking how narrow his escape had been. How nearly he had been a Masked One for life, the beautiful blue bird face bonded forever with his own. A few more seconds . . .

He reached for Jasmine's hand.

"No one but Barda and I were with you at midnight, Lief," she said in a low voice. "The Belt must have been stolen before then — while you were wandering alone in the crowd. Though how it could have been taken without you noticing, I do not understand."

Her words stirred a memory in Lief's mind. Bess, talking to Rust:

If he can take a purse from a man's coat without that man noticing, he can learn to deceive an audience with ease.

"Zerry!" he exclaimed.

"Who?" asked Steven, leaning forward.

"The little thief?" Jasmine cried at the same moment. "Of course! But Lief, how — ?"

"Some children jostled me in the field," Lief said slowly. "I remember now. Zerry was one of them. He must have taken the Belt then."

He stared across the field, remembering.

"Before that, I was feeling — confused," he said. "The Belt's magic, and the magic of the mask, were battling within me, I am sure of it. One minute I would think I was a Masked One. The next minute a voice inside me would remind me I was not. And I could not stop shivering. But after I was jostled by the children, all that disappeared."

"Because the Belt had gone," murmured Jasmine.

Lief nodded. Absently, he noticed that the bees had risen from the fence. Now they were swarming back towards the road in a ragged stream.

He focused on them. He stared.

"Zerry must have known exactly what he was after," Steven said thoughtfully. "An ordinary thief would have searched your pockets. That can only mean that, child or not, he is an ally of the guardian of the north — a servant of the Shadow Lord."

Jasmine swallowed the last of her tea and jumped up. "We can still catch him! He is on foot. No doubt he escaped from the field last night with everyone else — and went by the road, for fear of becoming lost."

296

"But which way did he go?" Steven asked, tossing dust on the fire to put it out. "Among the mass of tracks, how are we to find those of one small boy?"

"Look at the bees!" Lief said.

Steven glanced at him in surprise, then looked to where he was pointing.

A dark cloud of bees was swirling over the dust of the road.

"What are they doing?" Steven growled. "There is nothing for them out there!"

"Oh, but there is!" Lief could not help smiling, despite the stinging pain in his face. "Yesterday, Zerry stole honey from the store wagon," he said. "He must have hidden himself away and had a secret feast. When he jostled me last night, his hands were sticky with honey — and no doubt it had dripped on his clothes and shoes as well. Look! The bees can smell it!"

They were all on their feet now, shading their eyes, staring at the bees. The swarm was slowly moving west.

"You see?" Lief said softly. "The bees are following a honey trail. To find Zerry and the Belt, all we have to do is to follow them!"

✳

Lief rode inside the caravan so that his injuries would be protected from the dust of the road. He rolled up his cloak for a pillow and tried to sleep, like Barda, but sleep would not come.

Long hours passed. Then his heart leaped as he heard Steven calling the horse to a halt.

"Why have we stopped?" he asked anxiously, as Jasmine threw open the caravan doors with Filli chattering on her shoulder. "Is Zerry — ?"

"The bees have lost the trail," Jasmine answered flatly.

As Lief clambered to the ground, he saw that the road no longer ran between open fields. Now it was overshadowed on both sides by tall rocks and trees with pale, thin branches that clattered together like bones.

He walked with Jasmine to the front of the van, where Steven was pouring water into a bucket for his thirsty horse.

Immediately ahead, there was a road leading off to the left. It was marked by a signpost so faded that Lief could not see what it said.

Kree was perched on the signpost. The bees were swarming uncertainly behind it, where there was a large clearing. Wheel tracks crisscrossed the open space, leading off in both directions.

Lief approached the signpost, and looked at it.

Something stirred in his mind. He felt he had seen that name somewhere else, not long ago. But where?

"The boy met a wagon here, it seems," Steven said, moving up behind him with Jasmine. "And surely not by chance. We can follow — but which way?"

"The trees here can tell me nothing," Jasmine said grimly. "They are weak and ill — barely alive. The wheel tracks tell a story, however. Only one wagon moved west. And by the deep grooves it left behind, it had been standing here for a day or two before that."

"Indeed," Steven nodded, peering at the tracks. "All the other wagons came and went quite quickly. And they all went south to Riverdale. No doubt the boy is with one of those."

"I cannot see how a meeting was arranged," Lief frowned. "Zerry was travelling all day yesterday. And Happy Vale was deserted. How was the message passed?"

"You might as well ask how Zerry knew he must steal the Belt," Jasmine said impatiently. "Perhaps he saw it written in the sky! Perhaps the clouds formed letters saying, 'Steal the Belt of Deltora. Meet at the Riverdale signpost'! What does it matter?"

Lief's heart jolted. He had just remembered where he had seen the name Riverdale before! And with the memory had come a vivid picture — and an idea. A wild idea . . .

"It might matter a great deal," he exclaimed, kneeling and fumbling in his pocket for paper and pencil. "Remember the Happy Vale noticeboard? Everyone in the troupe saw that as we moved through the town. Did you, Steven?"

"Of course," Steven said gravely.

Lief put the paper on the ground in front of him. "The main notice is not important," he said. "But I want you both to help me remember all the small ones. Word for word, if possible."

"I did not read them all," murmured Jasmine, flushing a little. She still felt awkward because she read so slowly.

"You may not read fast, Jasmine, but you observe without even trying," said Lief. "That will be your part — and the most important one, if I am right."

Quickly, they finished the first notice, and the second. Jasmine could help no further after that, but Steven and Lief soon worked out the next three between them.

"I cannot help you on the last one," Steven said. "It concerned that villain Laughing Jack, the money-lender. I did not read it."

"It does not matter," Lief said. "I remember it. I noticed it particularly, because the first words — 'Seek the Nomad' — were odd."

"Ah, yes," said Steven sourly. "Laughing Jack is a great one for eye-catching notices. And he is a nomad, for he has no fixed home. He appears without warning outside one town or another, and in between it is as if he vanishes. Where was he camped this time?"

"Here," Lief said, writing out the last notice and drawing a border around it. "At the Riverdale signpost!"

12 - The Chase

Jasmine exclaimed with interest and craned her neck to see the words Lief had written. But Steven's frown had become a scowl.

"Ah!" he said in disgust. "So now we know whose wagon stayed so long! Laughing Jack never leaves a place until he has wrung it dry."

He shook his head. "No doubt most of the other tracks were made by the poor fools who came to do business with him."

"What is so wrong about lending money?" Jasmine asked, puzzled.

Steven snorted. "Nothing, if it is done fairly. But Laughing Jack preys on those who are desperate."

He saw that his companions did not understand him, and raised his voice slightly as he explained.

"Laughing Jack lends his victims what they ask, or more, and makes them sign a paper that half of them cannot even read," he said. "A season or two later he returns, demanding that the loan be repaid."

He paused. Dark shadows flickered in his golden eyes.

"And then?" Jasmine prompted.

Steven's fists clenched.

"And then his victims discover that they have sworn to pay back ten or twenty times as much as they borrowed," he muttered. "If they do not pay, which most often they cannot, Laughing Jack takes possession of their homes, their beasts, their furniture — everything they own."

"I have not heard of this!" Lief exclaimed.

Steven shrugged. "Laughing Jack has been a plague in the land for years without number, and dark rumors have gathered about him. His victims are too afraid to complain to anyone in authority."

"Afraid?" Lief murmured.

Steven grimaced. "He is an evil man, and when they have given him all they have, and it is still not enough, what else can he take from them, but their lives?"

As his companions exclaimed in horror, he shook his head. "I am wasting our time by speaking of things that we cannot change at present," he said gruffly. "Lief, what are we to do now?"

Lief spread his paper out before them on the ground. He had drawn borders around all the notices, shaping them as he remembered.

"Now it is your turn to test your memory, Jasmine," he said. "See the Happy Vale board in your mind. All the notices were pinned into place, were they not?"

Jasmine nodded. "Pinned untidily, too. The people who put them up had taken little care."

"I think they took a great deal of care," Lief said.

As she raised her eyebrows in surprise, he gave her the pencil. "See if you can remember where the pins were placed on each notice," he said. "Mark the places with a dot."

He crossed his fingers for luck as Jasmine bent over the paper and began to mark it.

She finished the first notice, and then the second. Now and then she would close her eyes, as if seeing a picture in her mind, before going on.

By the time she had finished marking the third notice, Lief knew he had been right.

He glanced at Steven. The big man's eyes were bulging with astonishment. He seemed about to speak, but Lief shook his head warningly. He did not want Jasmine's concentration to be disturbed.

Jasmine moved on with increasing speed. In moments, the work was done. She threw down the pencil and pushed the paper away.

"There," she muttered. "I have done it. Though I cannot see why — "

She glanced up and saw their faces. "What is it?" she asked blankly, looking down at the paper again.

304

"Read the words beneath the dots aloud," said Lief grimly. "Read them in order."

Haltingly, Jasmine did as he asked. "'The . . . three . . . are . . . with . . . you . . .'" she read, and caught her breath.

"Go on!" Lief urged.

"'Follow orders,'" Jasmine went on, her voice rising. "'Send goods . . . to . . . Laughing Jack . . . at Riverdale signpost.'"

"And that was how it was done," Steven exclaimed, slapping his knee. "The simple cunning of it! A message in plain sight, but perfectly disguised. 'The three are with you. Follow orders. Send goods to Laughing Jack, at Riverdale signpost.'"

Lief was only half listening. He was staring at the paper.

Something about it was still nagging at him. But what? The hidden message had been revealed. What further secrets could the notices hold?

"The 'three' are you two and Barda, of course," Steven went on excitedly. "The 'orders' must be Zerry's standing orders to steal the Belt of Deltora if you crossed his path. The 'goods' are the Belt itself."

He shook his head. "This guardian of the north must be well organized indeed, with a secret network of allies who go about their usual business unless and until they are needed. Zerry was used because he was with the Masked Ones. Laughing Jack was used because he was plying his evil trade in the north. No doubt he himself put the notices on the board just before you arrived."

"But how did the guardian learn that we were with the Masked Ones in the first place?" Jasmine frowned.

Steven was not interested in more mysteries. The one that had already been solved was enough for him.

"So Laughing Jack is in league with the Enemy," he muttered. "Why does that not surprise me?"

Abruptly, he turned and strode towards the caravan.

"Let us be on our way," he called over his shoulder. "We must make haste. Our quarry's wagon, I hear, is as fast as the wind."

"Then we will never catch him!" Jasmine cried anxiously, scrambling to her feet.

Steven reached the van, jumped up to the driver's seat, and began rummaging in a sack crushed into one corner.

"Certainly we will," he said, without looking up. "I have a trick or two up my sleeve."

He pulled a small green bottle from the sack, and nodded with satisfaction.

By the time Lief and Jasmine reached him, he had climbed down and was whispering in the horse's ear. The horse snorted eagerly and whisked her tail.

Steven smiled. "I am looking forward to this," he said softly. "My brother and I have long wanted to meet Laughing Jack."

He opened the green bottle and emptied it into the horse's bucket. The unmistakable apple smell of Queen Bee cider filled the air. The horse plunged its nose into the bucket and drank eagerly.

"Your horse drinks Queen Bee cider?" Jasmine asked in astonishment.

Steven was removing the strings of bells attached to the reins. "Only on special occasions," he said. "And, of course, Mellow is no ordinary horse."

Lief and Jasmine glanced at each other. Mellow certainly looked ordinary. Very ordinary indeed.

As if she knew what they were thinking, Mellow pawed the ground. She had nearly finished the cider in the bucket. They could hear the sound of her tongue rasping on the metal sides as she licked up the last few drops.

"I would climb into the van at once, if I were you," Steven said quickly. "Make sure the doors are locked."

"Steven, I think that Jasmine, at least, should ride with you," Lief objected.

Steven smiled without humor. "She would be very sorry if she did," he said.

Mellow raised her head. She bared her long yellow teeth and neighed.

Every bee in the clearing seemed to stop in midair. Then the swarm rose in a black cloud. Kree squawked and soared high into the sky.

"Make haste!" Steve said urgently. He snatched

up the bucket, threw the empty bottle and the bells inside it, and swung himself up to the driver's seat.

Lief and Jasmine ran to the back of the caravan. Jasmine jumped in. Lief was about to follow when Mellow neighed again. He looked around, and the hair rose on the back of his neck.

The swarm was upon them. The horse's head and neck seethed with bees. The reins were heavy with bees. And like a thick black carpet unrolling, bees were swarming back, back, towards the van.

"Shut the doors!" bellowed Steven.

His heart beating wildly, Lief leaped into the van and slammed the doors behind him. In moments the dimness had became darkness, and the walls and roof were vibrating with frenzied humming.

"The bees," Jasmine whispered.

And then they were moving. Slowly, at first. Then faster, faster, faster — until all Lief and Jasmine could hear were the faint clicking sounds of hoofs that seemed barely to touch the ground, and the wild humming of the bees.

13 - The Funnel

On they raced, the caravan smoothly rocking, its timbers creaking gently. Jasmine put more green cream on Lief's face, and the stinging pain eased a little. They ate traveller's biscuits and a little dried fish, washed down with water from their flasks.

After a time, Barda woke. He was confused and full of questions. Jasmine began telling him of all that had happened. And, incredibly, in the middle of the story, Lief fell asleep.

He woke knowing that something had changed. He could hear a muffled roaring sound, but it was not the humming of the bees. The gentle rocking had ceased.

"We have stopped," Jasmine's voice whispered.

Lief turned his head and saw her beside him, just

a shape in the dimness. Filli was sitting on her shoulder nibbling a fragment of biscuit.

"How long have I been asleep?" Lief exclaimed, sitting up.

"I do not know," Jasmine said. "I slept, too."

The doors of the caravan creaked open. Cold white light flooded in. Moonlight.

Steven's face appeared in the doorway, his finger pressed warningly to his lips.

"We have travelled far," he whispered. "We are in a valley in the foothills of the mountains. Laughing Jack's wagon turned in to a side path not far ahead. It seems he has stopped for the night. How is Barda?"

"Asleep again," Jasmine answered. "I gave him more honey. Filli will watch over him and come for us if he needs us."

Steven nodded, and beckoned.

Filli sprang nimbly from Jasmine's shoulder and importantly took his place by Barda's side. Lief caught up his cloak and his sword and followed Jasmine out into the night.

The moon sailed overhead in a sea of stars. It was almost as bright as day, but everything was black, white, and gray. There were no trees. The mountains glowered above them, black as the sky. Rocks rose all around them, glistening in the moonlight. A dull roaring filled the air.

"Waterfall," Steven breathed.

He led the way to the front of the van. Mellow stood there, placidly munching leaves from a scraggy bush. She had never looked more ordinary. There was not a bee to be seen.

"Where is Kree?" Jasmine asked, looking around in sudden alarm.

"Far behind, I fear," Steven whispered. "He could not keep up with us."

Mellow snickered, as if with satisfaction, and tore off another leaf.

Steven grinned. "Come on — and quietly," he said. "This villain is slippery. We must take him by surprise."

A few steps ahead, a path led up a gentle rise. Beyond the rise they could see the waterfall — a broad, foaming sheet of white, covering the cliff like a veil.

A wooden gate had once barred the path, but this had been pushed down and now lay flat on the ground. The sign fixed to it had been trampled by hoofs, but the words could still be read.

Quietly, the companions moved over the gate. As soon as his foot touched the path, Lief's body began to tingle. The Belt was somewhere ahead. He could feel it. He began to move faster.

"Why would such a beautiful thing have an ugly name like 'The Funnel'?" Jasmine whispered, looking up to where the waterfall began, high above them.

"That question will be answered when we see the bottom, I fear," Lief muttered.

In moments, he was proved right. They reached the top of the rise. The waterfall thundered directly ahead. And below . . .

They stared, awestruck.

Below them, at the base of the waterfall, yawned the foaming mouth of The Funnel.

It was as if the jaws of the earth had opened to receive the great flood of water pouring from the cliff top. Deep within the vast basin of rock the water was spinning like a gigantic whirlpool, swirling down into The Funnel's throat like water rushing down a drain.

"A pleasant place to spend the night, indeed," Steven muttered.

Lief tore his eyes away from The Funnel and scanned the gently sloping rock that surrounded it.

At first, he could see nothing but gleams and shadows. Then, suddenly, there was a tiny movement. His eyes focused, and he jumped.

Where before he had seen only bare rock and a mist of spray from the waterfall, he now saw four black horses yoked to a large wagon. A thin man was standing in front of the horses, a brimming bucket in his hand.

"I thought so," Steven breathed. "His wagon is protected by disguising magic. Like your cloak, Lief, though far more powerful. That is how he comes and goes unseen. The Enemy has given him some powers in return for service, it seems. We will have to take care."

"I cannot see Zerry," Lief whispered. "He must be asleep in the back of the wagon."

Cautiously, keeping low, they began to follow the path down.

They reached the valley floor and hid behind a boulder. Laughing Jack was still standing with his horses. They could not see his face, but they could see the bucket swinging in his bony hand, and hear his high, grating voice.

"Would you like a little water, you stupid beasts?" he was saying. "Ah, yes, of course you would. You have not drunk all day. You must be thirsty. Very, very thirsty. So — will I give you a drink?"

The horses stretched out their necks and seemed to groan.

"He is tormenting them!" breathed Jasmine. She was trembling with fury.

"Look!" cried Laughing Jack, swinging the bucket even more so that water slopped over the sides and onto the ground. "Water! Can you see it? Can you smell it? Well, you cannot have it!"

Cackling with laughter, he turned away from the horses and moved into view, still carrying the brimming bucket.

Lief stared at him with loathing. He was dressed in black from head to foot. A braid of greasy brown hair hung down his back, skinny as a rat's tail. His face was skull-like. Skin like old leather stretched tightly across his jutting bones, and his large teeth gleamed in a permanent grin.

A little distance from the wagon, Laughing Jack had made comfortable arrangements for his evening meal.

Bread, fruit, cheese, and some sort of sausage lay on a platter near a small camping stove. A plump red sack had been placed in front of the platter, for a seat. All of this was protected from the spray of the waterfall by a huge red-and-white-striped umbrella.

No doubt that umbrella once stood over the market stall of one of his victims, Lief thought.

He realized that his fists were clenched, and forced himself to relax. The important thing now was to find the Belt. Everything else had to wait.

Laughing Jack filled a kettle from the bucket. He lit the stove and set the kettle upon the flames. Then he sat down with a satisfied sigh and helped himself to bread and sausage.

"He can still see the wagon," Jasmine whispered. "We will never get to it unseen, even under Lief's cloak."

"You will if I distract him," Steven answered.

Alerted by the grim tone of his voice, Lief glanced at him uneasily. Dark shadows were moving in the golden eyes. Steven's brother, Nevets, was very aware of what was happening.

My brother and I have long looked forward to meeting Laughing Jack . . .

"Steven, take care," Lief pleaded. "Before — before anything else happens, I must find the Belt."

Steven gritted his teeth. "I know that," he said.

He stepped out from behind the rock, put his hands in his pockets, and walked casually forward.

"Good evening, sir!" he called. "A fine night, is it not?"

Laughing Jack stiffened. Slowly, he turned his head.

"Did I startle you?" Steven said cheerily, strolling towards him. "I beg your pardon. I thought you had surely heard me coming, but the waterfall is very noisy, of course."

Laughing Jack made no reply.

Steven paced admiringly around the striped umbrella. "Why, you are set up very nicely here!" he exclaimed. "May I join you?"

He sat down on the other side of the stove.

Laughing Jack was forced to turn away from the wagon to keep him in view.

"Now," Lief breathed.

He drew Jasmine close to him and wrapped her in his cloak. Together they began to creep towards the wagon.

"This waterfall is a fine sight indeed," Steven said. "It takes my mind from my troubles."

"Troubles?" murmured Laughing Jack, leaning forward slightly.

"Indeed," Steven sighed. "The cart I use to take my goods to market is quite worn out, and I have no gold to buy another. People say I should sell the jewels my old aunt left me. But I do not want to do that. They have been in my family for generations."

"Ah!" Laughing Jack leaned forward even farther. "Well, well. What a fortunate chance that we met. I may be able to help you."

Lief smiled wryly. Steven had all the moneylender's attention now. No doubt Laughing Jack thought he had found a perfect victim.

The horses did not look around as Lief and Jasmine approached. Blinkers shielded their eyes, and their heads hung low. Straining against their heavy harness, they were trying to lick water from the rock.

Lief's heart ached for them. *After this is over, we will help you,* he promised them silently.

As though he had spoken aloud, one of the

horses on the far side lifted its head. Fearful that it would make a sound, Lief tightened his grip on Jasmine and slipped quickly around to the back of the wagon.

He eased the door open, hoping against hope that it would not creak.

Steven and Laughing Jack were still talking.

"There is nothing I like better than helping those less fortunate than myself," Laughing Jack was saying. "Why, I *live* to do good. And you seem such a worthy fellow. Let me lend you the money for your cart! How much do you need? Twenty gold coins? Fifty?"

"Fifty!" Steven exclaimed. "Why, with fifty I could put a new roof on the house as well!"

"All the better!" cried Laughing Jack. And Lief could almost see his skull's grin broadening.

The cart door was now fully open. Lief and Jasmine looked inside.

A mattress covered by a glorious patchwork quilt took up most of the floor space. Around the walls, baskets of food and valuable objects of all kinds were stacked to the roof. An empty honey jar had rolled into the corner nearest the door.

But there was no sign of Zerry.

"Where is he?" Jasmine breathed.

Lief shook his head helplessly.

Zerry was not in the cart. And he knew that the Belt was not there, either. If it was, he would feel it.

He began to close the cart door. As he did, a scrap of paper fluttered from a fold in the quilt and landed on the floor. Jasmine picked it up and glanced at it. Her eyes widened in horror.

She thrust the note at Lief.

HIS NAME IS ZERRY. TAKE NOTHING FROM HIM. THROW HIM, AND EVERYTHING HE CARRIES, INTO THE FUNNEL.

14 ~ Choices

Understanding broke over Lief in a wave of burning heat. He stumbled away from the wagon, hardly knowing what he did. He heard Jasmine gasp out his name, but he did not turn. He could not face the horror in her eyes.

The Belt was gone — gone with Zerry, down, down into the terrible throat of The Funnel. Perhaps only minutes before they arrived.

That is why I can still feel it, he thought. *That is why I was so sure . . .*

Blindly, he stared at the thundering waterfall, the greedy, swirling water beneath.

Zerry, whatever he had been promised, had only been a puppet — a puppet used ruthlessly by people far more powerful, far more wicked, than himself.

He had just been someone who could steal the

Belt. Someone who could carry it safely, as a true servant of the Shadow Lord could not.

Someone who could be disposed of as easily as a scrap of paper or an empty honey jar.

"So," Laughing Jack was saying loudly. "All you have to do is sign this paper, my good fellow, and your troubles are over."

Slowly, Lief turned his head to look at the evil man who could kill a boy, amuse himself by tormenting his horses, then calmly sit down to eat his dinner.

Laughing Jack was holding a piece of parchment in one hand and a small money bag in the other. He shook the bag. The coins inside jingled invitingly.

"I fear I am not much of a one for reading," Steven said, staring blankly at the paper.

"Oh, this is nothing!" The thin man flapped the parchment casually. "Just a few words saying that Laughing Jack lent you fifty gold coins. It proves you came by the money honestly, do you see? You would not like anyone to think you had stolen it, would you?"

"No indeed!" Steven said earnestly.

"Excellent!" said Laughing Jack. "Now, I think I have a pen here . . ."

He put the parchment on his knee, and bent to look inside his coat.

Instantly, Steven glanced up. He saw Lief standing staring at him, and his eyes seemed to flash. Immediately, he looked back to Laughing Jack, his teeth bared in a savage grin.

Too late, Lief realized that he had given no sign of what had happened. Steven thought they had found the Belt, and that now he could deal with Laughing Jack.

The moneylender had brought out a large pen and a bottle of black ink. Carefully, he took the lid from the bottle and dipped the pen into it.

"Now," he said, his hand hovering over the parchment. "Your name?"

Steven's grin broadened. "Hank Modestee," he said softly.

Laughing Jack grew very still.

"Ah — you have heard my name before, I see," Steven said, still in that same, dangerously quiet voice. "Perhaps you have also heard of my aunt — Dame Henstoke?"

"Who are you?" Laughing Jack hissed.

The next instant, his long legs were kicking out, and the stove and the kettle were crashing onto his enemy.

Pen, paper, and ink bottle went flying as he sprang to his feet. He kicked the red bag he had been using as a seat, sending it rolling towards The Funnel. Then he bent double and scuttled towards the wagon like a great, lanky, four-legged spider, so fast that he seemed a blur.

Steven growled ferociously, thrusting the stove and kettle aside. His eyes were flashing gold to brown, brown to gold. His body was quivering . . .

And the plump red bag was tumbling down the sloping rock towards the raging water.

Lief shouted and hurled himself forward. Suddenly, he knew what was in the bag. Knew why Laughing Jack had kicked it before he fled.

The bag had reached the edge of the rock. It was tipping . . .

Lief dived for it. His arms and chest hit the rock. His hands caught the last corner of the bag just as it slid over the lip of The Funnel. He held on with all his strength.

"Jasmine! Steven! Help me!" he shouted, twisting his neck, searching for a sign of them. But he could only see Laughing Jack, standing on the driver's seat of the wagon, a long whip in his hand. Jack's hollow eyes were blazing as he stared at something beyond Lief's vision.

The bag swung over the greedy, spinning water, drenched with spray. It was moving now. Someone inside it was struggling and kicking. Grimly, Lief held on, his arms straining. He felt himself beginning to slide forward.

Desperately, he dug the toes of his boots into the slippery rock, trying to hold himself back. But little by little the weight of the bag was pulling him after it.

He heard Jasmine cry out, and moments later felt her fling herself down behind him, felt her gripping his ankles.

Her strength was not enough — not enough, with the red bag dragging him down. The only way to save himself was to let go. But he could not let go.

"Steven!" he heard Jasmine scream over the thundering of the water.

Lief's head and shoulders were over the edge now. Spray beat on his face, filling his eyes and his nose. He gritted his teeth, held his breath . . .

And then, miraculously, he felt hands gripping him around the waist, lifting him back. Still he clung to the sodden, bulging bag, though his arms felt as if they were being pulled from their sockets and his fingers were numb.

With joy he saw the bag rise, dripping, over the edge of The Funnel, and Steven's great arm reach out to gather it in. But still he did not release his grip.

Only when he was sprawled on higher ground, and the bag was safe, did he allow his fingers to be prized away from it. He lay back, trembling all over, as Jasmine cut the knots that held the bag closed.

Out rolled a squirming shape tied up like a parcel in a thick brown rug. Muffled shrieks reached their ears.

"Hold him, Steven!" Jasmine said sharply. She cut through the ropes and peeled the sodden rug aside. And there was Zerry, drenched, screaming and kicking.

Grimly, Steven held him down.

"Let me go!" Zerry screeched, twisting violently. The buttons tore from his skimpy jacket. The ragged shirt beneath it ripped like paper.

And beneath the shirt, something gleamed. Something bright was looped around Zerry's neck, hanging down over his chest like a giant necklace.

Lief reached out. The moment he touched it, the Belt of Deltora fell into his hands. Tingling warmth flowed through him as he clasped it around his waist.

He closed his eyes, dazed with relief.

It is safe. It is with me. Safe . . .

The roaring of the waterfall was throbbing in his ears. It seemed to be echoing. Louder, louder . . . how could it be so loud?

Lief opened his eyes.

The waterfall was filled with stars — stars twinkling on a bed of midnight blue. It was as though, by some miraculous trick of the light, the night sky was reflected in the foaming, falling water.

And then the reflection seemed to rush forward. Something burst through the veil of the waterfall, through the clouds of spray — something real, and gigantic.

Roaring, it hovered over The Funnel, its scales

sparkling in the moonlight. Its mighty wings were like dark blue velvet pierced with light. Its eyes shone like stars. Every one of its claws was like a new moon, curved and gleaming.

Zerry screamed in terror. He rolled over and covered his eyes. Jasmine, and even Steven, shrank back.

But Lief crawled to his feet and stood with his head up, his hands on the Belt of Deltora, his heart beating wildly. *So — the waterfall veils a great cavern in the cliff,* he thought, steadying himself. *A safe hiding place, indeed, for —*

"Greetings, King of Deltora!" thundered the dragon. "At last you have come!"

"Greetings, dragon of the lapis lazuli," said Lief awkwardly. "I — I came when I could."

The dragon swept gracefully to shore. As it settled on the rock, not far away from the companions, Lief realized that, despite its enormous size, it was smaller than the other dragons he had seen. Smaller, and more delicate-looking.

The dragon looked at Lief closely. "You are wet, and the poor, thin hide of your face is torn!" it accused, shaking its own dripping wings. "What has befallen you, in this land of good fortune?"

Its gleaming eyes fell on Zerry. "This boy is one of mine!" it growled. "I can smell it! Did he dare to do you ill, King? Shall I deal with him?"

Zerry wailed and clutched Steven's arm. "I did not mean it!" he gabbled. "I did not know! Fern said the Belt was of no value — just part of a Masked One's costume that Bess had given Lewin for himself."

He wiped his nose on the sleeve of his jacket. "She said I should steal it if I could. She said there was a man at the Riverdale turnoff who fancied it, and would pay well for it. She said it was my chance to get away from old Plug and her lessons, and go home to Rithmere with gold in my pocket. She wrote a note for me to give the man, but he — "

"The note said you were to be killed, you young fool!" Steven growled. "If you had let Plug teach you to read, instead of spending all your time idling and thieving, you would have known that."

"This boy of Rithmere laid hands on the Belt of Deltora?" thundered the dragon, baring its fangs.

"The boy is not our enemy," Lief said quickly. "Our enemy is — "

And for the first time since he shouted for help at the lip of The Funnel, he remembered Laughing Jack. The dragon was sitting where the wagon had been. He looked quickly at Steven.

"I had to force Nevets back, so I could come to your aid," Steven said. "Nevets and I cannot be long apart. We fight together or not at all. So Laughing Jack escaped. While I was still lifting you from The Funnel, he was up the hill and away. We will never catch him, or his poor beasts, now."

Jasmine looked stricken.

Lief swallowed. "Could not Mellow and the bees give chase and — ?"

"They cannot work their magic again so soon," Steven sighed. "No — this time Laughing Jack has escaped the fate he deserves. But there will be another time. We will not forget."

The dragon smacked its lips loudly, as if annoyed at being ignored.

"I am famished," it announced. "If you will excuse me, King, I will go and fill my belly."

"You will not take humans or their beasts, I hope!" Lief exclaimed, suddenly fearful.

"Unless you see a thin man driving four black horses," growled Steven. "You are very welcome to him."

The dragon looked down its nose at them. "Do you take me for a savage?" it demanded. "Whatever dragons of other lands may stoop to, the dragons of the lapis lazuli would never dine on warm blood. Ugh!"

It shuddered at the very thought.

"I beg your pardon," Lief said hastily. "But you will find little to satisfy your hunger, I fear. The land is poor."

"I have sensed that already, King," the dragon growled, delicately smoothing the scales of its chest with one slender claw. "It seems that the Enemy took advantage of my sleep."

"He took advantage of all the dragons' sleep,"

Lief said. "The evil thing that is poisoning your terri-tory is called the Sister of the North. My companions and I are journeying to find and destroy it."

"Excellent!" the dragon exclaimed, inspecting its claws one by one. "Before we leave, I will snatch a hasty meal in the Shifting Sands. It is not far, as the dragon flies, and no doubt Sand Beasts still thrive there. Ah, I well remember how they crunch between the teeth. Delightful!"

Lief exchanged glances with Jasmine and Steven. He cleared his throat.

"I fear you cannot come with us to find the Sister of the North," he said. "It is deep in the territory of the emerald, in a place called Shadowgate."

The dragon seemed to frown. "Indeed?" it said. "We are very near the emerald border here, as it hap-pens. But surely it will still take you quite a time to reach this Shadowgate?"

"Yes, it will," Lief admitted ruefully.

The dragon was still looking at its claws. "Cer-tainly, before I slept, I promised not to stray from my own territory," it murmured. "But surely Dragon-friend did not mean this to prevent me from aiding the king who awoke me."

It looked up, straight into Lief's eyes. "Especially if the king should *ask* me to aid him," it added.

Lief's heart gave a great thump. "You would carry us to Shadowgate?" he asked. "But what of the emerald dragon?"

"What of it?" The lapis lazuli dragon yawned. "It may be dead, for all we know. Its territory was infested with the Enemy's creatures. Any one of them would have destroyed it, if they found it sleeping."

It sounded quite pleased at the thought.

"So," it went on, its eyes sparkling. "Good fortune brought us together, King. And you should never turn your back on your luck. Do you ask me to break my vow and take you to Shadowgate?"

Lief took a deep breath. "Yes," he said. "I do."

15 - The Pass

A nd so, for the second time, Lief, Barda, and Jasmine flew with a dragon. But this time was very different from the first.

It was not just that this time they were flying with a dragon that sang merrily as it flew. Or that this dragon seemed to glide through the air like a shooting star, with barely a beat of its wings.

It was not just that this dragon knew exactly where it was going because, unlike the dragon of the ruby, it prided itself on having learned about maps from the man it called Dragonfriend.

It was because, this time, they were not beginning a journey, but hurtling towards a journey's end. Mingled with their thoughts about what might be ahead were their thoughts of what had passed — thoughts they did not wish to share.

Barda was cursing himself for allowing the

Masked Ones to overpower him when he caught up with them on the road to Purley. As a result of that failure, he had been useless to his companions just when they needed him most.

He scowled as he remembered waking in the caravan, with no idea where he was or what was happening. Kree had just arrived, and was screeching angrily at Steven's horse. Filli was chattering in his ear. His companions were nowhere to be seen. He had gone in search of them, but by the time he reached the waterfall, all the excitement was over.

Steven had filled his place admirably, of course. Without Steven, the quest would have ended in disaster.

But now, thought Barda, *Steven is back in the caravan with Zerry and I am flying to Shadowgate. All is as it should be. I will not fail again.*

Jasmine was thinking of the horses yoked to Laughing Jack's wagon. She was bitterly regretting that she had not been able to release them.

She had tried. If she had had more time, she could have done it. But Lief had called and she had run to him, leaving the horses to their fate.

Should she tell her companions the terrible thing that she had discovered as she followed Lief past the wagon after their fruitless effort to find the Belt?

No, she thought, hugging Filli and Kree closer, drawing comfort from their warmth. *I must keep it to myself. Why grieve Lief and Barda to no purpose? Nothing can be done about it now.*

Lief was fighting waking nightmares.

Again and again he relived the moment when the mask of Bede's adulthood settled over his face. Again and again he saw the Happy Vale noticeboard, its sad main message surrounded by the notes that Laughing Jack had left for Fern.

Again and again he saw the dread black shape rising above Otto's wagon, the green gleam that was its face, the smooth white fingers oozing back into its robes. Again and again he saw the Shadow Lord's brand burning on Fern's tortured face, and heard those last, whispered words.

Beware the Masked One . . .

He shook his head. Why could he not clear his mind of these things? They were in the past, and could not harm him now.

Bess was dead. Fern was dead. Laughing Jack had fled. And whoever had conjured up the deadly phantom was in the camp of the Masked Ones, far away. Farther away every moment, as the lapis lazuli dragon sped through the dawn, following the line of the mountains towards their goal.

But instead of fading, the visions were growing brighter. The feeling of something left undone, something not understood, was strengthening. The whispered warning was hissing more loudly in his ears.

Beware the Masked One . . .

And now another sound was mingling with the memory of Fern's dying breath. A faint, ringing tune — four notes, repeated again and again, like a birdcall or the chiming of bells.

The Happy Vale clock, no doubt, Lief thought. *The chime that comes before the striking of the hour.*

His skin prickled, and he shut the sweet notes out of his mind. But always they returned, calling him.

※

The sky was still dark when the dragon landed, in a dreary place of rock and dead, twisted trees.

The mountains rose all around them, black and brutal, capped with snow. Thick gray clouds smothered the rising sun. A chill wind moaned through the cliffs, bringing with it the howls of distant beasts.

Lief, Barda, and Jasmine slid to the ground, and stood shivering in the gloom.

"This is the place," said the dragon. "Or very near it."

It glanced over its shoulder and its skin twitched. Its eyes were no longer sparkling, but dull as stones.

"There is a small village through there," it muttered, jerking its head towards a gap between two cliffs. "I saw it from the air. It has a wall of sticks around it. I saw humans creeping about within, like sick mice in a cage. And beyond it, I saw . . . other things."

It shuddered.

Bess's voice seemed to whisper in Lief's mind.

There are beasts, deep in the mountains. Monsters beyond imagining. Things that crawl in the shadows. Things that growl deep below the rock . . . Shadowgate lies among them.

Lief drew his sword. He heard Barda do the same. He heard Jasmine murmur to Kree, and the clatter of wings as Kree took to the air.

The raw patches on his face stung in the icy wind. The four notes of music rang in his ears. Louder now. And again came the whisper . . .

Beware the Masked One . . .

He felt like screaming to drown out the sounds.

Will I never be free of this? he thought desperately. *Did that cursed mask change me forever?*

The dragon shifted its feet. "What will you do?" it asked. Grimly, Lief noted that it had not said "we."

"We will go to the village," he said. "It is the village of Shadowgate. You can guide us from there."

Silently, Barda and Jasmine came up beside him. Together they moved towards the gap. The dragon shuffled behind them, its tail rasping on the rock, its claws scrabbling.

The gap was long and straight, and broader than it had looked from a distance. The cliffs that towered on either side of it were pitted with holes and caves. The wind howled through it like a lost soul. And they could hear other sounds — growls, scratchings, and chitterings from deep within the rock.

Here the Masked Ones came, seven years ago, Lief thought.

He could almost see the wagons rumbling through the pass, the drivers sitting rigidly, alert to every sound. He could almost see Otto, Rust, Quill, Plug, and all the rest . . . and in the lead wagon, the mammoth figure of Bess, her beloved son beside her.

Jasmine's voice broke sharply into his thoughts.

"Lief! I beg you to stop humming that tune!" she exclaimed. "It is driving me mad! What is it?"

Lief clapped his hand over his mouth. The four notes had been ringing in his head, but he had not realized he was humming them aloud.

"It is the Happy Vale clock, I think," he mumbled. "It seems to be stuck in my brain."

"This pass does not smell safe, King," called the dragon behind him. "And it is too narrow for me. You must find another way."

"There *is* no other way," Lief said. "You will have to fly and meet us on the other side."

The dragon made an unhappy, gurgling sound, but spread its wings and soared upwards.

"I have my doubts about that beast," muttered Barda. "I would not be surprised if it deserted us."

"It is not in its own territory," Jasmine snapped. "Naturally, it is uneasy."

Barda hunched his shoulders and did not answer.

Lief looked up. Kree was sailing between the cliff tops, riding the wind, yellow eyes searching the ground. Above him soared the lapis lazuli dragon, almost invisible, its underside matching the dark gray sky.

Keeping close together, glancing often behind them, Lief, Barda, and Jasmine began to walk through the pass. Lief saw Jasmine frown at him, and realized that he had begun humming again. He pressed his lips together.

"That is not the Happy Vale clock chime, Lief," Barda said. "The Happy Vale clock went like this."

He whistled a quite different tune, a tune with five notes instead of four.

"You are right," Lief said, suddenly remembering. "But then, why do I keep hearing — "

"It is probably some tune Bess taught you!" Jasmine broke in impatiently. "What does it matter? With everything — everything else we have to think of!"

She turned her head away, biting her lips.

And at that moment, Kree screeched a warning.

Instantly, the three companions drew together, back to back. There was nothing ahead of them, nothing behind. Weapons raised, they scanned the cliff walls.

Eyes glinted in every hole, every crevice. The cliff walls were alive with stealthy movement. Here, a dripping, pointed snout poked out of a tunnel. There, a bundle of blunt claws scrabbled against the rock. Bubbles of gray slime frothed silently from cracks and slid downwards.

"Move on!" Barda breathed. "On!"

They began to run. But Kree was still screeching above them, screeching warning again and again. And suddenly there was a thunderous roar that seemed to shake the rock.

The eyes in the cliff face blinked out. The snouts and claws disappeared as if they had never been.

Kree swooped downwards like a black streak. The strip of sky between the cliff tops darkened. They heard the lapis lazuli dragon give a single, panic-stricken cry.

And then they could see it no longer, for there above them was a vast, roaring thing of glittering green, its fangs bared ferociously, its spiked tail lashing, its wings battering the air.

Lief went cold. He looked down at the Belt of Deltora. The great emerald, symbol of honor, was burning like green fire.

The emerald dragon had awoken. The emerald dragon, drawn to this place by the Belt, had discovered its land invaded by another.

"Oath-breaker!" a great voice thundered. "Thief! Invader! Betrayer!"

Paralyzed with horror, Lief saw the huge talons slashing — talons like knives — and heard the lapis lazuli dragon scream.

"No!" Lief shouted at the top of his lungs. "It is with us! It is helping us! Do not harm it!"

But his voice was drowned by the sound of the emerald dragon's fury.

"Flee, then, coward!" it roared. "You have no honor! Turn tail like the snivelling sneak you are! You will not escape me!"

The great mass of green turned in the air and in an instant it was gone.

Suddenly, there was nothing to see between the cliff tops but sullen gray clouds. They could still hear roaring, but every moment the sound grew fainter.

Barda let out his breath in a long sigh.

"The lapis lazuli dragon will escape," Jasmine said confidently. "It is smaller, but it flies very fast."

"No doubt," Barda said grimly. "But now they have both left us. What are we to do now?"

"We must go on alone," said Lief doggedly.

He was trying not to think of what this meant.

The ruby dragon had uncovered the Sister of the East. Then the dragon's power had joined with the power of the Belt to destroy it.

But what would happen if Lief tried to face the Sister of the North alone? And how, without the dragon, would they find it?

Kree squawked urgently. Filli chattered. Lief looked up and saw that slowly the eyes were appearing in the cliff faces once more.

"Let us move on," said Jasmine uneasily.

They ran the rest of the way to the end of the

pass, and with relief burst out into the open. When they looked back, they could see that the cliff faces were crawling with movement and bubbling with slime.

"We are well out of that," Barda said heavily.

But Lief's stomach was churning. His knees felt weak. Cold sweat was stinging his face. His head was ringing with sound.

Slowly, he sank to the ground.

"The village is ahead," Jasmine urged, pointing to a wall visible beyond the rocks.

Lief made no answer. He feared that if he spoke he would be sick.

He felt in his pocket for something to dry the sweat, and his fingers touched something hard. Dimly puzzled, he pulled the object out.

It was the little set of chimes Bess had given him. With it came the paper on which she had written the musical notes he was to learn, and the stub of a pencil.

Only half aware of what he was doing, Lief tapped a chime with the pencil. A soft, clear note rang out.

Yes, that is right, he thought. He tapped another note. And another. And then the second note again.

"Lief, what are you doing?" Jasmine was kneeling beside him, her face pale with strain. "That tune again! What is it?"

Again Lief tapped out the four notes.

Music is like another language, Lewin . . . This is how we write it down.

Blankly, he stared at the paper in his hand. Then, rapidly, he began to draw in the clear space at the bottom.

His pencil hovered over the paper. He glanced up at Bess's far neater writing. His face began to burn.

"What are you doing?" Jasmine repeated, frowning at the marks.

Lief shook his head. "Nothing," he mumbled.

This is madness, he thought. *It cannot be!* Quickly, he turned the paper over, to conceal it.

On the other side, there was a mass of his own writing. He realized that he had used the back of Bess's lesson to write out the notices on the Happy Vale noticeboard.

With glazed eyes Lief stared at the writing. It seemed to shimmer before his eyes. Then, suddenly, letters seemed to move around, slip into new places.

And then he saw it — saw what his innermost mind had been trying to tell him for so long.

The names! The final secret of the notices was in the names. And as slowly he realized what that meant, his blood ran cold.

341

16 - Shadowgate

L ief met Jasmine's worried eyes. He saw Barda crouching behind her, watching him in concern. He knew he had to speak, though his head was swimming and his face and neck felt bathed in fire.

"We did not understand," he whispered.

"Did not understand what, Lief?" Barda asked quietly, glancing at Jasmine.

They fear my mind is wandering, Lief thought.

He thrust the paper towards them.

"The names," he said. "They are not real names. Laughing Jack invented them."

Jasmine's frown deepened. "I daresay he did," she muttered. "No doubt his little joke amused him."

Lief shook his head. "Not a joke," he said. "A threat. A warning to Fern not to ignore — "

He swallowed. "All these names — Dean the Smoke, Dame Henstoke, Andos the Meek, Hank Modestee, Kate Mend-Shoe — are made up of the same twelve letters. Do you see?"

There was a puzzled silence as Barda and Jasmine scanned the names.

"Yes," Barda said at last. "It is true. 'Seek the Nomad' is the same."

"And do you remember the sign we saw on the way to the Broad River Bridge?" Jasmine exclaimed. "Someone had scrawled upon it, calling himself 'Mad Keeth Nose' — the same twelve letters again!"

"It was just after we passed that sign that Fern first spoke to us," Lief said in a low voice. "The sign alerted her — made her suspect who we were. The Happy Vale noticeboard told her everything else she needed to know."

"But — " Jasmine shook her head. "But I do not understand this! What is so special about those letters?"

Lief took a deep breath. "Arranged correctly, they spell another name," he said. "The name of the guardian of the north. The name Fern spoke with her dying breath. The Masked One."

His companions stared at him, speechless.

"But — but the Masked Ones fled!" Barda said at last. "I saw them all, on the road to Purley. And Bess — "

Lief nodded. "Bess is dead," he said. "Rust, Quill, and all the rest are far away, and know nothing of this. The evil being who calls himself the Masked

One — the enemy who commands Laughing Jack, as Laughing Jack once commanded Fern — is someone else."

Slowly, he turned over the paper to show the four musical notes he had written at the bottom of the page. He sang the notes one by one, as Bess had taught him. And as he sang them, he wrote down their names.

"*Bede!*" whispered Jasmine. "Bess's son? But — he is dead!"

Lief shook his head. "All we know is that he disappeared into the mountains here, seven years ago, and was never found," he said. "So close to the Shadowlands border, who knows what evil thing he met, and what promises of power were made to him?"

"Of course!" muttered Barda. "He was vain and spoiled, by all accounts. Once he grew tired of the poor girl he had lured away from her home, the Enemy would have found him easy prey."

Lief gripped the paper tightly. "The tune that makes his name has been ringing in my ears, louder and louder," he said. "Bess felt it too, I think. The farther west she travelled, the more thoughts of Bede haunted her. Somewhere very near, Bede is singing his name, over and over again."

"I hear nothing but the accursed wind," growled Barda. "And the beasts, howling in the Shadowlands. Perhaps you hear the tune because of the Belt, Lief."

"Or because I wore Bede's mask, if only for a little time," Lief muttered. "It does not matter which. What matters is that we do not need a dragon to take us to the Sister of the North. The guardian himself will guide me."

✳

Their path took them past the walled village, but they did not knock upon the gate, and no one challenged them. A few wisps of chimney smoke drifted over the wall, but these were the only signs of life.

"Life here was always harsh, no doubt," Barda murmured. "But how much worse it must be now! Surely, most people have died or fled."

Lief nodded. He wondered if the parents of Kirsten and Mariette, the two lost girls, lived on inside the wall.

What would they say if they knew that the faithless one who stole their daughters' hearts was still alive — and thriving like an evil weed within their land?

The sky grew darker as the companions began to thread through the maze of rocks and cliffs that lay

345

beyond the village. Soon the light was so dim that they were almost feeling their way. Jasmine called Kree back to her shoulder. They lit torches, and moved on.

The clouds seemed to be pressing down upon them. Lightning flashed, and thunder rumbled ominously.

"This storm is not natural," Jasmine breathed.

Lief stopped abruptly and held up his torch.

"Look there!" he whispered.

A few paces ahead stood a tall stone. It looked horribly familiar.

They crept forward. Torchlight fell, flickering, on the stone.

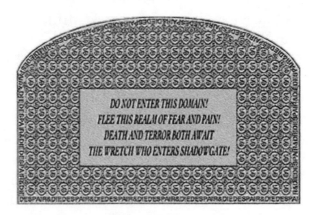

DO NOT ENTER THIS DOMAIN!
FLEE THIS REALM OF FEAR AND PAIN!
DEATH AND TERROR BOTH AWAIT
THE WRETCH WHO ENTERS SHADOWGATE!

Jasmine shivered. Filli had scurried beneath her jacket. Kree sat motionless on her shoulder, his feathers fluffed up, his beak slightly open.

"It is like the stone that guarded Dragon's Nest," she muttered. "The verse seems to say that Shadowgate is beyond. Yet we passed the village long ago."

"The village was named after the place, no doubt," said Barda. He wiped sweat from his brow and glanced at Lief. "Do you still hear the music?" he asked abruptly.

Lief nodded. The feeling of sickness had returned. His head was so full of sound that he could not speak. He moved past the stone, his face turned away from it.

Despair and die . . .

He heard his companions following him. *I am leading them to their deaths*, he thought.

Lightning cracked across the boiling sky, lighting up the flat sheet of rock upon which they stood, and a vast mass of jagged peaks blocking the way ahead.

Lief looked down at the Belt of Deltora. The ruby and the emerald had lost their radiance, but the topaz and the lapis lazuli were still glowing more brightly than the rest.

They shine because their dragons have awoken, Lief thought. *The ruby and the emerald would shine, too, if danger and evil were not all about us. Four dragons now fly Deltoran skies. But faith and happiness are far behind us. Luck has deserted us. Honor has turned its back on us. We are alone.*

"We are together," Jasmine said loudly behind

him. "We have the Belt of Deltora to protect us. We must not fear. We must not despair."

Lief knew that Jasmine was not talking to him. Jasmine was talking to Kree, to Filli, and to herself, defying the evil spell of the stone.

But her words cut through his haze of misery. He put his hands on the Belt. He felt the strength of the diamond, the calm of the amethyst, the hope of the opal flow through him. He felt his mind sharpen as the topaz glowed beneath his fingertips.

And as the lightning flashed again, he saw the mass of rock ahead shimmering and changing before his eyes. He caught his breath and gripped the Belt more tightly. He watched, astounded, as rocky peaks became towers, cliffs became high, sheer walls, hollows dissolved into barred windows . . .

A vast castle lay revealed before him. Evil seemed to stream from it like a vile smell.

He heard Jasmine and Barda gasp.

"You see it," he said huskily.

"Yes," Barda muttered. "Lead on!"

And Lief felt them move into place beside him.

✳

Nothing barred their way. No creature menaced them. But as they moved towards the castle door, thunder roared above them and lightning split the writhing clouds.

"The Masked One is waiting for us inside," Lief

murmured. "He knows we are here. He wants us to come to him."

"So it seems," Barda said. "He is proud, like his evil Master in the Shadowlands. And his pride will be his downfall."

He raised a great fist and banged upon the door.

"Stay out here and keep watch, Kree," Jasmine whispered. Kree squawked reluctantly, but left her shoulder and flew away into the dimness.

We have no plan, Lief thought. *We are walking into the web of this sorcerer with nothing but our wits and the Belt of Deltora to aid us.*

He glanced at Jasmine, and she smiled. *So be it,* he thought, and straightened his shoulders.

They waited in silence. They heard no footsteps. But suddenly there was the sound of a key turning in the lock.

Slowly, the door creaked open.

There stood a beautiful young woman in a long white robe.

A locket on a fragile golden chain nestled at the woman's throat. Her small feet were bare. A long, heavy braid of yellow hair, bound with golden thread, hung over one shoulder to far below her waist. Her eyes were wide and frightened.

This was the last thing the companions had expected.

Can this be Mariette? Lief thought in amazement.

Can it be that she still lives? Is her love for Bede so strong that she remains with him, even now? Can it be that Bede himself . . . ?

You will quickly tire of her. Why, only last year you were dallying with her sister . . .

So Bess had said to her son. Had she been wrong?

Barda was the first to recover.

"We are travellers, caught in the storm," he said, stepping forward. "We beg for shelter."

"We are not prepared for visitors," the woman murmured rapidly. "I fear we cannot — "

She caught sight of Lief and gasped. Her hand flew to her throat. Then she glanced quickly behind her. Soft music had begun, drifting from somewhere within.

The woman bit her lip and pulled the door wider. She watched silently as the companions moved inside. Then she closed the door behind them, turning the key in the lock once more.

The entrance hall was huge — as large as the entrance hall of the palace in Del. Hundreds of candles burned in great metal rings hanging from the ceiling. Streaks of emerald gleamed in the carved rock walls.

"Follow me, if you please," the woman said.

She turned and led them through the hall. At the far end stood two tall doors. The woman put her hands to the doors, preparing to push them open.

"Wait!" whispered Lief. "Please tell me! What is your name? What are you doing here?"

The woman turned. Her eyes were dark with misery.

"My name is Kirsten," she murmured. "And I am here because once I loved too well."

Before Lief could speak again, she pushed open the doors.

17 - The Castle

The companions moved into a vast room that was bathed in light. Its rocky walls gleamed green. Its stone floor was covered with exquisitely embroidered rugs.

A great fire blazed in a fireplace set into the wall that faced them. To the right of the fireplace was a vast table draped with a stiff white cloth and laden with food and drink.

And in the very center of the room, on a heap of cushions that gleamed with every color of the rainbow, lay a young man, hung about with gold and jewels.

The man had a small harp in his hands. He was playing softly. Emeralds glittered in his ears. A circlet of emeralds crowned his shining hair. Golden chains festooned his neck and his slender wrists. Beside him lay several pens and a scattered sheaf of papers.

As the companions entered the room, the music

stopped. The man raised his head and fixed them with burning eyes.

Then Lief knew he had been right. There was no doubt that the man lounging before them was Bede.

"He does look like you, Lief!" Jasmine breathed. "Why, you could be brothers!"

Lief did not like the thought. He stepped forward.

"Do not approach him!" Kirsten hissed behind him. "Kneel! Kneel, I beg you!"

Her voice was so full of terror that Lief did as she asked. Barda and Jasmine hesitated, then kneeled beside him.

"What is your will, my lord?" Kirsten asked.

Bede did not look at her. "Bring food and drink," he said, barely moving his lips.

"Yes, my lord! Oh, but do not stop playing! Your music is so sweet!" Kirsten scurried to the table and began putting wine and fruit on a silver tray.

Bede plucked softly on the strings of the harp. Sweet music filled the room. But he did not take his eyes from his guests, and neither did he speak.

In moments Kirsten was back. She kneeled in front of Bede and put a silver goblet of wine on the floor beside the sheaf of papers.

"Ah, you have finished the words of a new song, I see!" she said. "Is it your song for today? The one I am to copy into the book?"

Bede bent his head in a slight nod.

Timidly, Kirsten picked up a paper.

"How beautiful!" she murmured, looking at it. "Would you sing it for us, my lord? I long to hear it."

Is she trying to distract him? Lief thought. *Or is it part of her slavery that she must flatter him in the way he likes best?*

His mind was teeming with questions. Kirsten was plainly in Bede's power. She was terrified of him.

But did he control her by sorcery, or by some other means?

And how had she come here at all? It was her sister, Mariette, to whom Bede had lost his heart. Where was Mariette now?

Kirsten was coming towards them, carrying the paper and the tray. Lief reached out to help her, but she shrank back, her eyes wide with warning.

"Sing, my lord!" she called over her shoulder. "We will follow the words most carefully."

Slowly, she sank to her knees and put down the tray. She placed the paper on the ground where they could all see it. All the time her eyes were beseeching Lief, Barda, and Jasmine not to move.

There was a short pause, and then Bede began to sing. His voice was sweet, and mellow as honey. The music of the harp was like the soft rippling of a stream.

Lief listened, transfixed in spite of himself. It was only when Bede finished the song, and began at once to sing it again, that he began to follow the words.

He looked down at the paper lying on the rug in front of him.

> Fair as the day is my Kirsten.
> Sweet as a flower she is,
> Her goodness banishes evil.
> She is too perfect for one such as I.
> A poor plain man I am,
> Far, far beneath her.
> But her heart is my prisoner
> To me she can refuse no help,
> For she adores me.

Lief glanced at Kirsten. Her eyes were swimming with tears. Her hands were tightly clasped, the knuckles white.

Only then was the spell of Bede's voice broken. Only then did Lief realize how cruel were the words sung in those honeyed tones.

He felt Jasmine and Barda shifting uneasily beside him, and knew they saw it, too.

Bede was taunting Kirsten, rejoicing in his power

over her. No wonder she wept, remembering a time when his singing had filled her heart with joy.

Lief felt cold with fury. *Why do we kneel here?* he raged to himself. *Why do we not leap on him now and force him to take us to the Sister of the North?*

But he did not move, for in his heart he knew why. The room was thick with evil and menace. Delicate as Bede chose to appear, he was plainly powerful. Very powerful.

If they were to survive, and find the Sister of the North, they had to soothe him, flatter him, make him feel safe. They had to be cunning, and stealthy. They had to play his game.

Bede at last fell silent. He raised his eyes from his harp and looked straight at Lief. His gaze was intense and full of meaning.

Lief smiled, raised his hands, and began to clap. After a moment, Barda and Jasmine joined him.

Bede did not smile. He did not move, bow, or speak. When the applause at last died away, he bent his head to his harp and began to sing the song again.

Lief bent as if to pluck a grape from the tray.

"Kirsten," he whispered. "Where is Mariette?"

Kirsten stiffened.

"Is she alive?" Lief breathed. "Is she here?"

Kirsten nodded, very slightly. Her lips formed the word "captive." Her eyes were full of anguish.

And there is my answer, Lief thought, glancing at Jasmine and Barda, who were watching intently. *Bede controls this woman by a mixture of sorcery and threat. She is bound to him by fear for Mariette's safety, as well as her own.*

"We can help you," Barda muttered, leaning forward as if he, too, was choosing something to eat.

"No. He is too strong." Kirsten's voice was like a sigh. "His power is boundless . . . terrible . . ."

Clumsily, she began to pour wine. The jug clattered against the silver goblets as her hand trembled.

Lief looked over her shoulder at Bede. The man's eyes were closed. He was still singing his new song, softly, slowly, as if entranced by the beauty of his own voice.

He must feel the power of the Belt, as I feel his evil, Lief thought. *He is wary of us. He is biding his time, waiting for us to let down our guard. But he does not dream that Kirsten would dare to betray him. That is our strength.*

"Do you know where the source of his power lies, Kirsten?" he murmured.

Kirsten stared at him blankly.

Lief sighed inwardly and tried again. "Is there a place in the castle that Bede visits often?" he asked. "Somewhere you cannot follow?"

Kirsten shivered. She did not move her head, but her eyes slid sideways, towards a small arched door in a shadowy corner of the great room.

"He goes there," she breathed. "When he returns, he is — stronger."

"Then that is where we must go," Lief said. "How can it be done?"

Kirsten shook her head hopelessly.

"There must be a way!" Lief hissed. "Help us, Kirsten! If not for yourself, for Mariette!"

Kirsten bowed her head. Lief, Barda, and Jasmine exchanged rueful glances. Bess had called Kirsten a proud beauty. She was still very beautiful, but she was proud no longer. Bede had broken her spirit.

Then Kirsten raised her head again. Her eyes were still dark with fear, but for the first time a tiny spark seemed to glimmer in their depths.

"I will try," she murmured. She turned until she was facing Bede.

"My lord?" she called softly.

Bede's song broke off. He opened his eyes.

Lief, Barda, and Jasmine saw Kirsten's back tense. They saw her raise her hand to her throat. They prayed that she would not lose her nerve.

Stiffly, she gestured towards a door set in one of the side walls — the wall closest to the arched doorway.

"Your guests are tired and wish to rest, my lord," she said. "May I take them to a bedchamber?"

There was a long pause.

"If that is their wish," Bede said, without expression. He closed his eyes again and began to strum the harp once more.

Slowly, silently, her eyes fixed upon him, Kirsten

stood up and began backing towards the door that led to the bedchambers. Lief, Barda, and Jasmine stood up, too, and began backing after her.

Bede's golden voice followed them.

Fair as the day is my Kirsten,
Sweet as a flower she is . . .

Kirsten glanced quickly behind her and changed direction slightly. Now, instead of backing towards the bedchamber door, she was moving towards the arched door in the corner.

Lief's heart thudded. What a risk she was taking! At any moment Bede could open his eyes and see . . .

But Bede's eyes remained closed. He sang on, raising his voice, as if he wanted them to hear every word of his song one last time before they left him.

Her goodness banishes evil.
She is too perfect for one such as I . . .

Lief glanced over his shoulder. Kirsten had nearly reached the arched door. A few more steps . . .

"Perhaps poems do not have to rhyme," Jasmine whispered. "But surely the words of a *song* should rhyme. A song like that, in any case."

"It is no song at all," Barda muttered. "It sounds as if he wrote it in two minutes. Certainly, he took no care in writing it down. Yet he repeats it endlessly, as though it were the best song ever sung!"

Lief heard the tiny click as Kirsten lifted the latch of the door. He felt a cold breeze on the back of his neck. Again he looked over his shoulder.

The door was opening.

Inside was darkness. And from the darkness streamed a sense of evil so strong that his stomach seemed to turn over.

Kirsten met his eyes and beckoned, urging him to make haste.

Bede's voice rose again, echoing through the great room.

A poor, plain man I am,
Far, far beneath her . . .

Barda and Jasmine are right, Bede, thought Lief in disgust. *Your famous new song is very poor, and I wish I could tell you so. Bess boasted that your rhyming was perfect. But you have not even bothered to try. Every line ends with a completely different sound.* "Kirsten," "is," "evil," "I," "am," "her" . . .

His scalp prickled. He looked back at Bede.

Bede's eyes were open. He was staring straight ahead, at the paper lying abandoned on the floor beside the tray. He was singing the final lines of his song, his voice lilting, despairing.

But her heart is my prisoner,
To me she can refuse no help,
For she adores me.

Lief stared. He could not believe what his mind was telling him.

Taken together, the last words of every line of Bede's song formed a message.

Kirsten is evil. I am her prisoner. Help me.

360

18 ~ The Guardian

Lief stood frozen to the spot. Suddenly, shockingly, everything had turned upside down.

Images were flashing through his mind — signs that should have made him suspicious, but which he had ignored. The hasty writing on the paper. Bede's burning eyes fixed to his own. Kirsten shrinking back from his helping hand. The little arched door swinging open so smoothly at Kirsten's touch . . .

And now, from the back corner of the vast room, he could see what had not been visible to him when he kneeled in front of Bede.

The ends of the long golden chains which twined around Bede's neck and wrists were hidden beneath the cushions on which he lay. There was no doubt in Lief's mind that they led to strong steel rings fixed to the stone floor.

Nothing was as it had seemed. When he had

heard the four notes that spelled Bede's name, he had been hearing not triumphant boasting, but a desperate cry for help. Bede had been calling Bess, trying to tell her he was still alive, and needed her.

Bede was the captive. Kirsten was the jailer. The evil in the room was not his, but hers.

Why, then, had Kirsten shown them the arched door, and opened it? For Lief knew without doubt that somewhere within that foul darkness lay the Sister of the North.

"Make haste!" Kirsten hissed from the doorway.

Lief felt Jasmine tug anxiously at his arm.

"Treachery," he breathed. "Be ready."

He felt Jasmine stiffen. Her fingers tightened, then released him. She had heard.

Lief turned around to face Kirsten. She was beckoning urgently.

He moved to her side. Now that his eyes were opened, he saw how she slid quickly between the partly open door and the wall, to avoid his touch. He saw how tightly her hand gripped the doorknob.

"You first," she whispered to him.

And suddenly Lief understood her plan. Kirsten feared the Belt of Deltora. She knew that closer to the Sister of the North she would be far more powerful. That was why she wanted him to go through the door.

Once I am in there, she will slam it after me and lock it, Lief thought grimly. *I will be trapped with the evil in-*

side. Jasmine and Barda will be out here, unprotected. Kirsten will destroy them and then come for me.

His mind was racing. He had to foil Kirsten's plan — take her by surprise. But she would certainly recover very quickly. She might attack them, or she might use Bede as a hostage to force them to surrender.

He had to let Bede know that his message had been understood, so that he was ready to escape.

But how? How could he communicate with Bede without alerting Kirsten?

Then, suddenly, he knew.

He turned to Jasmine. *"Ay andastand!"* he said, loudly enough for Bede to hear. *"Ya wall bay frayd. Bay rady ta ran!"*

Jasmine's eyes widened in astonishment. Then, realizing what he was doing, she tossed her head as if in annoyance.

"I am not afraid," she snorted. "You do not have to speak the language of the forest to calm me!"

Blessing her quick wits, Lief glanced at Kirsten out of the corner of his eye. Kirsten looked impatient, but not suspicious.

Suddenly, he realized the room was utterly silent. The sound of the harp had stopped. Bede had heard. He was signalling, in the only way he could, that he was ready.

Kirsten raised her hand to her throat, in the gesture Lief had seen several times before. At once, the sound of the harp filled the air once more.

That is how she makes him do her will! Lief realized, with a jolt. *She touches the locket hung around her neck! It is a silent threat of some sort. But what — ?*

A strange and horrible idea struck him. His mouth went dry. Was it possible . . . ?

Whether it is or not, I can hesitate no longer, he thought.

He put one hand on the edge of the door and ducked his head, as though he was about to enter the passageway beyond. He took a deep breath. Then, suddenly, with all his strength, he thrust back at Kirsten, slamming her against the wall.

She shrieked and stumbled forward. Lief caught her in his arms and she screamed like a wild thing as he tore the locket from her neck.

With the locket clutched in his hand, he backed away from her, drawing his sword.

"Barda! Bede is chained!" he shouted. "Free — "

Kirsten's jaws opened. She howled. And from her gaping mouth thousands of tiny winged creatures flew, swarming into Lief's face, over his neck and hands, biting and stinging, blinding him.

Lief heard Jasmine cry out, and felt her rush forward. He heard Kirsten scream in pain and fury as Jasmine's blade found its mark. He heard Barda's sword clashing against metal behind him.

Then, suddenly, the flying creatures were gone.

Lief blinked and staggered, rubbing his streaming eyes. Through a haze he saw the arched doorway looming before him. Barda, Bede, and Jasmine were beside him.

"Kirsten is — protected," Jasmine was shouting. "The dagger barely scratched her. We — "

Her eyes widened in horror.

Barda roared in warning. Bede gave a sobbing, despairing cry.

Lief spun around.

Where Kirsten had stood, a huge black figure was rising — a black-robed being whose face was a shining emerald mask. Eyes burned through the mask's eye slits. Long white fingers oozed from the sleeves of the flowing robes — fingers without nails, lengthening, clutching, reaching . . .

The Masked One.

Lief did not hesitate. He ran through the doorway, into the darkness.

※

They stumbled along a pitch-black passageway, Barda half-carrying Bede, who was hardly able to walk.

"Mariette!" Bede choked. "Kirsten — has — Mariette." His breath was sobbing in his throat. After years in chains, it was a miracle he had been able to get this far. Lief guessed that Barda would soon be bearing his full weight.

"Kirsten will concentrate on us for now," Barda growled. "Hold on to me! Keep moving!"

Lief realized that he was still clutching the locket in his hand. He shivered, and thrust it deep into his pocket.

The passage began climbing steeply upward. Stairs carved into hard rock wound around and around in a dizzying spiral. The walls were raw, rough stone, slimy to the touch. Plainly, they were climbing up through one of the castle's towers.

Echoes of their hurrying steps, their labored breath, floated eerily from above and below. They could hear no other sound. But the Masked One was pursuing them. They could feel it. They could feel its cold menace behind them, like an icy wind.

Lief glanced behind him, as he had so often before. He saw nothing but inky darkness. No glimmer of white. No eyes burning through the gleaming mask.

It knows it can take its time, he thought. *There is only one way to run. No way out. And the closer it gets to the Sister of the North, the stronger it will become. Our only chance is to destroy the Sister before it reaches us.*

"The phantom — the creature of the night — was Kirsten!" Jasmine panted. "She killed Otto. And Fern — "

"In mistake for one of us," said Lief. "I am sure of it. Somehow she sensed us — sent her phantom out — to destroy us. But the distance was too great. The phantom was weak — it struck out, wherever it thought we were — killed whoever it found."

The stairway grew even steeper and more winding, and still they stumbled up, up, their legs aching, their knees trembling with the strain.

The air was thick and dead. It was faintly tinged with a sickening, musky odor that Lief had smelled before, though he could not remember where.

Filli whimpered in the darkness.

"This place smells like the City of the Rats," Jasmine muttered.

Snake.

Lief's stomach churned. Barda gave a muffled groan.

The musky smell became stronger. The sense of evil grew. All of them were fighting for breath. And little by little they became aware of a sound — a faint, ringing sound that seemed to seep into their souls and fill them with despair.

The song of the Sister of the North.

It seemed to Lief that the passage was growing narrower, pressing in upon them more closely with every step.

And every step was an effort. He felt weighed down. Weighed down by the heavy, musky air. Weighed down by dread.

They rounded yet another turn. The ringing sound grew louder. And there, in front of them, rose a straight, narrow tunnel, impossibly steep, with stairs that stretched like a ladder to a dim, distant point of light.

Groaning, they began to climb, heaving themselves up from one step to another, struggling towards the light. Up . . . up . . .

The patch of light grew larger. Lief realized that it was daylight. They were nearing the top of the tower.

Then Bede groaned — a terrible sound of anguished despair. A chill ran down Lief's spine.

Gripping the step above him, he turned and looked down.

He saw Jasmine behind him. Below her, Barda was clinging to the rock one-handed, his other mighty arm gripping Bede. And below them, floating in the darkness, was an emerald mask lit by two burning eyes, and white, tube-like fingers, snaking upwards.

The eyes seemed to flame. The slitted mouth hissed. The fingers seemed to stroke the walls of the tunnel.

There was a flash of brilliant light. And then it was as if the rock walls around Barda and Bede were melting, bulging into the center of the tunnel.

"Barda!" Jasmine screamed.

Grimly, Barda began scrambling upwards, heaving Bede after him. But the swollen rock was reaching out, covering Bede's legs, covering Barda's. Like vast, bubbling arms the rock enfolded their struggling bodies, greedily taking them in.

Barda raised his head. His teeth were bared, his

eyes staring. "Go on!" he roared at Lief and Jasmine. "Go! Do not — "

And then his head was covered in a groaning, billowing mass of rock. The rock surged upwards. Jasmine screamed again, kicking and struggling as it flowed over her ankles.

"Jasmine!" shouted Lief in terror. He began to scramble downwards, recklessly turning to reach for her.

"No!" Jasmine shrieked. "It is too late! Lief, go on!"

The rock had enfolded her to her waist. Desperately, she pulled Filli from beneath her jacket, whispered to him, and pushed him onto the stair above her.

Wailing but obedient, Filli bounded up the stairs towards Lief and leaped onto his shoulder.

"Go," Jasmine shouted. "Lief, you must!"

But Lief could not leave her. And when she saw that, Jasmine lifted her hands and let herself fall back, disappearing into the mass of rock as if it were quicksand.

Lief gave a cry of anguish. Below him the groaning rock bulged and surged upwards. He heard the hissing laughter of the Masked One.

A white rage such as he had never felt before boiled up within him. He flung himself back to face the stairs, looked up at the light, and climbed.

He no longer felt pain in his legs or hands or face. He no longer felt fear. He felt only that white-hot anger. It was as if it had burned everything else away. As if all that remained within him now was the will to destroy.

He reached the top of the stairs and hauled himself up into a round, stone-floored room. Only then did he look back.

Filli wailed, clinging to his shoulder. The little creature was grieving. Lief raised his hand to comfort him. He knew that was what Jasmine would have wanted. But he could barely feel Filli's fur. It was as if his fingers were numb.

He stared down into the tunnel, dry-eyed, feeling only a vast emptiness. It was like looking down a chimney — a chimney that was now almost completely blocked, about halfway down, by a misshapen lump of rock.

The tunnel wall had been released from its enchantment. The swollen rock had shrunk back as far as it could, then hardened once more. Its surface was oddly smooth, and it gleamed like a newly healed wound.

Through the narrow opening that remained of the tunnel, something green, black, and white was oozing like slime.

Lief stepped back and looked around. The musky smell was very strong. Through small, round windows he could see storm clouds boiling around the snowy peaks of mountains. He could hear the sound of thunder, and howling wind.

But neither of these was as loud as the song of the Sister of the North, ringing from the bottom of a pit which yawned in the center of the room.

Lief approached the pit and looked down.

The pit was writhing with snakes, hundreds of them, hissing and spitting, coiling one upon the other.

And the Sister of the North was among them. Lief could hear it. He could feel it.

Carefully, he lifted Filli from his shoulder. He walked to one of the round windows and put the little creature on the sill.

"You can climb trees, Filli," he said. "So you can escape from this tower. You can get down to the ground. Do you understand me?"

Filli stared at him with bright, unwinking eyes. Lief dug deep into his pocket and brought out the locket, still dangling on its broken chain.

"I want you to take this with you, and keep it safe," he said, pressing the locket into Filli's paw. "Keep it safe for me."

He had no idea if the little creature understood. He had no idea if there was any point in what he was doing.

He pushed the window open. Wind howled around the tower.

He nodded at Filli. "Go!" he said, waving his hand. "Find Kree. Take care."

Filli put the locket into his mouth and slipped through the window.

Lief closed it after him and walked back to the pit. He stared down at the snakes coiled within it. Rage still burned within him, but cold hopelessness had settled like ice in the pit of his stomach.

He had his sword. His arm was strong. He did not fear pain. He could kill many of the snakes, many . . .

But he would be dead before he killed them all. The Sister of the North would survive. The Masked One would live, growing in power and wickedness. Deltora would perish. Jasmine and Barda would have died in vain.

Again he looked down.

There was a slithering sound from the side of the room. Slowly, he looked around.

The Masked One was rising from the tunnel. Behind the emerald mask, its eyes glowed with triumph.

"So now I have you, King of Deltora," it hissed. "I have succeeded where others have failed. The Master has already rewarded me richly. Now I will have power beyond my wildest dreams."

Lief drew his sword. "I hope it is worth it to you, Kirsten," he said.

"I am the Masked One," the cold voice whispered. "Nothing can stand against me. Soon I will bend the whole of the north to my will."

"You are Kirsten of Shadowgate, hiding behind a

mask," spat Lief. "And you could not bend Bede to your will. You could not make him turn from Mariette. You could not make him love you!"

Behind the cold, green shell of the mask, the eyes flashed with hatred.

The black-draped arms rose. Tube-like fingers slid forward.

They struck Lief, burning like fire. And soundlessly he fell. Down, down into the pit.

19 - The Sister of the North

It was a nightmare. A nightmare of hissing snakes. And deep within the nightmare was evil so strong that it should have frozen Lief, mind and body.

But already he was empty of feeling. Already he was beyond fear.

He struggled to regain his feet, slashing wildly around him with his sword. Snakes thrashed around him, waist deep. He waited for the first, stinging pain that would tell him the fight was over. He wondered if it had already come, and he simply had not felt it.

The Masked One bent over the pit, the emerald mask gleaming, expressionless.

"Bede did not deserve my love!" the voice rasped. "Seven years ago he stumbled into my castle, with my sister fainting in his arms. How he stared when he saw me, and realized whose magic had led

374

him through the wilderness! He had his chance, then, to cast Mariette aside and pledge himself to me. He did not take it."

Lief could hear the snakes hissing in a frenzy, but the pressure around his waist and legs had eased.

He glanced down, and with slow surprise saw that the creatures were frantically arching their bodies away from him. Those that could were hurling themselves at the sides of the pit. They were trying to climb up the seeping walls, falling back, piling one upon the other in a tangled, squirming ring.

The Masked One had noticed nothing. Words were still tumbling through the cruel, slitted emerald mouth on gusts of panting breath.

"Even when Bede saw the wonder I had become in the year of my exile — even when I offered him a place by my side — he recoiled from me! He deserved to die."

Part of Lief's mind heard the words. Another part was still puzzling over why the snakes were fleeing him.

Then, like a dream, the memory of another hissing, dominating voice drifted in his mind.

Remove the thing you wear under your clothes. Cast it away.

It was a memory of Reeah, the giant snake which had once guarded the City of the Rats, in the heart of Deltora.

Lief grew very still. Feeling began to return to him. He pressed his fingertips to the Belt. They tingled. And at the same time, his mind awoke.

Reeah, for all its greatness, had feared the Belt of Deltora. Especially it had feared the ruby, the antidote to snake venom. How much more must these lesser snakes fear it?

And now that the ruby dragon had awoken, the gem was at its full strength. No wonder the snakes were being driven to madness!

There is still a chance, Lief thought. *A chance that I can live to destroy the Sister of the North. If only . . .*

He looked up at the Masked One hissing at the top of the pit. He remembered who hid behind the mask, and what he knew of her. He took a firmer grip on his sword and forced a mocking smile.

"So Bede deserved to die, Kirsten!" he said, putting all the contempt he could muster into his voice. "Yet you kept him alive for seven years. And why? Because his voice still had power over you."

"His songs entertained me," said the Masked One coldly.

"Oh, no, it was far more than that," jeered Lief. "It was because when he sang you remembered what it was to be human. You remembered how to feel. And that was what you longed for. Relief from the cold emptiness growing inside you. A chance to weep for all you had lost."

"I — " The Masked One seemed to choke. Then

suddenly it shimmered, and it was Kirsten who was leaning over the pit — Kirsten, in her white robe, her great braid of yellow hair dangling, her beautiful face twisted with rage.

"I regret nothing!" she shrieked, gripping the edge of the pit and leaning over even farther. "I was always more beautiful, more talented, more admired, than Mariette! How *could* Bede have preferred her? How *dare* he prefer her?"

Now, Lief thought, and thrust his sword upwards.

He moved fast, but something else was faster. Before the point of his sword was halfway to Kirsten's white throat, a huge snake had twined around her dangling rope of yellow hair and was wriggling upwards.

Kirsten screamed and tried to jerk her head back. But it was too late. Already another snake had caught hold of the braid, and another, and another.

In seconds, the rope of hair was a mass of snakes writhing desperately up to freedom. The weight dragged Kirsten's head down and pinned her, screaming, to the edge of the pit.

By the time Lief staggered back, stunned and horror-struck, she had become a living lifeline. The pit was emptying as snakes in the hundreds swarmed to freedom over her head, neck, and shoulders.

And as the pit emptied, Lief's strength ebbed away. He could feel it as surely as if it were blood draining from his veins.

His limbs were trembling and heavy. It was hard to keep his head upright. He could barely keep his eyes from closing. His mind was clouding.

The Sister of the North was being uncovered. Its song was growing louder. Its poison and malice were battering him like crashing waves.

Despair and die.

He forced himself to look up. Kirsten was covered in a wriggling, hissing mass of scaly flesh. And as she screamed and struggled, the panicking snakes struck at her again and again and again.

She is protected . . .

So Jasmine had said. But the snakes were striking in the hundreds. Their fangs were like needles. And with every tiny needle scratch, another drop of poison seeped into Kirsten's helpless body. She would take a long time to die.

Sickness churned in Lief's stomach. He looked down again.

There was only one snake left in the pit. And it was no snake at all. Pale and bloated, striped with thin lines of poisonous yellow, the thing thrashed mindlessly on the stinking, seeping rock.

It had no eyes. It had no tongue. It had no fangs. But evil radiated from it like heat. And from its empty, gaping mouth poured the deadly song of the Sister of the North, filling Lief's ears and his mind, forcing him to his knees.

He told himself he had to move. He had to raise

his sword. He had to try to smash the thing. Destroy it. But its evil was killing him. Its song of despair and death was ringing in his ears, drowning out all other sound. With a dull clang, his sword fell from his hand.

His fingers would not move. His hands felt as if they did not belong to him. Gritting his teeth, he lifted them. They felt like heavy lumps of dough attached to his arms. Clumsily, he pressed them against the Belt of Deltora.

He felt heat. Strong, beating heat. Heat far greater than he had expected. Not just in his hands, but in the Belt itself.

Confused, he looked down. His hands were shining green. A blaze of bright green was streaming between the fingers, lighting up the dark.

Dark . . . why was it dark? Lief forced his head back, looked up. The tower room was dim, as though the windows had been curtained by clouds.

He could just make out the figure of Kirsten slumped over the edge of the pit. And dimly he could see the snakes. They were fleeing, slithering off Kirsten's body and away, out of sight.

What . . . ?

Lief's heart was thudding like a drum in his chest. His fingers were hot, burning hot. He tilted his head a little more. He looked higher. Up to the high, dim roof of the tower.

Then, suddenly, astoundingly, there was an ear-splitting crack — and the roof was gone.

Suddenly, there was nothing above him but boiling clouds . . . and a vast, gleaming shape plunging towards him, green as the emerald glowing beneath his hands, roaring like thunder.

The emerald dragon!

The wind of the dragon's wings beat Lief down, flattening him against the floor of the pit. Mighty talons reached for him, closed about him, and lifted him into the air.

Weak as an infant, Lief rolled helplessly within the cage of the talons. All about him was open sky. The walls and roof of the tower room had been cracked away like the top of an egg, and thrown to the howling winds.

All that remained was the stone floor, Kirsten's sprawled body, and the pit.

The dragon did not speak. Its emerald eyes, burning like green fire, were fixed on the thing still thrashing in the pit.

But there was no need for words. For Lief could hear the dragon's heart beating, loud as thunder, thudding into his mind, crashing through the relentless song of the Sister of the North.

He took one hand from the emerald in the Belt of Deltora and seized one of the talons that caged him. He felt the talon's razor-sharp edge cut into his hand, felt the warm blood begin to flow. But he only tightened his grip.

And with fierce joy he saw green flame gush from

the dragon's roaring jaws. He saw the vile thing at the bottom of the pit writhing in a pool of emerald fire.

Again the dragon roared, and again, till the pit was a furnace of swirling flame. The rock blackened, then began to glow.

Searing heat billowed upwards. Lief cringed away from it, tried to roll himself into a ball to escape from it.

But still he gripped the dragon's talon with his left hand, and the great emerald with his right. And still the power flowed through him from one to the other. And still the dragon roared, and the pit burned.

The song of the Sister of the North rose to a cracked, piercing wail. It faltered. It stopped. A blinding flash of white light burst through the emerald flame.

There was a moment's breathless silence, as though the land was holding its breath.

Then there was a long, low groaning sound. And the next instant, the air was filled with dust — blinding dust as fine as powder, swirling in the wind. Lief screwed his eyes shut, coughing and choking.

He heard the dragon hiss, as if with satisfaction. Then he felt the wind rushing past his ears as it dropped down, straight down, to the ground.

✳

When Lief opened his eyes, he was sure that he was dreaming.

Above him, two dark shapes loomed against a

background of hazy blue sky. A gentle breeze blew on his face. Someone was holding his hand.

"Lief!"

He blinked. Slowly, his eyes focused and he realized that the shapes were faces. Smiling faces.

Jasmine and Barda were bending over him. Kree was perched on Jasmine's shoulder. Filli was nuzzling into her neck, his tiny paws clutching her tangled hair.

Lief stared. Now he knew he was dreaming. Tears burned in his eyes as he waited for the vision to tremble and disappear.

But it did not.

"It was an enchantment," Jasmine whispered, putting her arms around him. "The spell was broken. We awoke — here."

"And the castle was dust," said Barda. "Nothing but dust, blowing in the wind." He leaned forward. "Lief, surely this means — ?"

Dizzy with joy, yet still hardly daring to believe it, Lief nodded. "The Sister of the North is no more," he said huskily. "And I think Kirsten died at the same moment. It was because — the emerald dragon returned. It — "

"We saw it," Barda said grimly. "It dropped you onto the ground with us, then flew away. Perhaps we will see it again. But I would be more than happy not to. It had a stern, fierce eye."

"It is the dragon of honor," Lief muttered. "It came to clean its land of evil, as was its duty. But I fear it is still angry, because we brought another dragon to its place."

"It can be as angry as it wishes," Jasmine grinned. "It did its part, that is all that counts. It did its part, and you did yours, Lief! The Sister is gone. All Kirsten's sorcery is undone. And we are not the only ones to rejoice. Look!"

She pointed. Lief turned his head.

The castle of the Masked One had vanished.

Where its towers and turrets had risen to the sky lay a great sheet of smooth, flat rock powdered with fine dust. Two figures stood in the center of the rock, hand in hand. One was Bede. The other was a slender young woman with long, light brown hair.

"When the spell was broken, Mariette was freed, just as we were," said Jasmine. "The dust cleared, and she was standing there. She had been enchanted — imprisoned in her own locket, which Kirsten had taken for herself. But you must have known that, Lief, or why did you take the locket at all?"

The locket! Lief plunged his hand into his pocket and winced. He had forgotten that his hand was cut and bleeding. He felt around with his fingers, but the locket was not there.

"Filli has it," Jasmine said softly. "Do you not remember? You gave it to him for safekeeping, when you thought you would not survive. You told him to take it out of the castle. And so he did. He has been waiting to return it to you."

"Indeed," said Barda. "He would not give it up to anyone else — even Mariette. The emerald dragon is not the only one in this land who values honor."

Proudly, Filli climbed down from Jasmine's shoulder, uncurled his paw, and tipped the locket into Lief's waiting hand.

Lief opened the locket. Inside, as he had expected, was a small painting of Bede.

"Jasmine, your dagger?" he asked.

Jasmine passed the dagger to him. Gently, using the dagger's point, Lief prized the little picture out.

And behind it, pressed into the back of the locket, was a small scrap of tightly folded paper. Lief picked it out in turn and carefully unfolded it.

Together the companions stared at the grim name of their next goal, and noted how far away it was. They stared at the new lines of verse, wondering what they meant. But no one said a word, and after a few moments Lief folded the paper again and thrust it deep into his pocket.

They all knew that, all too soon, he would have to take it out again. Soon they would have to travel on, and face whatever dangers might come.

Troubling questions would have to be faced, too. How, despite all their secrecy, had the guardian of the north known where they were, almost every step of the way? Why did the Masked Ones hate the king so bitterly? Where had Laughing Jack gone? Would they see him again? Was he still a threat to them?

But this — this moment under the hazy blue sky — was not a time for plans and questions, but for rejoicing.

They were safe. The dread song of the Sister of the North had been silenced forever. At last, the land of the north could throw off its mask of death, and begin to live again.

For now, that was all that mattered.